A
TRICK
OF THE
DARK

WITHDRAWN

D1142779

Also by B. R. Collins

The Traitor Game

A TRICK OF THE DARK

B. R. COLLINS

BLOOMSBURY

LONDON BERLIN NEW YORK

Bloomsbury Publishing, London, Berlin and New York

First published in Great Britain in 2009 by Bloomsbury Publishing Plc
36 Soho Square, London, W1D 3QY

Page 29, line 33 and Page 30, lines 1 & 2 from
'La Belle Dame Sans Merci' by John Keats
Page 59, lines 4 & 5 from 'Peter Pan' by J.M. Barrie
Page 72, lines 25 & 26 and Page 308, lines 3, 7 & 8 from
'Death, Be Not Proud' by John Donne
Page 123, lines 11 & 12 from 'Pippa Passes' by Robert Browning

A CIP catalogue record of this book is available from the British Library

ISBN 978 0 7475 9915 9

All papers used by Bloomsbury Publishing are natural, recyclable products
made from wood grown in well-managed forests. The manufacturing processes
conform to the environmental regulations of the country of origin.

Typeset by Dorchester Typesetting Group Ltd
Printed in Italy by LEGOPRINT S.p.A

1 3 5 7 9 10 8 6 4 2

www.bloomsbury.com

Wake up. For God's sake, wake up. You've been asleep for more than twenty-four hours. Just lying there. I'm not sure you've even moved.

But I can't bring myself to come and look at you. I'm too cowardly, too sick of myself for letting this happen. All because you were trying to help me . . . I know you *will* wake up. You have to. But it's my fault, that you're lying there, dead to the world. Your hand's so bruised it's gone this weird shade of duck-egg blue round the knuckles, where it's not all cut and scabbed up from the broken glass. And there's that long cut down your forearm, the cigarette burn on your other wrist . . . it's going to hurt like mad when you do wake up. I'm not all that bothered about the bruises and stuff, mind you – because, well, they're mostly your own doing, anyway. Serves you right . . . It's just that you're there, like that, because you were trying to help. So asleep you look dead. It scares me, to think what might have happened, if . . . No, fuck that. You're going to be OK. You'll wake up. Of course you will. Any time now.

I actually stopped writing this for a second and went to peer out of my bedroom door into your room, because in any decent set-up you would have woken up the moment I finished that sentence. But guess what? You didn't.

The stupid thing is, I never in a million years thought I'd need your help. It was always the other way round, wasn't it? You'd be moaning about your maths home-work, and I'd waltz in and do it without thinking, taking the piss out of you for being so thick. Or – do you remember when I told your horrible little friend I'd scrag her if she wasn't nicer to you? (And yes, I did say *scrag*.) That's how it's always worked, anyway. That's just how it is: I'm the hero, you're the adoring hanger-on. And I hated – still do hate – the idea of needing *anyone's* help, let alone yours . . . Honestly. My little kid sister, for God's sake! Why would I need you, after all, when I'm bigger and stronger and – well, frankly, better-looking and cleverer and more proficient at just about anything you can name? It's all wrong.

Not that you actually *did* help. Not that you actually did anything useful at all. Sure, you made a sweet, valiant attempt to help. And you ended up comatose and covered in minor injuries, and it didn't do a blind bit of fucking good.

Sorry. Not the way I meant to start.

Oh Lord . . . I don't even know why I'm writing this. As an act of faith, maybe. If I write it, then you have to

2

wake up, so you can read it. No, that's too noble. I'm writing so I can keep telling myself I'm still here. Not faded, not yet. I'm still a person . . . just. As long as I can write, I'm human. I'm myself. Even if I look at myself in the mirror and don't recognise my own face.

I keep going back, remembering over and over. My head's a sort of whirlpool at the moment: I try to think in a straight line, but it won't let me go. I watch everything that's happened again and again, like a damaged DVD player. So all the worst moments keep coming back to me. The ruins; the day in St Jean-le-Grand; that night in the house when Mum and Dad were at the concert; the night before last, when Pete had to lug you to bed, unconscious, covered in blood and bruises . . . Or sometimes even the stuff before this all started – my last afternoon at school, or that fucking horrible morning last winter, when Dad decided to phone Cecilia (may she rot in hell) without checking who was within earshot . . . Whatever you're dreaming about, little sis, it can't be as bad. Everything churns round and round until my brain feels like a washing machine. And that's what's already happened; that's before I even start on what *will* happen. Jesus, I'm scared. I almost envy you, lying there. Almost. You've got no idea how much I miss sleeping.

What's odd, though, is that the thing that comes back to me most is something I hardly even noticed at the time. But now it seems . . . important.

We were driving down through France, about ten days

3

ago – Jesus, only ten days! – and Mum and Dad were arguing. Remember? Yeah, 'course you do. You were staring out of the window, kicking the back of Mum's seat, and every so often you'd put on your innocent look and say something like, Are we there yet? or, If we're lost, why don't we just go home? I was pretending to listen to my MP3 player but the battery was flat, so I could hear everything, right down to Mum grinding her teeth.

It was one of those arguments. The ones where, sure, they're arguing about getting lost and whether it's the map being out of date (Dad's fault) or slipshod navigation (Mum's fault), but *really* it's an argument about Mum and Dad and Cecilia (may she rot in hell). Like a snowball fight where every snowball has a rock hidden inside it. In any normal family, someone would have the sense to say, All right, I'm sorry, I probably *did* get confused in Périgueux, even if it wasn't true. But oh no, Mum couldn't do that, because *that* would mean she was admitting she might have been partly responsible for Dad having an affair . . .

And what makes it worse is that it's my fault that she knows. If I'd been wise enough not to say anything . . . And they both hate me for it. They keep it out of sight, most of the time – they wouldn't admit it, even to themselves – but they do; and I hate them back. Especially Dad. They love me too, of course. But they'd both be much, much happier if I'd kept my big mouth shut. So would you, probably. And when you add all the stuff about St Timothy's chucking me out . . . We might as well be honest about it. As far as they're concerned, I'm not a Good Thing. Not that I care, any more. In all honesty, it seems pretty trivial now.

4

Anyway. We're in the car at seventy miles per hour, bombing along a French motorway in what is quite possibly the wrong direction. And Mum's been grunting and sighing over the map in a sort of I-can't-work-in-these-conditions way, but finally she realises Dad's determined to ignore her, so she says something like, This road should be curving round to the left . . . And I watch you peer round the edge of her seat at the road ahead, and I don't even need to see it, because I know from the look on your face that it doesn't do anything of the kind.

And Mum says, I knew you'd turned off too soon on the last road. They must have built that motorway after the map was made. So yes, we're lost. Didn't I say we should have bought another map? Oh no, you said, don't worry, darling, I know the Dordogne like the back of my –

And Dad looks at her and gives her thigh a benevolent little pat with his free hand and says, Please, Helen, my love, there's really no need to apologise. You simply mustn't blame yourself for everything.

And Mum's jaw clenches and she says, I don't see why I should apologise for something that isn't my fault.

Dad doesn't answer, but – I'm not sure if he means to – he treads on the accelerator. I can't see the speedometer from the back seat, but the side of the road flashes by, faster and faster. In the corner of my eye I catch you looking out of the window, then back at the space between Mum and Dad, as if you're not quite sure whether you're imagining it . . . but the car is definitely speeding up, and Mum and Dad go silent, and it gets harder and harder to focus on anything going past outside. I've been in Elliot's car when he did 110 miles per hour, and . . . well, maybe Dad wasn't going as fast as that. But it was close. I'm sure it was close. And he doesn't take his foot off the pedal, and the car swerves into the fast lane (except that it's on the wrong side of the road, so it feels like the slow lane) and we're driving way, way too fast and *no one says anything*.

I see you holding your own hand as if it's someone else's. Mum's curling up the corner of the map, so the car's full of this weird papery scratching, like something trying to break out of a wasps' nest. And underneath that there's this silence, like no one wants to be tactless and ask Dad if he's trying to kill us all . . .

And suddenly I'm furious. With Dad, Mum, you, me, everyone. We're sitting in the car while Dad drives like a maniac, and no one has the sense, the guts, the – oh, hell, I don't know – the *humility* to say something. We're just pretending it isn't happening. I remember thinking, And if we *die*? Do we just pretend *that* isn't happening, either?

And I'm so fucking sick of it that I press my hands against the back of Dad's seat and will him to go even faster. I tense my whole body like I'm pushing us forward, and imagine the needle on the speedometer creeping past 110, up to 120, 130 . . . And I pray for a tyre to blow, something to hit the windscreen, Dad's concentration to go – anything. I'm so angry I mean it. I say, Crash, crash, *crash* . . . under my breath. I imagine a spectacular skid, the car slewing across the road, a burst and fireball of flame as it flips over, a quick, violent end to all of us. I close my eyes and pray. *Crash*.

The car wobbles. The momentum pushes me against the window as the car swerves, like a hand on my shoulder. And for a second I think, I've done it. This is it. We're going to die. I hear you make a noise that isn't quite a yelp. Mum says, Edward, for God's sake, keep your eyes on the road! There's real panic in her voice. I stare at the green blur going past the window and I feel the excitement rising, and it's not just serves-them-right (although it is, a bit), it's another feeling too, like flying, like the moment before an aeroplane lifts off, when you feel the speed and the danger and think, yes yes yes –

Just for a second. Then Dad sneezes. The car noses back into the right lane, and he sniffs and says, Sorry. Then he slows right down, and Mum relaxes again, and you lean back, and everyone except me takes a big breath. And even though we must still be doing seventy it feels like a crawl.

And I'm so fucking disappointed I could cry.

I lean my face against the window and stare out, at the verge ahead. And that's when I see these people standing at the edge of the road. At least, I *think* they're people, at first; until we get closer and I realise that they can't be. They're too still, too *flat*, somehow . . .

They're dark shapes, life-size, but blank, like black cut-outs . . . two tall ones, two smaller ones, like a family. Like our family. They stand frozen by the side of the road, watching, waiting . . . They give me the creeps. I don't know why they're there. It feels like they're looking at me, even though they don't have faces. Trying to tell me something. *Beware.* Or, *go back.* Shadows without people to cast them, warning me.

Coincidence, of course. I worked out later that they mark places where people have been killed. I suppose

7

the French government puts them up, as a macabre sort of way to tell you to drive carefully. Anyway, they're all over the place. So – coincidence. Of course.

But I first saw them – *then*. At that particular moment. Maybe that's why it seems so important. Just as I was thinking, Yes. Yes, I want to crash. Yes, I want Dad to kill us all. Yes, I want to get killed. Maybe – if there was something – if . . .

Oh, fuck it. Even if it *was* a warning . . . it didn't do much good, did it? Well, did it? Anz?

Jesus, Anz. Why don't you *wake up*?

One

If she looked at it the right way, it was beautiful. Annis could see that. The long curve of the valley below her, spirals of mist coming up from the trees like smoke, and on the other side the rise of the fields, bleached summer-yellow, and the long road, and the towers of the chateau opposite . . . Yep. Very nice. Picturesque. She said to herself, *Wow, countryside*, hitting the first syllable like a hammer. *How lovely. As long as I don't turn round, I can pretend I'm in a painting or something*.

Of course, if she moved her head, the whole picture-postcard thing fell apart. On her right, in the grass in front of the house, there was a pile of the rubbish they'd cleared out of the barn, which was definitely *not* picturesque. And if she looked straight ahead, towards the trees and the bulge of the hill . . . Not that it wasn't pretty, but you could just see the chimney of the derelict house, and . . . It felt like a kind of blot on her retina, a sort of dark patch, making her uneasy. She thought, *Stop it! This is nonsense, just because Mum and Dad have absolutely forbidden us to go down there* . . . But it wasn't that. She was obedient, fair enough, but not *that* obedient, not enough to make her feel on edge, just seeing the ruin through the trees. There was something . . . She didn't like looking at it, that was all. It didn't fit in with the rest of the landscape; it wasn't pastoral and summery and aren't-we-middle-class, converting-a-barn-in-the-Dordogne? like everything else was . . .

She made herself stare into the trees until she could make out the ragged edge of a wall, and the white flash of the *DANGER: DEFENSE D'ENTRER* sign. Nothing moved. *See? Nothing to be scared of. Anyway, Zach's always down there. He likes it.*

She finished the last of her bread and cheese, and leant her head back against the cool stone of the wall, wondering whether it was worth going inside for some more food. It was so quiet she could have fallen asleep; except that quiet wasn't a good thing, because it meant the builders weren't here, and that meant –

Somewhere behind her, Dad shouted, 'Helen! *Helen!* What's the French for guttering? This bloody idiot is pretending not to understand –'

Annis heard the measured, cool murmur of Mum's voice, too low to make out what she was saying.

'Fine. Where's the dictionary? You had it last night – you remember, when you were –'

Mum's voice again, slightly louder now. 'I'm trying to work, Edward. Find it yourself.'

'Oh, so that's *proper* work, and talking to the builders isn't?'

A pause. Annis put her chin on her knees. She wasn't hungry any more.

Dad cleared his throat. 'Look, Helen, love, if you could just find the dictionary for me, we really need this sorted out by – *fuck.*' A dull crash, like he'd kicked something. 'The fucker's just hung up on me. For fuck's sake.'

Mum said, 'Edward.'

'What? Stupid fucker. I mean, we're *paying* them, for fuck's sake, they ought to at least fucking talk –'

'Please don't swear like that. Annis might hear you.'

Annis almost got up and went inside, just so she could point out that she had, in fact, heard the word *fuck* before. But that would only make things worse, so she stayed where she was. She heard Dad come out of the front door on to the grass, on the phone again, talking French so slowly it sounded like his batteries had gone. That was him trying to be polite. She pressed herself back against the wall and pretended she wasn't there.

Mum called after him, 'And did you speak to Zach? Edward? Did you . . . ?' but Dad didn't answer. Annis heard him kick the rubbish as he walked past it, and the slow slither of something falling off the top of the heap. Then it was quiet again. *Only now*, she thought, *it isn't even approaching idyllic sunlight-and-birdsong-filled silence, it's the same bloody silence we had in London. The we-hate-each-other silence. Silence like someone's* died.

That was the worst thing. Not the fights – although they weren't much fun either. The silence, that filled the whole house and settled on everything like a layer of grime, thickening and thickening until she thought it would bury them. It was even worse here than at home. She kicked at the grass, digging a trench with one heel, and thought, *For God's sake! Whose bright idea was this, anyway? I know, we're a dysfunctional family, let's go and renovate a barn together. Never*

11

mind that we can't stand being in the same room for five minutes . . .

She wouldn't have minded so much if Zach –

No. She was determined not to think about Zach. She was sick of thinking about Zach, frankly, because it just made her miserable, and it wasn't as if she could *help* . . . He'd made that perfectly clear, those horrible weeks after he got expelled. Those awful, awful weeks, while Mum had taken him round all the private schools she could find, trying to get him a place for next year . . . It was scary; like someone else had taken over his body, and didn't know what to do with it. He didn't smile or speak. He used to hold himself rigid, as if anyone coming too close would give him some appalling disease. He stopped coming into her room to help her with her homework and take the piss out of her posters. Once, she asked him, did he really want to sell drugs, or . . . was it because, did he really do it because of Dad . . . ? For a second, when he looked at her, she thought he was going to tell her properly. Then the ice formed again over his expression and he shut his bedroom door in her face. All those weeks she watched him not eating and not talking and thought, *I have never seen anyone so unhappy. He's dissolving.*

And . . . She thought, *If it was anyone but Zach . . .* Sure, she'd have been sympathetic. But for it to be Zach . . . She couldn't bear it. It made her feel physically sick, to see him like that. *Zach.* Zach, her brilliant, funny, popular brother . . . it was all *wrong*.

And Mum and Dad made it worse. Mum treated him like a five-year-old who'd stepped out in front of a car, furious and solicitous at the same time, when even Annis could see he just wanted to be left alone. And Dad . . . he was so *polite* to him. Polite and distant and official, as if he couldn't remember what it was like to be Zach's father and had to settle for being his bank manager instead. As if Zach had betrayed him so totally there wasn't even any point being angry . . . She felt a wave of anger herself, thinking about it, because – for God's sake – what was Zach *meant* to do? Say, 'Yes, fine, Dad, I won't tell Mum, 'course not, hope you and Cecilia-the-tart are really happy together . . .'? It was so unfair she wanted to scream. But Dad probably wouldn't notice if she did.

He didn't really bother with Annis, these days. No one did. They didn't even see how nice she was being. That might have made her feel better, but no one had enough room to notice. Mum was too busy being obsessed with Zach's chequered school career and Dad's love life, and Dad was too busy feeling guilty and hating everyone for making him feel guilty and worrying about whether his bosses at the ad agency knew that he'd been having an inappropriate relationship in the workplace . . . and Zach . . . After a fortnight she'd said to Zach, trying to make a joke of it, '*You* can still see me, right? You know, 3-D and everything?' The old Zach would have looked round blankly and said, 'Hello? Hello? Is someone there?' but the new Zach just looked straight through her and nodded.

You had to hand it to him, though. He'd never, ever blamed anyone else for getting expelled. It was like he thought he deserved it; like he'd *wanted* it, almost, although that didn't make any sense. Annis remembered overhearing Mum and Dad arguing, a few nights after Zach had split on Dad; Mum shouting, 'You bastard, this is all your fault, how can you have done this to our family?' – and Dad yelling back, 'Jesus, Helen, if you weren't such a frigid bitch, do you really think I'd have needed to go to someone else?' She hadn't meant to listen, and she'd clapped her hands over her ears and pelted upstairs again, afraid Dad might say something about Zach. But she couldn't get the words out of her head. After that, she was almost too scared to eavesdrop, the evening Zach got expelled, but he didn't say anything except, 'Yeah, I screwed up.' That was all. 'I'm sorry. I screwed up.' And then, over and over again: *I'm sorry, I'm sorry*, until the words stopped meaning anything.

She bit the top of her forefinger, remembering the expression on his face as he came upstairs that night, walking past where she was sitting on the landing as if he didn't even see she was there. A year before – three months before, when no one knew about Cecilia-the-tart – he'd have taken a good long run up and thrown a kick at her, stopping just short; she'd have rolled her eyes, grinning, said, 'Zach, you tosser,' and reached for his ankle, trying to grab him before he had time to step over her . . . But then, three months before she wouldn't have been sitting on the landing, listening to Mum bawl him out for drug-dealing. And she wouldn't have seen that look on his face, strained, desperate, only – somehow – *vindicated* . . .

She bit harder, until she realised how much it was hurting and took her hand hastily away from her mouth. Shit. She was thinking about Zach, *again*.

After being so determined that she wouldn't . . .

Dad was stamping back towards the house. She heard his phone snap shut; he started to shout before he got into the house. 'Helen! Tuesday! That's the soonest they can do, because of the weekend, which evidently extends through Monday. Tuesday for the barn, but the guttering'll have to wait. OK?'

A murmured answer. Annis yawned. When she opened her eyes she was looking right at the chimney of the ruined house; she felt something inside her flinch. She narrowed her eyes, squinting through the trees. The sun had moved, fractionally, so she could see it quite clearly. It was just a chimney – just a perfectly normal, if rather badly maintained chimney . . . but it made her feel odd, looking at it. Zach would be down there somewhere. He'd listened to Mum and Dad do their that-ruined-house-is-very-dangerous-it-could-collapse-at-any-time spiel, deadpan; then the first time they turned their backs he'd been off to explore it, more excited than she'd seen him for weeks. Now he spent most of his time down there, reading and chain-smoking, probably. He didn't let Annis follow him – which was fine, because she didn't want to, anyway. She had better things to do than hang around in death-trap buildings. Like . . . er, like . . .

Oh, for heaven's sake . . . ! It wasn't fair. It really wasn't fair. Everyone else was in Majorca. Jenny, Suze, Caitlin, Penny . . . They were probably on the beach at this very moment. Jenny was probably writing her a postcard. *Dear Annis, sorry you couldn't come, hope you are having fun and lots of fit French boys are helping your parents with the barn.*

Embrasse-les from me! Garçons, I mean, pas tes parents! J xxx.

Annis had bought a bikini especially. She'd tried it on in the shop, and Jenny had said, 'Hmm, well, pale and interesting and your bikini line needs a teensy bit of attention, but otherwise, wow, you are *gorgeous*, sister.' And when Annis turned round and looked at herself, she had to agree. It made her feel like a model or something. When Mum told her she couldn't go to Majorca after all, she was going to take it back to the shop; until Mum said she'd give her the money for it – 'And in any case, the house has a swimming pool, so you'll be glad to have it anyway, darling.' But it was so *unfair* . . . After Zach's GCSEs he'd biked round Morocco for three weeks on his own, and Annis couldn't even go to Majorca. OK, to be honest, Mum and Dad *thought* he was staying with a friend on the Isle of Wight – she remembered the row there'd been afterwards, and grimaced – but it was the principle of the thing. Her first holiday with her friends, and it got cancelled because she had to come to France and help *renovate a barn* . . . She had a mad, uncontrollable urge to storm into the house, wait until Mum looked up from her computer, and say, 'So, Dad had a bit of posh tottie on the side, and Zach got chucked out for selling hash to his mates, and, Mum, you're a complete emotional mess . . . so what am *I* being punished for?'

But she didn't move.

Voices, again. Although not shouting, this time. Mum: '. . . not the baguette, the other loaf, I think it's going stale,' and Dad: 'Yes, fine, whatever. I just need to try Pascale again . . .'

Then Mum was coming round the side of the house, towards her. 'Annis! Lunch! Where's Zach?'

Annis said, 'I'm not sure.' Which wasn't quite a lie. 'He didn't tell you where he was going?'

Yeah, because he just adores the way you try to keep track of him . . . She said, 'No. I don't know, maybe he's gone for a bike ride or something . . .' She could see Zach's bike leaning against the wall of the barn, her rucksack draped over one handlebar. 'Or he could be having a swim.'

'That boy! I'm at the end of my tether.' Mum said it on the edge of a laugh, but it sounded true. 'I *said* lunch would be at two – I wanted us all to eat together.'

Annis said, 'Oh, yes,' and tried surreptitiously to brush the crumbs off her T-shirt.

'It really isn't much to ask!' Mum stood with her hands on her hips, staring down at the valley. 'If only he'd start taking responsibility for himself! Honestly –'

Which means, Annis thought wearily, *doing what you tell him* . . . She said, 'He'll come back when he's hungry, Mum. It doesn't really matter, does it?'

Mum swung round. 'How dare you tell me what matters and what doesn't!'

'I only meant –'

'Don't you *dare* talk back to me, young lady! I have worked *so hard* for this family. Don't you dare try to tell me what to do – who the hell do you think you are? I am giving Zach *parameters*, trying to impose some *discipline*, because he's clearly in need of some, and I don't have time for you to undermine me, do you understand? Don't – you – *dare*!'

17

Annis blinked. For a second the sense of injustice blocked her throat like a bud opening; then she swallowed and it faded. There wasn't any point trying to defend herself. She muttered, 'Sorry, Mum.'

'I should think so.' Mum looked across the valley again, but Annis could tell she wasn't really seeing it. 'As it happens, Annis, I've been meaning to talk to you. I think it's the worst possible thing for Zach, the way you worship him.'

Annis felt the air go out of her. Her lungs paused, frozen, as if she'd never need to breathe again. She thought, *I can't believe she said that –*

'You can see what he's like. If it wasn't for your influence . . . oh, I know, there've been other things going on –'

Like Dad having an affair, you mean? Like the way you hate each other? But she couldn't even move her lips.

'– but you need to see, Annis, you're not helping! Zach isn't perfect – he isn't even *close* – and it's not good for him, the way you –'

'Mum!' Annis found her tongue, quite literally, as if it had suddenly sprouted in her mouth. 'What do you mean, Zach's not even *close* to being perfect? He's your *son* – you're supposed to love him!'

'Oh, don't be so absurd! I *do* love him, Annis! That's what this is all about. I don't like seeing you with him, it's positively unhealthy, no wonder he –' Mum stopped.

'He *what*, Mum? Sold drugs to his friends? Got expelled? Or told you about Dad and Cecilia? That's his fault as well, right?'

'You see! You always stand up for him –'

'And it's not *my* fault, either —'

Mum said, 'I'm simply saying —'

'Well, don't!' Annis scrambled to her feet, not sure where she was going.

Zach said, 'Are we having lunch, or not?'

They both spun round. He was there, at the corner of the house, a book in his hand, his index finger marking his place. Annis felt a hot, prickly rush of embarrassment, because if he'd heard . . . But he looked straight through her, his eyes blank.

Mum said, 'Where have you been? I told you lunch was at —'

'Two. Yes. And it's —' He made a show of consulting his watch. 'Gosh, Mum, I'm sorry! It's almost *three minutes* past.'

Mum stared at him, chewing her lower lip. Then she said, in a tight, careful kind of way, 'All right. We'd better go in.'

Zach said, in exactly the same tone, 'Yes, we better had, hadn't we?' He started to walk back the way he'd come, round the side of the house. As he went round the corner he said, 'Oh —' and stepped backwards and sideways, because Dad was coming in the opposite direction.

Dad said, 'What's going on here? Family reunion, without me?' He sounded like he was trying to be jocular, but his voice was just off-centre.

Mum said, 'Let's go in and have lunch.'

Dad said, 'Yes, well, I've been *waiting* . . .' but he caught Mum's eye and stopped. Something flickered in his face — a kind of childish resentment, Annis thought, like he was younger than Zach. Then he smiled and turned to peer at the book Zach was holding. He said, 'Good book, is it?'

Zach narrowed his eyes. He held the book out, silently, so Dad could see the cover.

'Ah. *The Poems of John Donne*. One of mine, isn't it?'

Annis said, trying to break the tension, 'God. Heavy. Is that for –' and then bit her tongue.

Zach shot her a glance. 'For school? Obviously not.'

Dad put his hands in his pockets and rocked back on his heels. 'I said, that's one of my books, isn't it?'

'So what?'

'I don't think you should borrow my books.'

Zach blinked, frowning, his mouth partly open, as if he was trying to make sense of what Dad had said. Then he said, 'But – I'm *allowed* – after my GCSE results, you said I could –'

'Not if you're not going to take care of them. Look!' Dad snatched the book and flipped it open, riffling through so that they could all see the dog-ears on the pages. 'It's an abuse of the privilege, Zach. Taking them outdoors, writing in them . . .'

'I *haven't* written in –'

'I just don't think you can be trusted with them. Look at this. It's in a state. You've spilt something on it, here, and the pages are starting to fall out. If you convince me you'll look after my books, in future, then you can read them. Otherwise you can ask before you borrow them, like Annis does.'

Zach was squinting at him, his whole face screwed up, as if he was trying to read something a long way away. 'You can't – I haven't *done* anything to – I can't believe – just because –'

Mum said, 'Edward . . .'

Dad said, 'No, Helen, you're right. Zach needs to take some responsibility. Well, he can learn that privileges have to be earned, and kept.' He was still looking at Zach. 'Don't you agree, Helen?'

'I *did* earn it – my GCSE results – you were proud of me, you said I'd get as much out of your books as you did . . .' Zach stopped, swallowed, and took a long, slow breath. 'Oh, Jesus . . . It's not about the book at all, is it? You don't give a toss about the book. Fuck me, Dad . . . what are you *like*? You sad, sad man. You think this is some kind of *gesture*, like suddenly you've got the moral high ground – all self-righteous, like cracking the spine of a shitty paperback classic is worse than fucking your evil bitch of a secretary –'

'That's *enough*, Zachary! Edward, Annis, it's time for lunch –'

'Well, I'm sorry, Dad, I'm sorry I screwed up your life, I'm sorry for everything, I'm *sorry*, OK, but if you want a gesture, well, here's your fucking *gesture* –'

Annis thought for a mad split second he was going to punch Dad. So did Dad, probably, from the way he flinched away from Zach's hand. But Zach was only grabbing the book back. He held it for a moment on his palms in an odd, archaic way, like it was alive. Then he opened it and ripped out the first page.

Mum said, '*Zachary!* That's your father's –'

Dad didn't say anything, but he stepped forward, reaching out.

'Sorry, Dad, am I jeopardising my *privileges*? Oh well.' Another page, and another; getting quicker, so that now he was taking whole handfuls of pages, tearing them easily away from the binding and dropping them. Already there were yellowing pieces of paper drifting across the grass. *Rip. Rip. Ri-i-i-ip.*

Annis thought Mum would say something else, but she didn't. They stood in silence until Zach dropped the empty binding on the grass. It flipped over as it fell. Annis could read *Edward Randall, June 1978*, in the corner.

Zach looked at Dad; staring and staring, as if he was looking for something in particular, some specific response . . . but whatever he wanted to see, it wasn't there.

Then he turned and ran.

Two

Annis didn't mean to move; it just happened, as if her body had a will of its own. She glanced at Mum, then at Dad; and then, when neither of them met her eyes, she started to run after Zach, stumbling as her foot hit a clump of grass. She was shaking, her stomach burning with an acid surge of fury. The way they just *stood* there – as if they couldn't see how desperate, how miserable he was – as if it was his fault . . .

Mum shouted, 'Annis! *Annis!*'

She slowed to a walk, and turned round, reluctantly.

'Come back here, now! Where on earth do you think you're going?'

Annis felt her mouth get ready to say, *After Zach, of course*, but her vocal cords had frozen in outrage.

'It's time for lunch. I've made it, and we'll sit down and eat it like civilised people, whether or not Zach has decided to throw a tantrum.'

Throw a *tantrum*? She said, 'Mum, he's upset, shouldn't someone – I think I should go after him, just in case –'

'Oh, please, Annis! You know he won't want to talk to you, any more than he wants to talk to us.'

She felt that register inside her, and knew it was true. Zach probably *did* want to be on his own. He hated people talking to him when he was upset. It was just . . . she couldn't bear to sit down and have lunch, as if nothing had happened.

Dad said, 'Well, I'm starving.' He smacked his lips. 'That brie looks wonderful, Helen. I don't think we need to worry about Zach.' His eyes flickered towards Annis and away again.

You bastard, Annis thought, *pretending it's nothing to do with you, all genial and innocent, when it's all your stupid fault.* She bit her lip, in case she said it aloud.

'Come on, Annis.' Mum gave her a tired, unexpected smile, and for a heartbeat Annis felt bad, because you had to admit Mum was having a horrible time, too, and she was trying her best.

'Fine.' Annis walked slowly back to them. There was such a weight of gloom in her stomach she was sure she wouldn't be able to eat anything, but she followed Mum and Dad obediently into the house.

Any normal family, she thought, as she tried to force down enough soup so that Mum wouldn't be offended, *would realise it was a lost cause, trying to act all friendly and cheerful over lunch . . . but we're so used to pretending, we've completely lost track of what any normal family would do. So we make small talk about the weather and the concert they're going to tomorrow in Limoges and whether someone needs to put more chemical* chaussettes *in the swimming pool . . .* She picked the cherry tomatoes carefully out of her salad and wondered whether Zach was OK, while Mum said, 'Well, Edward, the pool filter's *your* area of expertise.'

'I'm sorry, Helen, I don't remember volunteering for general maintenance.'

'You were here when Jamie came to talk you through it, while I was in London. If you recall.'

Oh, for goodness' sake, Annis thought, *why are they such children? How come they can tell me what to do, when they act like they're younger than I am?* She had a wild, babyish impulse to lean forward, open her mouth, and let all the chewed-up cheese slide very slowly over her bottom lip on to the tablecloth. But that wouldn't achieve anything.

'Pudding, Annis? There's crèmes caramel in the fridge, and some lovely apricots.'

'Yeah, thanks. I'll eat it later. I'm just going outside for a bit.' She started to stand up, and saw Mum's mouth open. 'I can put some *chaussettes* in the pool, if you want, when I go past.' It was a cheap tactic, especially as she didn't have any intention of doing it, but it made Mum's expression soften.

'Oh. Oh, all right. Thank you, darling.'

She would have felt bad about leaving them alone together, but it wasn't as if they liked having her around . . . She took a handful of apricots and tore a hunk off the bread when no one was looking. She would have taken some cheese, as well, except that it was practically liquid and she didn't think Zach would fancy sucking it off her fingers. At least she hoped not. She thought, E*w, yuck, Annis, that's really gross* . . .

Dad said, 'If you see Zach –'

But she was out of the door before he finished the sentence, and she definitely wasn't going back to hear the rest. She unhooked her rucksack from the handlebars of Zach's bike and jogged round the edge of the house. She checked quickly that no one had followed her, and then walked straight towards the trees, ignoring the fist of unease that clenched slowly under her diaphragm as she got closer to the ruined house. *Don't be silly. It's fine. Zach'll be down there.*

As she found the path that led downhill into the trees she felt a shudder go over her skin. *It's the shadows*, she thought. *That's all. Just the sudden shade, after coming across the field in broad daylight. It's cooler here, out of the direct sunlight. That's why you're shivering.*

The ruins were just ahead, the fence sagging rustily. She'd never climbed over, but it looked easy – maybe four metres high, but full of holes, so evenly spaced and suitable for footholds they looked like an invitation . . . And you could probably cling to the edge of the *DANGER: DEFENSE D'ENTRER* sign, if you needed an extra handhold. *Zach must do it all the time*, she thought, *unless he's found an easier way in . . .*

She pressed her hands gently against the wire netting, feeling the way it sagged under her weight, and stared through. There were a few bushes, and a grassy line between them that must have been a path once. And there was the house, in a clearing, although from here she could only see a dark doorway, the edge of that ragged wall, and something that might have been a window. Just a house. Nothing terrible, or scary. The kind of house anyone might live in . . . except that –

She didn't know what it was that made her skin creep. It was just a feeling in the air. As if all the tension from Mum and Dad and Zach was collecting here, seeping into the brickwork, until . . . She thought, *Shut up! Shut* up. *You're spooking yourself out for no reason.*

She wished she could see Zach, though. She knew he'd be there, but she would have felt better if she could see him. She didn't like being down here on her own. It was weird, that he *did* . . . But then, he'd always been braver than she was. He liked anything that felt dangerous – roller coasters, rock-climbing, skiing, drugs . . .

Something moved in the ruins. She saw a flash of white – something so white it had to be man-made, like a plastic bag, or a sheet of paper. She craned her head to one side, staring, but she couldn't make it out. Whatever it was, it disappeared behind a thick screen of leaves. She said, 'Zach? Zach!' but the air swallowed her voice, and nothing answered.

She laced her fingers through the netting, and started to climb. It *was* easy; at least, it would have been if she hadn't felt so shaky. She half swung, half slid down the other side of the fence, and followed the path into the clearing where the house was.

She hadn't seen it up close before. It looked . . . could something look powerful, when it looked like you could knock it down with a teaspoon? Her eyes told her it was fragile – no wonder it was *DEFENSE D'ENTRER*, those walls could come down any second – but her skin told her it was strong, stronger than she could imagine. Not the walls, but the place – the feeling of it – the *danger* . . .

She blinked, pushing the irrational fear away, and took a brief mental inventory. Small, derelict house.

27

One door, two windows on the ground floor, two above. Hole in the roof, end corner missing and wall irregular and half fallen down. Top section of wall hanging outwards at precarious angle. No ivy or undergrowth to speak of. Very old-fashioned front door wedged open by damp (presumably) but bizarrely still intact. No graffiti, animal shit, rubbish or similar. Just the walls, bulging threateningly, as if there was nothing holding them up except will power. Zach.

He was standing in front of the ruins, just beside a great green, overgrown hump that might have been a woodpile once. He had a cigarette in his mouth, and a lighter held in both his hands. Annis could hear the click of the flint, again and again, as if he was having problems getting a spark. As she watched he turned slightly, as if he wanted to shelter the flame, and she saw his face.

He was so *white* . . . so white she closed her eyes, automatically. But when she opened them again he hadn't moved; and she hadn't been imagining things. He was so pale it could have been his skin that she'd seen, flashing through the trees. It made her eyes skip when she looked at him, as if her brain couldn't believe it. *No one goes* that *white* . . .

But he was. She saw him manage, finally, to light his cigarette. He looked round, letting his gaze drift, until he saw her and his face changed. He said, 'Anz . . . by Jove . . .'

There was something odd in his voice. She said, 'Zach? I thought . . . I'm sorry, I hope you don't mind, I brought you some lunch . . .' She started to swing the rucksack off her shoulders, to get at the food, but something in his face made her stop. 'What?'

He was smirking. He didn't normally smirk, but that was the only word for it. He said, 'No, nothing, yeah, great, that's, that was really, yeah, really . . .' He gave his head a quick shake, like he was trying to get water out of his ears. 'I mean, nothing. That was kind of you. Thank you.' Then he started to laugh.

Annis kept her voice level, with an effort. 'I thought you might be a bit . . .' You couldn't say *upset* to Zach. He took it as an insult. But she couldn't think of a better word. 'A bit . . . upset, and . . . after what happened, with the book –'

'The . . . ? Oh. Oh yes.'

'So . . .' What was *wrong* with him? 'I take it you're not upset, then.'

He took a drag of his cigarette, scowling at it determinedly as if he was trying not to giggle. 'Not now, thank you. I was a bit . . . you know, miserable, but, no, thanks, I'm fine now, fine, absolutely, yeah, totally fine, yeah –' He cleared his throat suddenly, as if he was making an effort to stop talking.

'You're sure? You're really OK?'

'Yeah, I'm . . . I'm really, *really* OK, I mean, this wonderful thing hap—' He shook his head again, grimacing. 'No, I mean, I'm fine. Fine, fine, fine. Yeah.'

She stood there, watching him. She could feel one of Mum's expressions on her face – suspicion and anger and distrust – and took a deep breath.

Zach gave a loud spurt of laughter. It echoed off the ruins. Annis saw a tiny drift of dust unfurl from a crack in the nearest wall, like smoke. 'Oh, Jesus, sorry, Anz – but you look so serious, standing there like a – like, oh I don't know, but hilarious, oh what can ail thee, knight-at-arms, so haggard and so woe-begone –'

'Zach, for God's sake!'

He caught her eye and pressed his lips together, in a kind of parody of sobriety. 'Sorry. Sorry, Anz.'

'What's the matter with you? I thought – the way you were, with Dad, I thought you'd be all . . . all silent and wintry –'

'Got over it. Like a miracle. Absolute fucking miracle. I feel fine.'

'Right.'

'Come on, then, why don't we go back to the house, have a swim, you fancy a swim? No point moping about here all day, bit of healthy exercise . . .' He took another long drag on his cigarette, winked at her, and strode towards the path to the fence. Annis stepped aside to let him past, but he mirrored her, and when she stepped in the other direction to get out of his way he'd already moved and they were face to face again. 'Hey, Anz, is this some kind of dance? Brilliant . . .'

He launched himself at her. She dodged, out of habit; and he stumbled, caught his foot in a tree-root and fell forward. She heard the breath go out of him, the impact as he hit the ground, cracking his chin on another root. Her own spine tingled in sympathy. She bent to help him up, but stopped before she touched him, because he was laughing helplessly. It wasn't shocked, reflexive laughter – that would have been perfectly normal. It was amazed, mirthful, hiccuping laughter, as if he'd suddenly heard some good news. Or as if . . .

She couldn't believe she'd been so slow. She said,

'You're stoned. You're high.'

'No – no, really, I'm not, not exactly . . .' He carried on trying to say something, but the giggles submerged the consonants and the vowels were left floating meaninglessly on top.

She said again, hearing the words, 'You're stoned.' She took a deep breath. 'You shit. You selfish *shit*.'

'No – seriously, Anz – it's not, don't be, honestly, I'm just a bit –' This time the words dissolved into a noise like steam escaping from a pipe.

She almost kicked him. It took an effort to turn and walk away. She felt the apricots rolling around in the bottom of her rucksack and wanted to cry with fury. She'd been so *worried* – she'd thought, that look on his face as he ripped up the book, like despair, like utter, utter misery, worse than anything – she'd been desperate for him to be OK, she'd wanted to help . . . And all the time, he'd been here, smoking dope until he was off his face. She almost changed her mind and went back to kick him after all.

She climbed the fence, anger giving her movements a kind of unexpected fluency. She hoped Zach was watching. He ought to be impressed.

He shouted, 'Anz! Anz, come on, don't be like that –'

She dropped on to the patch of bare earth on the other side and stood there, listening but not letting herself turn round. Stupid git. She couldn't believe it. She'd never imagined that things could actually get *worse*, but if Mum and Dad caught him like this . . . She couldn't help herself. She spun round and shouted back, 'You bastard, Zach! You promised Mum and Dad – you said you wouldn't take any more drugs! You selfish bastard.'

He laughed. 'Calm down, Anz, nothing's wrong, I'm not even stoned –'

'Oh, yeah, like hell!' She glared at him through the fence. Just looking at him made her eyes ache. It was because he was standing in the sunlight. No, he *wasn't* standing in the sunlight. It was because –

'I promise, cross my heart, hope to die, haven't taken anything, oh no, tell a lie, had a paracetamol yesterday evening.'

She shouted, 'Screw you! *Screw you*.' She heard the echo bounce off the walls, like someone agreeing. Another tongue of dust flicked out from the wall and dispersed, raining slowly to the ground.

'Hey . . .' He gave her a you-know-you-love-me-really grin.

She felt a hopeless surge of warmth, in spite of herself. She couldn't help it; just to have him back, cocky and charming – and infuriating, because she *did* love him really . . . But there was a core of resistance that didn't quite give in. She shook her head, silently.

'Oh, fine, whatever.' The grin widened and he turned away, sauntering back towards the ruins, kicking at the stones on the ground. He *was* stoned, definitely. She could tell from the way he was looking round, peering at everything. He held up one hand in front of his eyes with a kind of awestruck expression. She could have sworn he said, 'Wow . . .' It was like he'd forgotten she was there. In the end he collapsed against the wall, leaning his head back, staring beatifically at the specks of grit showering down from the stonework above. They glinted as they dropped through the sunlight.

32

Annis said, 'Zach . . .'

He smiled, but he didn't answer or turn his head.

'Zach.' She saw something move between the blocks of stone, over his head. It could have been a lizard, or a trickle of sand. She wanted to shout, but suddenly she didn't dare. 'Zach, I think you should come away from that wall.'

'Really? Why?'

'Because it's – look at the way it's *bulging* – it's not *safe* –' She raised her voice, catching herself just too late. It *was* sand, gushing out of the wall like water; she could see it sparkle as it fell. '*Please* –'

He looked up. For the first time he seemed to register the bloated curve of the wall, the way it leant out over his head without any means of support. He said, 'Oh. It's fine, Anz, it's been like this for hundreds of years, I expect, it's not going to –'

'*Zach!*'

There was a movement in the top of the wall above him. Annis's eyes flicked automatically to the place, following the motion, before she understood what she was seeing. A nudge, as the stones settled; a second of stillness; and then, with horrible slow-motion intent, a fragment tumbled forward, out of its mortar. She watched, frozen with horror, as it slid down and out, caught by the arc of the bulge, gathering speed, and flipped down into space, small but deadly as a pebble from a slingshot. She heard her own voice catch in her throat, lost her breath, couldn't think anything but *No, please, it's going to hit* –

It fell, harmlessly, a couple of metres away from Zach's legs.

She felt the sweat start out under her arms and in the small of her back.

Zach laughed. He said, 'You see? I've got a charmed life. You need a silver bullet to kill me . . .'

She managed to find enough air from somewhere to say, 'Zach, please, can you come away from the wall, it's making me nervous.'

He grinned at her, shaking his head, and for an odd, snapshot moment she had time to feel happy again, because he looked the way he used to, carefree, casual, the old balance of affection and mockery in his eyes. Then he pushed himself to his feet and took a deliberate step closer to the wall, craning his head to look at the absurd angle of the stones. He said, 'Look. It's fine. Look, it's fine.' He wasn't exactly shouting, but his voice rang out like a bell. Another trace of dust fell across his face and he brushed it away with the back of his hand. He stretched out, leant a cool, purposeful hand on the stonework, and said, 'Look. Watch me push . . . oh my God, looks like the whole wall's going to go – does it? Or – oh well. Maybe not.' The grin flashed again. 'Yep – I think we can safely say you're shitting yourself for nothing, because –'

She whirled round in disgust and started to walk away.

So she didn't even see it, this time.

Only heard it. Only heard a kind of rattle, a noise like the world shrugging its shoulders, felt the new, cool lick of air on her back, realised mid-step that something was happening, behind her, and she'd better turn round and look . . . Only she took so long turning her head that by the time she was looking in the right place there was nothing moving except a

34

blank, dense veil of dust. She could just see a few slow blades of grass drawing themselves back up to their full height, the last little fragments of stone finding somewhere to sit. It was as if somewhere in the space between hearing and looking round she'd missed the middle of it. There must have been a moment . . . A whole *wall*, collapsing – it must have shaken the ground, must have been so loud anyone would know, just from the noise . . . It must have been huge, dramatic, a hundred years' worth of weight finally letting itself go . . . but she'd missed it.

And perhaps there'd been a moment, too, when Zach had screamed, or at least there would have been the noise of the impact, stone hitting something weaker than itself . . . Even – she thought, with a strange clarity – even the noise of bone crunching inwards, or flesh giving under pressure, or the air coming out of his lungs. But all she'd heard was that innocuous, *courteous* rattle, like the wall clearing its throat; as if all the really bad things happened in silence. As if the silence in her head was so loud it drowned out the noise.

She stood still and looked at the place where she could see Zach's T-shirt, half blanked out by the dust, like a drawing behind tracing paper. She could just see the shape of his body, behind the scattered stones. She thought, *I knew that was going to happen. I knew it.*

The side of the house gaped open. The end wall had gone.

And she never knew, for sure, what she'd done, in the next few seconds. She could only guess, later.

She must have screamed Zach's name. Screamed

and screamed, as if the sheer power of her voice could turn back time. She must have launched herself forward, praying, *believing* that if she ran fast enough she could get there before the stones hit him and knocked him flat, she could pull him away before the wall collapsed, she could shield him from the impact . . . She must have run towards the fence, must have run faster than she'd ever run in her life, falling and stumbling, gasping for breath, still screaming his name. She must have thrown herself at the wire mesh, clawing at it, fighting it. And somehow, through the haze of momentum and desperation and pain she must have managed to drag herself up, staring towards that blue-red shape of jeans and T-shirt, got high enough to see –

She must have known, then. She must have seen the huddle of stone at the base of the wall, or rather where the wall had been; must have seen the chunk of rock, bigger than a football, that lay beside Zach's hand, as if he was reaching out for it. And she must have understood, must have heard the silence spreading out, telling her the world had changed; must, *must* have seen the impossible angle of Zach's neck, the way his head didn't match up with his shoulders, before she even got halfway up the fence.

Then she knew. She knew.

Three

She stopped where she was, hanging halfway up the fence, staring at Zach's body until the blotches of colour shimmered and ran together. She hung there, fingers laced tight through the wire, face pressed against the mesh, until the pain in her hands got too much to bear and she let herself slide back down.

She closed her eyes. But when she opened them again she could still see the scattered debris, and the blue of Zach's jeans, the crumpled red of his T-shirt. That lump of rock, just beyond his reach – jagged, sitting in a dent in the ground as if it had been there for years . . . She took a deep breath and started to climb the fence again. This time it was harder. Because she had time to think about it, probably; or because she was taking her time, taking it slower than she needed to. Zach was going to sit up, any minute now, before she got to the top. There was no point climbing over, because he was fine. He was going to move, roll over, start to swear . . .

She swung herself carefully over the last bit of fence and slithered down, landing awkwardly. The sounds she made were very distinct, like they'd been pre-recorded. She took a step forward. It felt weird that she had to walk, moving her feet one by one. And that the ground stayed where it was, so steady. It was almost like this was all *real*.

She picked her way through the debris, threading her way towards him. There was a thick smell of dust in the air. She could feel tiny traces of grit between her teeth and on her eyelashes. Then she knelt down next to him, took a deep breath, and made herself look.

His head was bent horribly to one side, his eyes closed. One hand was thrown out sideways, as if he was stretching for something on the ground. The other was trapped underneath him. It looked uncomfortable. And his face – the shape of his skull . . . Annis stared, feeling nothing. There wasn't much blood; only a dark wetness in his hair above his temple, and a long trickle from his mouth that seemed such a cliché she caught herself looking over her shoulder for the hidden camera. And his face was still that strange colour, full of light, only not daylight. He didn't look how Annis had imagined dead people would look, but –

He wasn't dead. She saw his eyelids flicker.

For a second she froze, watching the tiny, miraculous movement. Then, suddenly, she was herself again, liquid with relief. *Oh, thank God!* she thought. *Thank God . . .* but when she looked back at his face the warmth drained away. The angle of his neck, the contour of his skull . . . He was all broken. Annis forced her eyes downwards. She stared at the loose ends of his shoelaces, trailing, undone, underneath his shoe, and thought: *He's going to die. He's not dead yet, but he's going to die. He's hurt too badly. There's nothing anyone can do.* A voice in her head added distantly, *How weird, that I can tell that just from looking at his shoelaces* . . .

She knew she should do something. But she couldn't move. She thought, *I can't leave him. I should go for help – but he's my* brother – *I can't leave him to die here, on his own* . . . She didn't believe in God, but she prayed: *don't let him die. Please. I'll do anything. Anything at all. Please don't let him die.* But it was like she was falling, grabbing helplessly at nothing. *Zach . . . please, Zach, don't die, please* . . .

His hand moved, opening into the air, like he was letting something go. Even his palm had that same elusive pallor, like it was transparent. Annis stared at it, her thoughts moving too slowly. *My brother Zach is going to die. Right here, right now, in this awful sinister place. I can't do anything. No one can.*

But he's my brother . . . please, please . . . She reached out to touch his hand; then drew back, feeling sick all the way down to her knees. *Zach* . . .

I can't let it happen. I won't, I won't – no –

Her brain jolted back into normal speed with a shock. God, what was she *thinking*? Just sitting here, staring, while –? Go, go, go! She sprang up and ran, struggling up the fence again, scrabbling in her pocket for her mobile before she even got down the other side. She flipped it open, half stumbling when she took her eyes off the ground, throwing out her other hand to the side to steady herself. 999. No – *oh God* – what was the number, in France? She thought, *Oh Jesus, you* idiot, *Annis, you bloody* bloody *idiot, how can you not know the number for an ambulance?* She heard herself panting in great sobs and didn't know if she was crying. *Come on, then, run. Get up to the house, to Mum and Dad* – or anyone, anyone would do. *Mon frère – il est mort.* But no, he wasn't, not yet, he *wasn't* . . . She was halfway up the hill, throwing herself forward, knowing she *was* crying now, only there wasn't time to think about it. Zach was going to die, and she couldn't do anything. *I can't bear it*, she thought, *I need him, I can't live without him, can't bear it, if he dies . . . And I'll never forgive him, he knew the ruins were dangerous, Zach, you stupid bastard, how could you, get high and then lean on that wall, pushing it like that, you were showing off, you stupid, you stupid, stupid –*

'Annis!'

She carried on running, sobbing, feeling tears and spit and snot splash down her T-shirt. She thought, *I have to get an ambulance. I won't think about anything else. Just the ambulance. I have to –*

'Annis! *Annis!*'

She twisted her head to look, mid-step, not pausing. *I have to get an –*

Zach.

She stumbled and found her balance again, still staring at him. He stood there, a little way away, not even out of breath from running after her . . . She stared for so long it felt like the sun had moved, like all the shadows in the wood had swung round, deepening and lengthening. *Thank you*, she thought. *Thank you.*

Then she said, 'But – what – you –'

He said, 'Where the hell are you off to?'

It took a long time for the words to make sense. Annis had to repeat them in her head, slowly, syllable by syllable, before she understood what they meant.

All the time Zach was glaring at her, eyebrows raised, like he'd caught her running off to tell on him.

'Ambulance.' She cleared her throat and took a deep breath, trying to remember how to construct a sentence. 'I'm going to get an ambulance.'

'What for?'

Annis blinked. She thought hazily, *Maybe it's* me. *Maybe* I'm *on drugs.*

He said again, 'What do you want an ambulance for, Annis?' His voice was too loud, hitting a strident note.

'For – for you.' She tried to keep her own voice steady.

'For *me*?' He laughed, like an actor pretending to cough, and held his arms out wide. 'Look, no problems. I'm fine, Anz. Why would I want an ambulance?'

Because you should be dead, Annis thought. *Because you were smashed to bits by the wall collapsing. I saw you, you had blood on your* – and there still was blood on his face, starting to dry and crack like red paint. She frowned, craning to see the side of his head, where the dent had been, the wet spines of hair . . . but he moved, shifting backwards into the shade of a tree, so she couldn't make it out. She said, 'The wall . . . Zach, the wall collapsed . . .'

'Yeah. Cool, right?' He smiled. Then he scrubbed at his face with the back of his arm, as if he'd suddenly felt the blood caking on his skin.

'The wall collapsed and . . .' Her vocal cords stalled and she had to start again. 'The wall collapsed and – and, and –' Oh, for goodness' *sake*! 'Zach, the stone must have hit you, I saw you on the ground, you were –' Thirty seconds ago she would have said, *You were dying*. But now . . .

'Yes. I got out of the way just in time. One of the stones gave me a bit of a clonk on the head, but nothing serious.' His smile stretched wider and wider until she knew he was lying. But he *couldn't* be – because he was standing there, after all, he *wasn't* dying . . .

She felt the wetness on her cheeks, suddenly, the damp fabric of her T-shirt sticking to her front. She wiped her forearm over her face, taking longer than she needed to. When she lowered her arm he was standing with his hands in his pockets.

She said, in a rush, 'Stop it, Zach, I saw you – the blood – stop mucking around, it's not funny.'

'I'm not mucking around. I'm fine. Look –' He held out his arms theatrically, did a kind of little dancing twirl so she could see. 'No marks.'

And he was right. Almost. Apart from the darkened blotch of hair, sticking up spikily into the air. Everything she'd seen – everything that told her he was hurt, badly, *badly* hurt – it had gone. Or she'd imagined it.

She said, very slowly and clearly, 'The wall fell down. And a bit of rock – that big piece of stone – hit you. You were lying on the ground with a broken neck.'

He laughed. Jesus, he *laughed*. 'Oh, come on, Anz! With a broken neck? I don't think so, somehow. The stone just glanced off me. I wasn't even unconscious.'

'Just glanced off –?'

'Did you *see* it hit me? Did you?' A pause. He wasn't laughing any more. 'Well then. Stop being stupid. And don't you dare tell anyone about this. Mum or Dad. If they find out we've been down here they'll –'

That made her look at him sharply; because he'd stopped short before he said, *kill me* . . .

He didn't meet her eyes. 'Let's go. I'm bored.' And sauntered away with his hands in his pockets, with the casual slouching walk that was a put-down in itself. She felt her breathing hiccup and falter, as if she was going to start crying again. It was the heat, and the confusion, and having sprinted all this way, uphill . . . She turned away from Zach and took a moment to calm down, looking down through the trees at the fragments of the house that showed through the leaves. It would have been beautiful in the sunlight, if it wasn't for the power coming off it, like cold . . .

There was someone inside.

She saw the movement first; something catching her eye, something that wasn't just the tremble of leaves or a bird . . . She narrowed her eyes and leant forward, putting up her hand to block the sunlight. Someone there – a shadowy shape, moving. He was in the doorway, looking round, standing in the darkness so she couldn't see his face.

'Zach. Zach!' She took a step, squinting through the branches. 'There's someone down there. There's someone in the house.'

She heard the twigs crack underfoot as he turned and ran back to her. He said, 'No. There isn't. There can't be.'

'Look. *Look*, Zach, there –' She pointed. But she couldn't see properly. There was only the shape of a person, dark against the darkness inside the house;

43

and her sense, clear as a bell, that someone was looking back at them. 'We should –'

'We should what? Anz, there's no one there, you're imagining things.'

She shot him a glance, hissing at him through her teeth. 'Zach! Look – can't you see?' But when she looked again she couldn't see anything. She thought, *Oh God, maybe he's gone back inside* . . . 'If there's someone – I mean, there's someone down there, and it's *dangerous*. The wall collapsed, Zach, anything could happen – and he's inside, whoever it is, the floor might be rotten, or . . . oh, for heaven's *sake*!'

'There's nobody there, Annis. There's nobody.'

His voice. Something in his voice. And when she turned round it was in his face, too, whatever it was; something that didn't make sense.

'I'm going back down,' she said. 'There's someone in that house, and it could go any minute. I don't care if you're too selfish to let them kill themselves, but I don't want it on my conscience. OK?'

'Don't – don't – you can't –' It was desperation, suddenly showing through, like metal under paint, for no reason. 'Annis! You can't go back down there – there's nobody, I promise, I was in there, I'd have seen them – it's too dangerous, and you're only imagining – come on, Anz, don't be so fucking stupid.'

It wasn't like she *wanted* to go. But there was someone there, whatever Zach said, and those walls . . . She said, 'Sorry, Zach. But you can't stop me.'

'You stupid little cow! You don't have a clue, do you?' He grabbed for her, closing his fingers roughly round her wrist. 'You listen to me –'

There was a crack, like a glass breaking, and a flash

that made the trees stand out like a stage-set, even in broad daylight; and pain that shot down her side into her toes. She pulled away, caught her breath, and started to laugh with the shock. 'What was *that*?'

Zach blinked. He glanced down at his hands. Then his jaw clenched and he put them back in his pockets, pushing down so hard his fists dragged at the denim. He said, 'I have no idea.'

Annis had the sudden conviction that it was the first true thing he'd said, since she saw him running after her. She squeezed her hand between her knees, trying to lessen the sting. 'Ow. *Ow*.'

'Static, I guess.'

It had been stronger than any shock she'd ever had from static electricity. It was more like the electric fence she'd touched when she was small, which stung and jolted her backwards and gave her nightmares. But she was too busy getting her breath back to argue.

Zach said, 'It's probably nothing. I mean . . . it's nothing. Lots of storms round here, I expect it builds up . . . or maybe it's my trainers . . .' He frowned into the space behind her shoulder. 'Did it hurt?'

She straightened up, staring at him. 'Yes. Why, didn't you –?'

'I – yes. Of course. A bit. I mean, yeah, sure, I just wondered if it hurt you too.'

She thought, *He's lying again. But why would he lie?* She said, 'It hurt quite a lot, actually.'

'Yeah. Me too. I *said*.'

She flexed her wrist, rolling it back and forth until it felt normal again. He was watching her. In the end he gave her a smile that didn't reach his eyes and said, 'I didn't mean to shout at you.'

45

''Course you didn't.'

'Just don't – don't do anything stupid, will you, Anz? I mean, I had a – a close shave down there . . . Please.'

She bit her lip and wondered when he'd last said *please* to her.

'Promise me you won't. Please. Just keep away from the place. Mum and Dad were right.' He laughed, without amusement. 'Much as I hate to admit it.'

'I . . .' She looked involuntarily over her shoulder. She was so sure she'd seen someone. 'Zach . . .'

'Please.' He tilted his head to one side and put on his pleading look. 'I'm only thinking of you, Anz.' He reached out for her shoulders, as if he wanted to pull her closer to him. For a split second she felt his fingertips graze her skin; but before they had time to grip there was a sickening jolt, and another deep flash of pain stabbed right down to her feet.

She recoiled, hissing through her teeth. 'Bloody *hell*, Zach!' She leant forward, trying to get her breath back to normal. This time he didn't say anything.

When she straightened up again she saw that he was gazing past her, at the ruins. She thought, *He's so white . . . really, really white, so white it's uncanny . . . Normally when he's ill he goes pale green.*

Zach said, 'I'm going back to the house.' He didn't wait for her to answer before he strode off. He was moving oddly, as if his coordination had gone. He didn't look behind, but there was something in the set of his shoulders that told her he wanted to, desperately; that every step forward was an effort.

But he'd forgotten to make her promise not to go back down to the ruins.

Not that she wanted to. She didn't like doing it. As she walked towards the fence she felt the same menacing heaviness in the air, the tension building up like a storm. And knowing there was someone there – someone who'd been watching them from the doorway, standing in the darkness, so they couldn't see him . . . well, that didn't help. But she was determined, because it was dangerous inside the house, and it wouldn't be fair to let someone have an accident, when she could help. It just wouldn't be *fair*. She swallowed the taste of cowardice that rose like acid into the back of her mouth and made herself keep going.

Although, when she got to the fence . . . the house was empty. She could tell from the quality of the quiet in the air, the way you could tell whether someone had just left a room. There wasn't anybody there. It wasn't just that she couldn't see anyone; she could feel it on her skin, that she was alone. Apart from birds, and lizards and trees. *I suppose*, she thought, *what I mean is, there's no one human* . . .

So she wasn't sure why she climbed the fence, except that she would have felt pathetic just turning round and going back up the hill. And once she was on the other side, she wasn't sure why she walked towards the door until she was standing in the shorter grass in front of it, like a guest about to ring the doorbell. She wasn't sure why she said, 'Hello? Is there – I mean, *est-ce qu'il y a quelqu'un* . . . ?'

There wasn't any answer, anyway.

She hadn't been expecting one. She really hadn't. It was just to check – just in case. *'S'il vous plaît* . . . ? *Je pense que, la maison, c'est dangereux* . . .'

Nothing. Nobody there. No movement, no shadowy shape in the doorway. Maybe there had been – yes, there *had*, she'd *seen* him – but he'd gone. He'd probably realised for himself that the house was in danger of falling down. It wasn't exactly a revelation. A wall collapsing was a bit of a giveaway.

The memory of it came back to her, with an odd, nauseous jerk. She'd almost *forgotten* . . . no, not forgotten, but it had sunk to the bottom of her mind. It surfaced now, unwelcome: that insidious patter of the stonework loosening, the green of leaves in her field of vision as she swung round, the colours of Zach's clothes, half hidden by the fallen debris . . . It couldn't have happened the way she remembered it. Zach was telling the truth. *Well, of course*, she thought, *why would he lie? And he's walking and talking, when according to you he should be dead, so, on balance, I think his version of events has the edge, don't you?*

She walked over to the fallen wall, very gingerly – although she knew this was probably the safest place to be, now that it was only a heap of rubble. When she closed her eyes she could still see Zach's body, the angle of the neck, the broken face, like a dropped dinner-plate, the blood . . . the blood was real. Yes. The stone had glanced off him, he'd said; so the blood was OK, she could work with the blood . . . and the rest of it was only her imagination. *And after all*, she said to herself, *I was in a bit of a state. I'd been shouting at Zach for getting stoned, and I knew the ruins were dangerous. I was expecting Zach to get hurt, so that's what I saw.*

She took another step; reached out to touch the stones . . . but she couldn't do it. Her whole body protested, forcing her to draw back. She thought, *I can feel . . . this place . . . It's – it's not malevolence . . . but something wrong, somewhere, like a kind of dislocation, a gap that ought not to be here. Like there's something switched on, when it shouldn't be . . .*

OK. That was it. She was going back up to the house to have a swim and a nap before dinner. She'd had enough.

She looked round, taking her leave of the place, feeling so relieved that she wouldn't ever have to come back that she almost didn't mind being there. *And,* she thought smugly, *chances are Zach won't come back, either.* She smiled at the thought. He'd learnt his lesson. Which was good, because she'd never been quite at ease, all those afternoons, knowing he was down here on his own. From now on maybe he'd be more sociable, and Mum and Dad would see he was making an effort, and . . .

That was when she knew there was someone behind her.

She didn't know which of her senses told her, or if any of them did. She only knew that there was someone in the doorway. Knew it as clearly and precisely as if someone had tapped the back of her neck.

She froze. She wanted to turn round, but she wasn't brave enough. She didn't think she was brave enough to move at all, but her legs surprised her, with the purposeful way they took her towards the fence and lifted her feet into the holes in the wire. She was scared she'd panic, so she started to do her eight-times-table in her head, clinging to how ridiculous it was that she couldn't remember whether three eights were twenty-four or twenty-six. She knew, in a weird detached way that was separate from the fear, that she wouldn't have been so afraid if she hadn't felt so alone, before – alone with the birds and lizards, the only human being in the place . . .

She was over the fence. *Good. Now walk. That's all. Walk. Five eights are forty. Easy. Six eights are forty-eight. Seven eights are –*

He was coming after her.

Oh God, oh God . . . The detached voice in her head wanted to know how she knew it was a boy, but she didn't care, she *did* know, a boy, definitely, she'd seen . . . It wasn't important, anyway, he was following her, that was all that mattered. He was coming for her – he was going to catch her . . . she felt a mad, irrational rush of horror. She couldn't hear him climbing the fence, but she knew he was there, right behind her. She could almost feel him breathing.

She felt her knees drop to the ground. Her legs were folded underneath her. *No, no, I have to run, please* . . . She sensed the boy behind her, close, so close –

She couldn't bear it. She was nearly sick with terror. She closed her eyes.

When she opened them he was going up the hill in front of her, the way Zach had gone. He didn't look back.

The world wavered and went dim, like someone had covered the sun. She felt numb. Everything was draped in a kind of veil, sparkling, but dark, like black gauze . . . lovely, but . . . she felt weird. Sleepy, with relief.

It was the heat. She'd got dehydrated. She put her

head on her knees and took deep breaths.

She stayed like that for a few minutes, then raised her head and looked round. Her eyes were back to normal; she felt tired, but OK. She thought, *You stupid girl, letting yourself get too hot, all that running, up and down and up again, no wonder you're feeling funny. Running away from shadows* . . . She stared at the path leading up through the trees, the way the patches of shade flickered and solidified. She must have imagined the boy . . . otherwise, where was he going? Yes, that was it. Maybe the first time she had seen someone in the doorway, but when she was down there on her own . . . She thought, *Well? Did you see him, that time? No, you didn't. You thought you sensed someone standing behind you. And then you thought you saw someone overtake you, but it was only the trees moving, casting shadows on the path. Look. Doesn't it look like someone running?*

She laughed, weakly, because really, when it came down to it, she was just scared of the dark.

She took her rucksack off her shoulders and rootled in it for an apricot. Low blood sugar, that was her problem. The velvet of the skin felt reassuringly real under her teeth.

And then she stopped, staring up the hill, the way the boy had gone.

It wasn't anything, really. But . . .

The grass, at the side of the path . . . As she watched, the long blades curled downwards, wilting, shrivelling, in a kind of accelerated movement that didn't look real. And the leaves on the trees above . . . browning, curling, starting to drop already, although the branches further from the path were still green. As if someone had poured weedkiller along the path, and the plants were soaking it up. Even then, surely it would take longer for something to die? No, it was more like the grass had been scorched, the moisture sucked away so quickly from the leaves that they rattled in the wind, desiccated. There was something eerie in the noise they made.

She shivered, dropping her apricot half-eaten, staring at the withered grass. It had to be some kind of natural phenomenon. But she couldn't quite make herself believe it.

She raised her head and stared along the path. But there was no one there.

Four

The field behind the house was full of pages, yellowing with age, as if they were growing in the grass. As she sat where she'd sat that morning, Annis could count eleven – no, twelve – sheets of paper. One of them lifted into the breeze, flipping over and dropping again. There was another, at arm's length, and she reached out for it. The poem on it looked like it was unravelling. 'A Lecture Upon the Shadow.' She started to read it, but she couldn't concentrate, and anyway it was all in old-fashioned spelling. When she turned the page over there was another poem – 'The Expiration' – and a vertical note in pencil. She turned the page through ninety degrees to read it. It said, *cf Marvell, p. 26*. Then there was a space, and a scrawled addition: *Helen train 8.30 TAKE NOTES HAMLET LECTURE & tea bags*. It made her smile, thinking of Dad, when he was a student, grabbing the nearest book to write on and never even bothering to rub it out. It was funny, how similar Dad's handwriting was to Zach's; you could see why Dad thought Zach had been writing in his books . . .

She folded the page into a square and pushed it into her pocket, suddenly not wanting to look at it any more. She could remember the day of Zach's GCSE results, when Dad told Zach he could borrow his books without asking. It was an announcement over dinner, as Dad was opening the second bottle of champagne. He'd filled Zach's glass, then he'd swapped a smile with Mum, and said, 'Well, Zach, your mother and I have discussed this, and we both think you're a responsible adult, and so I'd like to give you a little token of my esteem . . .' Zach had sat up straighter, looking hopeful, so Annis could tell he was crossing his fingers for a car. When Dad announced that – ta-*dah*! – Zach could read his books without asking, there'd been a tiny moment of silence, while they looked at each other. And then, simultaneously, they'd cracked up, laughing uproariously until Mum caught Annis's eye and shook her head. Annis was amazed. If she'd been in Zach's position, she wouldn't have laughed like that. She'd have said, *What? That's a token of your esteem? What would you have given me if I'd* failed? But Zach thought it was hilarious; and later, when he'd calmed down, Annis thought he was pleased, even if it wasn't a car . . . He never said so, but you could tell from the way he grinned to himself when he didn't think anyone was looking. As if Dad letting him read his books really meant something.

We were happy. Weren't we? Zach was happy . . .

She couldn't bear it. She leapt to her feet, ran towards the nearest piece of paper and picked it up. Then the next, and the next, and the next, until she was standing in the middle of the field holding a handful of ragged pages in a hot, damp hand. She glanced down at the top one – 'A Valediction:

Forbidding Mourning' – and shoved the whole lot into her pocket. It made her hip bulge, like a tumour.

And all of a sudden, for no reason, she could see the way Zach had lain there, a few hours ago, his skull knocked out of shape, the trickle of blood running sideways down his cheek . . . She said to herself, *He's fine, you saw him, he's fine* . . . but she couldn't get rid of the picture. A wave of panic came over her, as if she was back there again, crouching next to him. He was *dead* . . . no, he wasn't, of course not, but – if he really was dead, if he really had died, what would she *do?* It made her start to shake, just thinking about it. *I couldn't bear it*, she thought, *if Zach died, I'd – I'd . . . He can't die. He's the clever, talented one. He's brilliant . . . if it was just me left – the dull, ugly one.*

For heaven's sake, Annis! She clenched her fist and hit the wad of paper in her pocket, hard. *Oh yes. That's right.* He's *the perfect one, the one that everyone adores, with his exam results and floppy hair, fooling everyone, all charismatic and witty and so charming . . . It's not fair, it's not* fair *– I can't win, either way . . .*

If only it was just exam results – or just being talented, or just being charming. She could have coped with that. If there was *something* she could be better at – if she was brave, or exciting, or just somehow *worthwhile* . . . but there wasn't. She thought, *So what do you expect me to do, Mum? I've* got *to worship him. It's either that or hate him. And you and Dad seem to hate him already.*

And anyway, Mum had only said that because of Dad – because they all hated one another, these days.

It was different, before Cecilia-the-tart. Back then, Mum and Dad had worshipped Zach just as much as – *I don't* worship *him*, she thought, *but if that's what Mum thinks, well, whatever* – they'd *worshipped* Zach as much as she did. More. And they weren't the only ones. Like the night of the school play, when the whole audience was on its feet – and everyone knew, even though the whole cast was bowing, you *knew* they were applauding Zach, because of the way they'd coughed and shuffled before he came on, and then the electric, pin-drop silence as soon as he appeared. That roar of applause – and Penny whooping right in her ear . . . Annis had had a fight with Zach a few days before, because she'd said *Peter Pan* was babyish, honestly, why would anyone choose it for a second-ary-school play . . . but at the end she'd been too shaken to do anything but clap, as hard as she could, until her hands stung. Mum had leant over and shouted, 'Wasn't he *wonderful*?' above the noise, but she hadn't even been able to open her mouth to answer.

And afterwards, when Zach came out to speak to them, still in make-up, and there was a rush of people, Zach's mates and a couple of Upper Sixth boys, all giving him congratulatory punches, slapping him on the back, making jokes . . . 'Nice one, Randall, love the make-up – give Tiger Lily one from me, mate – so, if we want fairy dust, we come to you, right?' But they weren't taking the piss out of *him*; they thought he was fantastic. *And he was*, Annis thought. *He was extraordinary. He flew* . . .

Penny had been there at her elbow, trying to catch Zach's eye, but Zach turned straight to Annis, with a level, intent look on his face like he cared what she thought. She hadn't managed to do more than nod, and mumble, "S really good, Zach,' but he'd watched her and smiled, like he'd understood. She was so relieved at not having to say anything else that when Elliot Scott came down the corridor towards them and Penny leant in and whispered, 'He's so fit! 'Course, not as fit as Zach, I mean, but . . .' Annis could roll her eyes and grimace, like she felt normal. She couldn't decide whether to say, 'Yeah, liked him better with the hook, though,' or, 'Penny, that's *revolting*, Zach's my *brother*, hands off,' but in the end she didn't have time for either before Elliot had barged through the other boys and grabbed Zach playfully by the back of the neck. 'Oi, you coming to Vanessa's party –' he shot a quick grin at Annis and Penny – 'er, the, er, the party, where you'll be drinking *soft drinks* all night, because you're *under age*, right, Randall?'

Zach twisted out of his grip, laughing. 'Yeah, sure.'

'Great. Let's go.' Elliot made a sweeping gesture with his hand and leered at Penny and Annis. 'All right, fans, I know you're keen, but we have to live our lives, you know? Time for little girls to go home to bed while the big boys go out to play . . .'

Annis clenched her jaw and gave him a big wide great-white-shark smile. Penny said, 'Yeah, Elliot, we're just going, but we just wanted to say you were *amazing*, you were so, you know, you were so *amazing* . . .'

'Oh, well, you know, just comes naturally . . .' He winked at her. 'You must be Zach's sister, right?'

Annis saw Zach snort, then straighten his face again, hurriedly. She said, 'No, that's me. I'm Annis.'

'Anyway,' Penny said, 'you were just –'

'Amazing, yeah, you said,' Elliot said.

'Yeah,' Annis said, smiling up at him sweetly. 'You were really, *really* good. Almost as good as Zach.' She caught Zach's eye; he shook his head slightly, but he was trying not to laugh.

Elliot blinked and frowned, as if he thought he'd misheard. 'Oh. Right. Thanks.' He glanced round at the other boys, his face turning red. 'Er . . . Let's be off, then, gents, shall we? Time and limited amounts of beer wait for no man . . . See you later, girls.' He gave Annis a final stare, then swaggered off down the corridor.

Penny hissed, '*Annis.* That was so *rude.*'

'True, though.'

'That's not the *point* –' Penny stopped, because Zach was still standing there, waving at the others to go on without him. 'Oh, *hi*, Zach.'

'Come to the party, Annis. I mean, and you, too, Penny, of course,' he added, but then his eyes flicked back to Annis. 'It'll be fun. You know Vanessa, anyway, don't you? She won't mind.'

'What, us?' Her cheeks flared with a great surge of pleasure. She willed the blood inwards, away from the skin. 'But isn't it time for little girls to go home to bed?' she said, as witheringly as she could manage.

Zach shook his head, grinning. 'I know, he's a tosser, what can I say? But you should come. It'll be fun.'

Penny said, 'That'd be great. We'd love to.'

Annis shrugged, pressing her lips together, playing it cool, so she didn't show how proud she was that he'd asked her. 'Yeah, might be OK, I suppose . . . I'll phone Mum, let them know we're with you.'

'Great. Come on, then. *Fans*.' He jogged down the corridor, whistling to them over his shoulder. 'Follow me. Second to the right, and straight on till morning . . .'

And she'd thought – she remembered thinking: *I don't deserve this, I'm so, so lucky, that he's my brother* . . . feeling it like heat on her face, basking in the glory like a cat in sunlight. Even if it was only *reflected* glory – it didn't matter, did it? He was her brother. He wanted her to come to the party. He didn't mind her tagging along. She could have cried with gratitude.

Penny said, 'Wow, he is so *cool*. You're so *lucky*, my brothers hate my guts.'

And then they'd gone to the party.

Annis watched a last errant page of *The Poems of John Donne* drift across the grass, carried by the wind until it slipped down the hill in a current of air, towards the valley. It looked beautiful, in the evening light . . . sort of carefree.

All right, she thought. *So I worshipped him. So I still do. So bloody what?*

'Annis! Aaaa-niiiis!'

Mum, calling her in for dinner. She turned away from the dipping sun, trying to keep the sky inside her head, like a gold screen in front of her thoughts. It shielded her from the pictures that wouldn't leave her alone: Zach, on stage, glittering in the spotlight; Zach ripping Dad's book, tearing it apart. And Zach dead, on the ground, his head tilted at that sinister angle . . . She thought, *Shut up. Zach is not dead. You know he isn't. Stop it.*

'Darling, did you hear me? Time for dinner!'

She shouted, 'Yes, I heard, I'm just coming,' and ran towards the house.

The silence was back again; like the room was filled with hundreds of invisible glass balloons. Annis sat as still as she could and looked down at her plate, keeping her elbows tucked in, in case she moved too quickly and smashed one of them. *Why is it*, she thought, *that we have lost the ability to make noise? Just ordinary, amiable, not-really-listening-to-each-other noise. It's either silent or a battlefield, there's nothing in between . . .*

Mum said, 'Did you have a nice afternoon, sweet-heart?'

There was a pause. Annis waited for Zach to answer; but he stayed silent, his face turned slightly towards the window, eyes narrowed as if he was listening for something. In the end Annis said, 'Are you asking me? Or Zach?' *Presumably not Dad*, she wanted to add, *because you don't call him* sweetheart *any more*.

'Yes. Well, both of you, really. How was your walk?'

Zach turned to look at Annis. She didn't mean to look back, but suddenly she was staring straight into his eyes. She choked on a bit of pasta.

'Are you all right, darling?' Mum leant across the corner of the table. 'Can you breathe? Do you want me to bang you on the back?'

Annis spluttered, gasping for breath, then said, 'No. Fine. Thanks. Nice weather. Walk fine,' which was all she could manage. She took a gulp of red wine and hoped Mum would drop the subject.

'How about you, Zach, darling?'

Zach shrugged, loading his fork with penne as if he was trying to see how many he could spear at once. 'Same. Uneventful.' He glanced at the window again edgily, as if he could see something outside.

'Splendid,' Mum said, beaming as if *uneventful* was the best possible thing Zach could have said.

There was a pause. The noise of chewing was so loud it was starting to put Annis off her food. She fiddled with her fork, not looking at anyone.

Mum swallowed and took a sip of water, and another, like she wasn't thirsty, just uncomfortable. In the end she shot a sidelong look at Zach, went back to her food, and said, with a kind of strained casualness, 'You look a bit peaky, love. Are you all right?'

Zach shut his eyes, so briefly Annis thought she might have imagined it. Then he said, 'I'm fine.'

Dad said, 'Your mother's right. You look off-colour.'

'Well, I'm not ill. OK? I said I'm fine.'

'You're as white as a sheet.' Dad made it sound like an accusation.

Zach didn't answer. He shrugged tightly and stared at the clump of compressed pasta on his fork.

'Strange,' Dad said, in his I'm-not-drawing-any-conclusions voice. 'Nice healthy lifestyle, swimming, no pollution, good food . . . And somehow you manage to get ill.'

Zach hissed through his teeth, then looked up. 'What are you saying, Dad? My immune system is ungrateful? Not exactly my fault, is it? Unless you think I've *made* myself –' He stopped, with a quick mirthless laugh, like a hiccup. 'Oh, I see. Right.'

Mum shot a quick glance at Dad, then back at Zach. 'Darling . . .'

Dad said, 'I suppose you thought we wouldn't notice?'

Mum said, 'Edward –'

'I'm sorry, Helen, but I'm sick of it. I'm fucking tired of it. We slave our guts out trying to sort things out, and the snotty little fucker –'

'*Edward* –'

'– thinks he can smoke himself shit-faced without us even noticing. Well, let me tell you, you rude, selfish little git, we're not fucking stupid, OK? You've got a fucking nerve, after everything we've done for you, you *dare* to sit there like you haven't done anything wrong –'

Zach tilted his head to one side, tapping his fork on the side of his plate. His knuckles had gone even whiter than before. 'After everything you've done for me, Dad? *After everything you've done* . . . ? Like –'

Annis shouted, 'Stop it! Stop it, Dad, you've already – just shut up, please, both of you, just *shut up.*'

And they *did* shut up. It surprised her; she hadn't really expected anyone to notice her. She looked around at their faces – shocked, like, *Wow, Annis can talk* – and took a deep breath. 'We went for a walk and then we had a swim, and I'd know if he'd taken anything, and he hasn't, have you, Zach?'

Zach didn't say anything.

'Come on, Mum, Dad, please, stop getting at him, he's been feeling a bit rough all day, haven't you –' she didn't dare to catch Zach's eye – 'and it's just the weather or something, we, um . . .' She struggled for plausible detail. 'Maybe it's the sun, because we were, I noticed how ill he looked, we'd been in the ruins, and –' Oh no. Oh *bugger*. She started talking again, as rapidly as she could, without taking a breath. 'Then we came up and the weather was, I mean the sun was really, I think maybe –'

Mum said, 'You went down to the ruins? You've been in the ruins?'

Too late.

Dad said, 'You stupid little *idiots*! I can't believe – after we told you – those ruins are –'

'Dangerous . . . ?' Annis started to laugh. She couldn't help it. She knew it was a bad move, but she just couldn't help it. Dangerous? *Really*? The kind of place where a wall might collapse at any moment?

'Shut up, Annis.' Zach glared at her. His pulse was racing in his temple.

She took a deep breath, trying to master her giggles. *Come on, Annis, it's not funny, you know it's not funny*. 'I'm sorry, Mum. Dad. Sorry. We just had a really quick look round, you know. We won't go back or anything.'

'You – after what we said – you – good Lord, I can't *believe* –' Dad spluttered and stopped, like he'd run out of petrol.

Mum had gone almost the same colour as Zach. She banged her hands down flat on the table; but when she spoke her voice was level, and icy cold. '*Zachary Randall*. How *dare* you drag your sister into danger? What a foolish, irresponsible, *arrogant* . . . If the place had collapsed on you, or Annis had fallen, or – whatever happened, it would be your fault. You know, for once your father's right – I have had just about enough of you. I don't understand how you could be so reckless, so *cruelly, callously* reckless, not only to put yourself in danger, but lead Annis –'

'He didn't lead me –'

'– into that kind of danger, when you know perfectly well how naive she is. It was a despicable thing to do. Do you understand?'

Zach raised his head. 'So you don't care about *me*?'

'I've done more than enough caring about you, Zachary.' A silence. Someone – Annis wasn't sure who – breathed in sharply through their teeth. Mum bit her lip and looked down at the table, colour coming and going in her face; but she didn't take it back.

Zach stared at her. Then he swallowed, and nodded, jaw clenched. 'Right. Thanks. That's good to know.' He cleared his throat, as if he was about to say something else, but then he looked away, glaring at the wall. Annis thought, *Oh God, he's trying not to cry*.

She said, 'Mum – it wasn't his fault – it was my idea –'

Zach twisted to look at her so violently his chair skidded on the floor. 'Shut *up*, Annis! For God's sake, you stupid cow, you make everything *worse*, can't you keep your mouth *shut*? Sitting there like you've got a fucking halo –'

'Zachary, don't you *dare* talk to your sister like –'

'See? Your fucking fault –' His voice cracked. He leant towards her, clenching his fist on the tablecloth, so that Annis's wineglass tilted and rocked. 'Why can't you just leave me alone? Stop sticking your nose in, trying to *help*, you sad little –'

She grabbed for her wine glass before it overbalanced. 'I'm not –'

'Then fuck *off*.'

She threw her wine straight into his face.

She felt the smash of glass down her arm, the impact stinging her fingers. He shouted something, reeling back. There was purple liquid dripping off his face – and red mixing with it, running opaque down his forehead – a jagged cut over his eye – oh no – oh no –

She couldn't breathe. *No. Dear God, no, please, I didn't mean to do that, oh God oh God I hit* him, *with the glass, I've hurt him, oh* no –

Someone was shouting – Mum – and Dad, too – the noise of chairs, people standing up, running, Dad reaching for Zach's arm –

Zach spun, so he was facing the wall, and took a few stumbling steps away from them. He held one hand over his eye, then looked at the red smears on the palm of it. He said, 'Oh Jesus, oh *fuck* –'

Then . . .

Annis was staring at him. She was staring so hard she couldn't move. And she saw . . . No, she didn't. She couldn't have done. She *thought* she saw . . .

His face healed. Smoothly, like a clever piece of animation, the skin coming together, the blood stopping. The cut evaporated off his skin. There wasn't any bruising. No scarring. No marks. As if it hadn't happened. There was blood on the neck of his T-shirt, on his face, mixed with wine; but no cut. The skin wasn't broken.

Annis squeezed her eyes shut and opened them again. He was digging at his forehead with his fingertips, biting his lip. There were wet smears of red over his eye, clogging up his eyebrow. But she hadn't imagined it. The cut was gone.

Dad said, 'Let me see – Zach – take your hand out of the way.'

Zach staggered, twisting backwards before Dad could touch him. 'Dad, it's fine, I'm OK –'

Mum said, 'I've got the antiseptic, just stand still and let me –'

Zach said, 'I'm *fine*. Look, I'm fine, Mum, there's nothing wrong with me.'

'But there's all this blood, darling, please, let me have a look –'

'It must be Annis's or something. Maybe she cut herself on the glass.'

Mum turned to look at her, holding the bottle of antiseptic in both hands. 'Annis? Did you hurt yourself?'

My blood? she thought. *For God's sake, it's* Zach's, *didn't they see his face?* She looked down; she was still holding the wine glass in her hand. The bulb had broken into a jagged edge. There was red wine dripping on her jeans. For a second she stayed still. Then she shoved her chair back and ran, dropping the glass as she went. She heard the smash as it hit the floor but she carried on going.

Dad shouted, 'Annis! *Annis!* You come back here, young lady!' but that didn't stop her either.

She ran up the stairs into the bedroom and slammed the door, breathing hard. Oh God, oh God. She slumped down and put her head on her knees, trying to get her heartbeat back under control.

The memory replayed itself and another wave of

nausea hit her. His face – it just *melted* back to how it was before . . .

No. No, it couldn't have. She held her hands up to her face, expecting to see her own blood – because it must have been, it *must* have been her blood on Zach's face – but her skin stared back at her, blank, only the red wine darkening the creases on her palms. She couldn't think straight. There had to be a rational explanation. Of course there was. It was just that she couldn't quite think of it.

She kicked off her shoes and crawled into her bed fully clothed. It was too hot, but she didn't care. She rolled into a ball under the duvet and closed her eyes. Downstairs she could hear talking, then a door slamming; then a silence until Mum and Dad started to shout again. Annis couldn't hear any of the words. She rolled over on to her side, drew back the duvet a bit until she could breathe properly, and stared at the wall. There was still pale, post-sunset daylight from the window. She took deep breaths and let her eyes blur. In, out, in, out, as slowly as she could . . .

She didn't know what woke her. It was late. The only noise was the crickets chirping outside: everything else was completely silent, completely still. She could see the window, a patch of bluer, blacker dark in the wall, and a pale-skinned silhouette in front of it. She started to sit up, her breath tight in her throat. But it was only Zach. He was sitting at the end of his bed, leaning forward, elbows on his knees. She gazed and gazed, but he didn't move. He hadn't got undressed; she could see the outline of his T-shirt and jeans. After a while he got to his feet and went right up to the window, letting his forehead rest on the glass. *There must be a moon*, she thought; *a full moon, because his skin is so bright.*

She said, 'What time is it?'

Zach looked round, then turned back to the window. 'About three.'

'What are you doing?'

'Watching.'

'Watching what?'

He didn't answer. Annis rolled over until she could stare at him without having to raise her head. He rubbed his face with his hands, briefly, then tilted his head forward again towards the window. *Watching . . .*

'Go back to sleep, Anz.'

She stayed awake for as long as she could, but he didn't move from the window. Then she closed her eyes for a moment, and she was asleep.

It's late. So late it's early. I'm watching the sky get brighter and the reflection fade out of the window and I'm saying to myself, Today will be the day she wakes up. Today.

I used to watch the sun come up after I'd been clubbing. I used to go to one of the parks, whichever was closest to the club we'd been to. I'd climb over the fence if I had to, and sit on my own, watching the sky go from orange-black to purple to perfect breathtaking blue. Once the sun had come up I'd know I had to get a night bus or the first tube home, but before that, while I was just waiting, I used to feel so happy. I guess it helped that I was generally still high, but there was something about watching the sky change colour . . . It wasn't the dawn I liked, but the bit just before. The bit when it's supposed to be darkest. And I'd feel great, having been up all night, seeing the sky light up before anyone else was awake. It felt special. Like I was the only person in the world. Like I was a god.

But it doesn't feel good any more. Now I feel like I've

taken something by mistake – I'm wired and edgy and paranoid and I want to sleep and I can't. I've been drinking and it hasn't had the slightest effect. Except that I stink of alcohol, of course. Pete came in here a while ago and gave me a look of absolute contempt. Which is particularly devastating from Pete, who is the kind of person who'll pick up a wasp with a glass and a post-card and take it outside instead of swatting it. He's been sitting with you. All the time, pretty much. Watching at your bedside, the way I would be, if I were a decent human being. He hasn't said, Zach, you pathetic speci-men, why the hell am I suddenly responsible for your sister? but I know he would, if he was just a bit braver. And he's right. Why the hell aren't I there with you, instead of writing this?

The same old question. And the same old answer: because I'm scared. I want to pretend this isn't happen-ing. I thought maybe the whisky would help with that, but I've had the whole bottle and I'm still completely fucking lucid. Maybe I should take it back to the off-licence, as soon as it opens. Excuse me, Mister, this whisky isn't an intoxicating beverage. I'm going to write a strongly-worded letter to the *Guardian*. What do you think?

Nothing, of course. You don't think anything. You're asleep.

I remember the first night I couldn't sleep. I didn't know then that it would carry on. I thought it was just because I was so wound up.

It was after that argument with Mum and Dad, when

you hit me with your wine glass. Remember? 'Course you do. You went straight to bed, so you didn't hear them rowing after we'd gone. I managed to get out early on. I wasn't sleepy, and I couldn't concentrate on my book, so I went for a swim in the dark. At least, I was going to. I meant to. But when I got there . . . I stripped off and stood at the end of the pool, on the steps . . .

And then I felt someone there. I mean . . . of course, I knew who it was. Even then, I knew. But I tried not to, if you know what I mean. I said to myself, Come on, don't be stupid . . . but I was so sure he was there, watching me, coming closer. And I panicked and grabbed my clothes and sprinted back to the house. I was panting and dripping pool-water everywhere and I have no idea how I managed to sneak in without Mum and Dad hearing, but I did. I ducked into the bathroom and got dressed again. I was shaking so hard I could hardly do up my flies.

Then I came into our bedroom, and for the first time I didn't think, Why the hell can't I sleep on my own in the barn, the way I asked? and I was glad you were there. I could hear your breathing and it felt like maybe I'd imagined all the stuff about him following me. And I took my shoes off and sat on the end of my bed, staring out of the window, waiting to feel sleepy.

And I didn't. I just didn't feel sleepy. I thought, OK, whatever, I'll just sit and wait. Eventually I'll nod off. I'll stare out of the window into the darkness and tell myself to stay awake, and then I'll fall asleep. But then . . .

I saw him, outside. Waiting for me, or calling me. Standing there . . . and I don't know how I saw him, it was so dark. I leant forward, and I put my forehead on

71

the glass. I could see my reflection, so bright, as if there was a light in the room, but behind that, or through it, or inside it . . . in my eyes . . . oh, hell, I don't know. I just knew he was there. And I knew I wasn't going to sleep; and I knew that the only way to keep him away was to watch at that window like a sentry, keeping him at a distance. I think I would have run away – don't know where, or how – to the ruins, perhaps – if you hadn't been there. But you were there, so I stayed. I don't mean I was protecting you. I mean knowing you were there made me feel stronger.

I stayed there until the morning. I stayed awake, watching and watching.

And I told myself he was a trick of the light. I was seeing things. There wasn't anyone there. I said to myself, Just a trick of the light, that's all. I said it over and over again: a trick of the light, a trick of the light . . . I said it to myself, under my breath, until I was sick of it. But that didn't make it true.

I wonder where he is now.

I've got lines in my head from some poem. It won't leave me alone, and I can't remember what it's from. 'From rest and sleep, which but thy pictures be, Much pleasure, then from thee, much more must flow . . .' Whatever it is, I wish it would piss off. I've got enough to worry about.

The sun's come up. Look.

Five

Zach was at the table, staring into his bowl. He was sitting in a shaft of sunlight, so that his skin gleamed unhealthily with that whiter-than-white sheen, like he was actually *emitting* light. His fingers were tapping out restless patterns on the tablecloth, as though he was on edge, waiting for something, but he didn't look up when Annis came into the room.

She stood still, looking at him, trying to get hold of a thought that kept slipping out of her fingers like a sliver of soap. There was something wrong – something *really* wrong . . . but she couldn't work out what. Looking at him made everything seem slippery.

She gritted her teeth and sat down opposite him. *Come on*, she thought, *stop being so hysterical. Just because you had a weird day yesterday . . . Look, he's 3-D, he's moody, he's even eating . . . urgh, yuck . . .* There was half a soggy *tartine* on a plate next to him, and when Annis followed his gaze she noticed tiny platelets of grease floating on the surface of his coffee. *See? If there's anything weird going on, it's that anyone would want to dip their bread into their coffee . . .*

She said, 'Good *morning*, Annis, how absolutely

73

delightful to see you, I *do* hope you had a pleasant sleep.'

Zach raised his head. He said, 'Good *morning*, Zach, I am *so* sorry, I absolutely *must* apologise for breaking my wine glass over your head last night.'

Then I didn't dream it, Annis thought. She stared at the smooth white skin over Zach's eye and said, 'But –'

'You're lucky it didn't split my head open. Well – *I'm* lucky it didn't split my head open.' He went back to looking at his coffee.

'Zach –'

'Don't mention it. Let's just forget all about it, shall we?'

Right. Great. Annis took a bite of her croissant and chewed it slowly, watching Zach. OK, so she *had* bopped him on the head with her wine glass. So . . . 'I thought I – Zach, I thought it *did* split your –'

'Well, it didn't.'

'But there was all that blood –'

'For God's sake, Anz, what is all this I-thought-you-were-dead stuff? Would you rather I *was* dead? Were you *trying* to bash my head in? Are you disappointed?'

'No, but –'

'Then *shut up*.'

She probably wouldn't have done, except for the way he said it. She took a long gulp of hot chocolate, keeping her head down. He looked terrible. Normally when he was tired his eyelids went a funny colour and he had a permanent frown, like that was the only way he could keep his eyes open. But now . . . she tried to

74

think of something that was as pale as Zach's face, but she couldn't.

Dad came in, flipping his mobile shut. 'Good morning, kids.' He paused at the end of the table, then went to hit Zach on the upper arm with the palm of his hand. It was probably meant to be a hearty man-to-man slap on the shoulder, but Zach flinched before Dad could touch him. Dad tugged at his nose, as if he'd *meant* to swipe uselessly at the air, and said again, 'Good morning. How's it hanging?'

Zach glanced sideways and shrugged, without saying anything.

Annis said, 'Hi, Dad. How are the builders? Still disappointingly French?'

'I think I'm making progress.'

'What, they're getting *less* French?'

Dad gave her an insincere ad-agency smile. 'Coffee, anyone? Zach?'

Zach pushed his chair away from the table and stood up. 'I'm going outside.' He went out, shutting the door heavily behind him. Annis saw him go to the corner of the house and sit down against the wall, looking out over the field, towards the walnut tree. She craned round to see his face, but the edge of the doorway was in the way.

Dad shouted, 'Don't go far! We're going into St Jean-le-Grand in twenty minutes or so!'

Annis carried on eating her croissant. 'What for?'

'Go to the market, buy another dictionary, your mother wants some espadrilles, and you kids can have a look round the place.'

'What's there to look at?'

Dad pushed the plunger of the cafetière down so

hard coffee grounds spurted on to the worktop. 'Don't push it, Annis.'

'I didn't mean –' God, that was so unfair. It was a perfectly innocent question – for once. She shoved the rest of her croissant into her mouth and said, chewing, 'So we don't have a choice, right? We have to come?'

'Your mother thinks we should get out more as a family.'

Oh, fantastic. It wasn't enough that they were stuck in a house together, they had to *get out more* as well . . . and Dad thought it was a rubbish idea too, you could tell by the way he said *your mother* . . . *Then again*, Annis thought, *maybe it'll do us good. I need to get out of this house – get away from the ruins*. It was like something rotting in the corner of her mind, something black and sticky seeping out and staining the rest of the world. As if everything that was wrong – all the stuff with Zach – came from the ruins, as if that was the heart of the dark . . .

Dad said, 'You'd better go and get dressed. We're going as soon as your mother has checked her emails. It's best to get to the market early.'

'I *am* dressed.'

Dad gave her a cursory look. 'Oh.'

She thought, *Great one, Dad. You are so observant you can't even tell the difference between my pyjamas and my proper clothes. No one has even noticed that I was so freaked out last night I went to bed at about eight-thirty, fully dressed. Excellent.*

She left her hot chocolate and went back upstairs, had a shower, and got dressed again. While she was pulling her jeans on she hopped over to the window to look out, but Zach was too close to the house for her to see anything but his feet. She stared at the walnut tree, not quite knowing why, except that she had that feeling again, like there was someone there . . . Someone standing in the shadow of the trunk, watching . . . And the tree itself looked diseased, the lower leaves warping into brown shrivelled fingers, pointing at the ground. Like the grass that had withered on the path . . . She felt her pulse speed up, a shot of panic going straight into her bloodstream. *No, please, no* . . . She craned to the side, trying to get a better view. But there was only the shadow of the trunk, thick darkness that could have been shadow or solid. She couldn't see properly. *And, oh, for God's sake*, she thought, suddenly infuriated, *why* should *there be someone there? Why the hell* should *there be?*

Mum called, 'Annis! Zach! We're going now!'

Normally they would have waited ten minutes for Zach to clean his teeth or gel his hair or something; but he was already there, hovering by the car, by the time Dad came out with the car keys. He kept looking round, his jaw clenched. Even outside, in the sunlight, he looked luminous and ill. Annis watched him out of the corner of her eye. There was still something . . . *Come on, Anz, what is it?* Something – *missing* . . . But she couldn't figure it out, and once they got out of the sunshine into the car the feeling faded. Zach huddled in the corner of the seat, hands clasped in front of him so tightly she could see the outline of every bone. But as they drove off he seemed to relax. He peered over his shoulder at the house, staring fixedly, but as soon as the car turned off the gravel track on to the road he took such a deep breath Annis could have sworn she felt the air swirl round her. Then he sagged sideways, leaning his face on the window.

Mum said, 'How are you feeling, Zach, darling? Any better?'

'Yeah, a bit, thanks.'

Annis said, 'You don't *look* any better.'

Dad said, 'He'll be fine. Won't you, Zach? He can have a bit of a wander, get some fresh air, practise his French . . . a bit of ordinary activity will work wonders.'

Zach closed his eyes and didn't answer.

The drive didn't take very long. *We could have walked it*, Annis thought, *except that it would mean half an hour of one another's company, not just five minutes*. As they got out of the car she looked round, grudgingly liking the look of the place. *Very quaint*, she thought. *Very touristy. But nice.*

Mum said, 'The market's just down that alley. There's a lovely little church a couple of streets away – that's worth a look. There are some exquisite finials.'

Dad got two five-euro notes out of his wallet. 'Here you go, Annis, Zach. Bit of extra pocket money. Buy a souvenir.'

Annis said, 'Dad, this is about *five quid*.'

Dad opened his mouth and shut it again. Then, without a word, he took two ten-euro notes out and shoved one at Annis and one at Zach. Annis grabbed hers before he had time to change his mind, but Zach wasn't even looking. He was breathing deeply, with his eyes closed and his face tilted towards the sun, like he'd just come out of prison.

Annis took Zach's ten-euro note as well. She said, 'Thanks, Dad.'

Mum said, 'Are you coming to the market? Or shall we meet you back here in a couple of hours?'

A pause. Zach opened his eyes and said, 'We may as well have a look round the market. Right, Anz?' He sounded almost normal.

'Yeah. Sounds good.' She looked at him covertly, wondering why the tension had dropped out of his face so quickly, but he caught her eye and smiled, and she smiled back and forgot to wonder any more.

The market was smaller than she'd expected, but busy, so that within seconds Mum had disappeared into the crowd. Dad swore under his breath and plunged after her, shouting, 'Helen! *Not* the loaves with poppy seeds, you know I hate them,' and Annis and Zach were left standing next to a fruit-and-veg stall.

The rigidity in Zach's shoulders had eased; if he hadn't still been so pale, he would have looked like his old self. Annis felt such a rush of warmth that she looked away, scuffing at the pavement with her toe. He said, 'Come on, then. Shall we buy thirty euros' worth of . . . er . . . peaches? And goats' cheese? And local wine?'

'Dad would approve.'

'Yeah. Oh, well. Maybe not, then.' He reached out and draped one arm round Annis's neck. 'OK, Randall Minor –'

There was a bang like an explosion. The world flashed white, blinding her with brilliance. And then there was a wave of pain that rolled down her backbone into the soles of her feet, leaving her bent over, gasping and bathed in sweat. When the ground steadied again she heard herself saying hoarsely, 'Ow, *shit*, ow, bloody hell –'

'Jesus – are you OK? Anz? *Annis* –'

'Don't touch me!' She leapt away. 'Don't – stop it – don't *touch* me.'

'OK, OK!' Zach held his hands up, like he was surrendering. 'All right! Calm down, I'm not going to touch you.'

Annis felt involuntary tears welling up. She smeared them away with the heel of her hand. 'You're like a – pylon, or a – an *eel*, or something.'

'I'm sorry. Really, Anz, I'm sorry. I'm not doing anything.'

'Well, whatever you're not doing, just *don't*.' They stared at each other. Zach was the first to look away. The strain had come back into his face.

There was silence, except for the noise of the market. Finally Annis said, 'So, shall we have a look at the local produce?' She moved purposefully towards a cheese stall and stared blindly at lots of little cloned cheeses. As soon as she sensed Zach at her shoulder she moved on. Peaches. Dead chickens. Saucissons. Cherries. Walnuts. Courgettes.

Zach said, 'Annis. Annis, wait.'

She turned round. He was standing a little way away, hunched over, as if he was trying to make himself as small as possible. He said, 'Look, this is . . . I can't do this. I'll wait for you, yeah?'

'You can't do what?'

'I . . .' He stopped. Then, in a quick, low voice, he said, 'There are too many people. I'm scared I'll – if I brush against someone, by mistake –' He bit his lip.

'Oh.' Annis felt a current of dread run up the back of her neck. She said, 'You should really stop wearing those trainers. It's the rubber soles, or something.'

'I'm wearing flip-flops, Anz.'

'Right. Yeah,' Annis said. 'Right.'

'I'll wait for you over there, OK?' He pointed and walked off all in one movement. Annis watched him go, then turned back to the courgettes, feeling her heart pounding. God, what was *wrong* with him? *Calm down. It's just static electricity, Annis. Like at school, when you rub a balloon on your hair and stick it to the wall* . . .

She didn't want to be here any more. She wanted to go home. All the tension had come back into her stomach; the food stalls everywhere were making her feel queasy. One more minute, just so Zach wouldn't think she was being clingy, and then she'd go back to him and they'd find somewhere else to go. She moved determinedly towards a bread stall and stared at the loaves.

The girl behind the stall broke off what she was saying and turned to look down one of the side streets. Her hands froze in the middle of putting a round loaf into a bag, and she peered sideways, frowning. Automatically Annis followed her gaze.

There was someone there. Someone . . .

It shouldn't have made her look twice, but Annis stared, paralysed. A boy, standing on his own, watching. A boy with . . . but he was standing in the shade, and it was too dark to see his face. Annis blinked. No. The sun was overhead. There *wasn't* any shade. But . . . *come on, this is stupid. He's about Zach's size. He's wearing . . . he's got . . .* She narrowed her eyes, squinting at him. *He's . . .*

She took a step backwards, involuntarily. Her nerves were tingling. *I can't see him properly*, she thought. She fought a surge of panic. *It's like he's in the dark. But it's broad daylight. Something's wrong . . .*

She looked back over her shoulder. Zach was still standing near the wall, his hands in his pockets. He met her gaze and shrugged, in a kind of greeting, unsmiling. Annis felt an irrational rush of relief. He was there. He was OK. Whoever the dark boy was – it didn't matter – he wasn't anything to do with Zach. Zach was fine. She glanced to the side street again. The boy was walking towards her – towards the market. There was something about the way he moved . . . as if Annis had seen him before – *knew* him from somewhere. No. That was stupid. He just had a kind of ubiquitous teenage slouch, that was all. But it still made the back of her neck tingle. And he was looking at . . . No, no, *no*. How could he be *looking*, when she couldn't even see his eyes?

She felt a wave of unease run up and down her spine, prickling her skin. She thought, *Look. Zach's fine. You are worrying for no reason. Pull yourself together. Look at him. He's absolutely –*

Zach wasn't there.

For a second she couldn't believe her eyes. She thought, *He's disappeared into thin air.* She looked from side to side, scanning the crowds. No. He had to be there somewhere – of course he did . . . *Come on, get a grip, girl, he's just wandered off . . .*

There was a shout, so panicked and desperate she didn't know whether it was English or French – didn't know whether it had words, even – didn't recognise Zach's voice until she caught sight of him . . . A few heads turned to stare towards the middle of the square, where Zach was weaving and sliding between people, glancing back over his shoulder. Annis caught a flash of his face. He said something, stammering, flailing with his arms like he was trying to push past someone without touching them. The man in front of him looked round, surprised, a peach in both hands, and opened his mouth to speak.

Zach said, 'Please, *please*, there's someone – please . . .' as if he was too frantic to speak French. When he glanced backwards again Annis followed his gaze, already knowing what she'd see. The boy in black. He was staring at Zach, as if no one else was there. He took a step towards him, into the corner of the marketplace.

Zach said, 'Please – *please* let me past, please.'

The man in front of him frowned, said something rapid in French and turned back to the stallholder, holding out the peaches.

Zach said, 'Just – let me *past*.' He glanced over his shoulder again, turned back to the man with the peaches, and pushed him out of the way.

When the flash came it was so bright Annis had to blink. It made a noise like a gunshot; and when she opened her eyes the man was on his knees, gasping, and Zach was running towards the corner of the mar-ketplace. Everything was quiet, except for Zach hissing, 'Sorry, sorry . . .' as he ran.

Nobody moved. There was a moment of stillness, except for the man struggling for breath, sagging on to the cobbles. He still had a peach clutched tightly in one hand, and it split and oozed juice as he coughed.

Annis looked sideways, forcing her eyes to focus. The boy in black was already stepping forward, past the stall on the opposite corner of the marketplace. She watched him, frozen. Yes, she recognised the way he walked. Who *was* –

Then, suddenly, there was a wave of noise, as people all started to speak at once, swapping looks, peering round at the direction Zach had taken. A woman shrugged and turned to her neighbour, obscuring the boy in black.

Once Annis couldn't see him any more, she could move again.

She ran after Zach, as fast as she could. For a minute when she got to the other side of the square she thought she'd lost him. But just in time she saw a glimpse of his shirt and the sun glinting off his hair as he turned the corner. She pelted after him, dodging round people, swearing through her teeth until she ran out of breath. He swerved left, and she followed, forcing her legs to keep going. When she got round the corner he was halfway down the street, just managing not to collide with a fat man with a camera. He glanced back; and she glanced back, too, scared she'd see the boy behind them. But they'd lost him. There were only the tourists, and the empty rectangles of shadow on the pavement.

Zach faltered and stopped dead, outside the church. He looked round, twisting so quickly he staggered. He didn't seem to see Annis. There was a wild, lost expression on his face. Suddenly he ducked sideways through the doors, so Annis was left hovering stupidly on the pavement. The tourists were staring, but she didn't have time to care. She ran into the church after Zach.

The light from the windows was dim grey-green, so that it was like being underwater. Zach was leaning against a pillar, facing the entrance, so that Annis met his eyes as soon as she came in, but he didn't seem to notice her. He carried on staring, intently, his mouth moving; if she hadn't known better she would have thought he was praying. In the weird aquatic light he looked like he was glowing. When she walked up to him he didn't acknowledge her, only shifted so that he was looking over her shoulder. Annis thought, *He wants a clear view of the door. He wants to see who else comes in . . .*

She said, 'Zach?'

'Don't.' That voice again: stretched too tight, close to snapping.

She took a few moments to catch her breath, because she didn't know what to say. Zach, she noticed, wasn't even *sweating*. Or flushed. Or panting. He was luminous and still and tense as a wound spring. And he hadn't taken his gaze off the church door.

She pitched her voice carefully, so it was matter-of-fact, and casual. 'What happened?'

'*Nothing*. I just –' He turned his head, suddenly, as if he'd heard something. His hand jumped to his mouth and he pressed his lip with one knuckle until it went as white as the rest of his face. 'Oh Christ –'

'Zach,' Annis said. 'What's wrong?'

'Nothing – really – I . . .' For the first time he caught her eye. He took his hand away from his face, flexing the fingers, and gave a brittle gulp of laughter.

'Obviously. Can't you tell? Everything's just dandy.'

Annis went to touch his arm; then she stopped herself and pulled back. Zach registered the movement. His eyes flicked to her face and away again; but he didn't say anything. She said, 'It's that boy, isn't it?'

'That –?' His face was unreadable. For a second it was as if he couldn't speak. Then he breathed out, spilling words like water. 'Yes. That boy. He was coming after me, and that man, he got in the way, wouldn't let me past, and I didn't mean to hurt him, I just . . . and – Anz, I can't – you wouldn't –' He spun round to stare at the door, his face blank with a kind of frozen panic. 'Oh, fuck, fuck, *fuck*.'

Annis felt her heart miss a beat. She followed his gaze. Was someone –? But the church was still quiet, almost empty. She looked round, but there was nothing – no one who could possibly scare Zach like that. One woman was standing near the font; there was a man and a woman staring up at one of the statues. No one else. She laughed shakily and said, 'You sound like Dad.' But he didn't answer.

Then, as she watched, he slid slowly down the pillar until he was crouched on the floor, his hands covering his face, hissing something through his teeth. Oh God, oh Christ, he was *crying* – was he? She knelt down next to him, ignoring the woman turning to gape at them. 'Zach? Zach – please – what's wrong?' She really wanted to touch him; but when she lifted her hand towards his shoulder she remembered the look on the man's face, when he was on his knees, struggling for breath, and her fingers tingled.

Zach looked up. No. He wasn't crying. But the flat white fear on his face was almost worse. He shook his head, as if he was trying to clear it, and dragged his fingers over his forehead. 'Sorry, Anz. Sorry, I'm sorry . . .' Then he swallowed.

'Can I help? Is there anything . . . ? I'll do anything you want,' Annis said. 'Please, Zach. Whatever it is. There must be something.'

He shook his head again. His face still shone with that pale, uncanny radiance. Then he squeezed his eyes shut, as if he was listening for something. His lips were moving, making the same shapes over and over; and when Annis leant closer she realised he was whispering. It sounded like, *go away, go away, go away.*

'You don't have to tell me what's happening,' she said, her voice scraping in her throat. 'If you don't want to – I don't mind – but let me help, please, Zach, please let me help.'

For a second he was quiet. Then he looked up. 'There's nothing, Anz. You can't help. I don't think anyone –' He broke off, and sat up straighter. 'No, wait. OK. Go and find Mum and Dad. Make them bring the car. I'll stay here. Will you do that?'

'Make them bring the car? Here?'

'Yes. You said you wanted to help, Anz,' he added, before she could open her mouth. 'So will you do it?'

'I'll do my best,' Annis said.

'Go on, then. Hurry.' He turned his head, as if the conversation was over.

'OK. See you in a bit, then,' she said, pushing herself to her feet. Right. Make Mum and Dad bring the car. How hard could it be? *I'll lie*, she thought, *I'll lie through my teeth if I have to. I told Zach I'd help him, and I will . . .*

She went outside and started to run, blinking in the

sudden sunlight. They weren't in the marketplace, because they would have seen . . . so they'd be . . . she'd find them. Somehow, she'd find them. She ran, faster now, because she couldn't get rid of Zach's face in her mind's eye. It was hard to look up because of the sun in her eyes, so she kept her gaze on the pavement. She felt people move aside for her and caught sight of their shadows sliding out of the way. OK – right at the end of this road, then back to where the car was . . . There was someone in front of her. She swerved – *Oi, get out of the way!* – and almost lost her balance. She staggered and looked over her shoulder to swear. *Bloody stupid boy, don't just stand there –*

It was him. The boy in black.

He hardly seemed to see her. He was looking towards the church, standing still, waiting and watching. She could feel the force of his stare, like a bullet going past her face. She opened her mouth, but she couldn't speak. And her eyes weren't working properly; when she tried to look at him something blurred and darkened in her head.

Her knees gave way under her.

Literally. Just *gave way* . . . She sank on to the pavement, staring at her legs, folded in front of her, grimy strands of frayed denim dragging on the ground. *I didn't think knees actually* did *that*, she thought, dizzily. *God, I feel strange*. She raised her head and tried to focus on the street in front of her. The cracks on the paving stones doubled and split apart. *I just want to lie down here, never wake up . . . No. Stop it*.

She looked round, blinking as hard as she could. All the tourists had gone. There was only the boy in black, a few steps away . . . only not black, exactly, more a sort of . . . no, the word was gone . . . the boy with . . . *that* boy . . . *and whatever's happened to me*, she thought, *that was* him, *he did it, somehow, it sounds stupid, but I know it was* –

She stood up, fighting the giddiness. The boy didn't even look at her.

She thought, *He's waiting for Zach. He can't get into the church – or maybe he doesn't know exactly where Zach is, or . . . But he's followed him here, and sooner or later . . .*

She thought, *Run.* Her knees shook and protested, and the ground was still rocking under her feet. But she ran.

Six

Mum said, 'Zach's ill? *How* ill? What's wrong with him?'

'He's really . . .' Annis forced tears into her eyes, her voice cracking. It was pathetically easy. 'He's in a real state, Mum, please won't you get the car, *please* . . .'

Dad said, 'What's the matter with him? Is he throwing up?'

'He's . . .' Annis gave a little sob, to gain time. Oh, shit. *Come on, Annis, think! What's the matter with him?* Nothing too bad or they'd take him to hospital . . . She said, 'He's feeling a bit, um, dizzy, and sick, but he's not throwing up. He's – he thinks he's got dehydrated,' she added, suddenly fluent. 'Like when he was in Morocco and they had to put him on a drip. Sunstroke or something. But not as *bad*, obviously, he just isn't up to walking anywhere.' That had to do the trick. Surely.

Dad rolled his eyes. 'He was fine an hour ago.'

'It came on really suddenly.'

Mum said, 'He *did* look peaky.'

'Yeah, he's really ill, Mum, please, he made me promise to come and get you, he can't walk anywhere on his own . . .' *And he's there, in the church, while that boy waits outside, and I'm afraid for him* . . . but she didn't dare to say that. She let two big fat tears roll down her cheeks and gazed at Mum. *I'm not really crying*, she said to herself, *it's only for Zach's sake* . . .

'Well, we'd better go and get the car,' Mum said.

Dad said, 'Will there be somewhere to park?'

'You can just stop in the street,' Annis said. 'I can get him out of the church, if you wait in the car, it'll be fine, you won't even have to stop for very long –'

Mum was already walking. 'Come on, then. We shouldn't leave him on his own, Edward. Not if he's ill.'

As they walked to the car – Mum trotting in front, digging her keys out of her pocket before they even got to the right road – Dad muttered, 'If he's mucking us about I'll slaughter the little . . .' but Annis pretended she hadn't heard. When she got into the car she collapsed on the back seat. Her body felt numb, as if something had sucked the life out of the top layer of her skin; and she felt like the car was rocking from side to side, making her feel sick and sleepy at the same time. It was lucky Mum knew the way round the one-way system without Annis having to explain where to go.

Mum said, 'Annis! Wake up! Is this the right place?'

Annis could have sworn her eyelids sucked at each other, resisting her when she tried to open them. She stared blearily through the car window. 'Yeah.' She undid her seat belt. 'OK, I'll go and get him.' Every step, every movement was an effort. She couldn't even imagine what she'd do if he wasn't there.

But he was. He was crouched by the pillar, where she'd left him; and when she came through the door he looked up as if he would rather have seen her than anyone else in the whole world. He leapt to his feet like an athlete. 'Thank God, I thought – did you – did Mum and Dad bring the car?'

'Mmm. They're outside.' Even her tongue felt sluggish. *This can't be from running past that boy*, she thought, *that's absurd, it* can't *be* . . . She swallowed, and made herself speak. 'They think you've got sunstroke. You feel sick and dizzy, OK? And you can't walk on your own, so you'd better lean on me –'

'But I can't touch anyone without –' Zach stopped. They looked at each other.

'You don't know it happens every time,' Annis said. 'Want to try?'

She rubbed her eyes. 'No,' she said. 'You had a quick drink from the holy water stoup or something and now you can walk. Miraculously.'

Zach's face moved, like he would have laughed, if he could. 'OK. Right, then.' He squared his shoulders; for a second, in her mind's eye, Annis saw the boy in black, the way he'd stood so still, outside, waiting . . . 'We go straight to the car and get in. No fannying about.'

'Fine – I wasn't intending to *fanny about* –' But he'd already marched to the door and was waiting for her, hand flat on the wood. She followed, careful to keep a reasonable distance between them, just in case. Then they went out together into the sunlight.

But Zach didn't go straight to the car. He stood in the sun, his face as bright as a mirror, and looked at the boy at the other end of the street. Annis wondered how he'd known exactly where to look, because she hadn't said anything, and yet Zach's eyes had gone straight to the right place. And while they looked at each other, there was a feeling in the air like before a storm, a kind of tension building up. She thought, *It's not just that he's scared, it's something else as well – a feeling like* . . . something so familiar, and yet she couldn't quite put her finger on it. That intensity – a feeling like –

Then the moment broke, and Zach spun round and raced to the car. Annis almost called out to him, 'Zach! Slow down! You're meant to be *ill*, remember?' But by then he'd opened the car door and thrown himself on to the seat, and she didn't want Mum or Dad to hear. It was too late, anyway. Dad's eyes had followed Zach, then flicked away, and his face was set and rigid, like he was struggling not to say anything.

Annis jogged towards them and got in the other side. She was determined not to look back at the dark boy, but she couldn't help it. What was he *doing* there? What was going on? When she sneaked a look at Zach he was staring straight ahead, his jaw clenched.

Mum said, 'Darling? Annis said you were ill –'

'Please let's *go*. Now. Please, Mum.' Zach leant forward, digging his fists into the back of her seat. '*Please*.'

'But, sweetheart, what's the matter? Are you going to be sick?'

'No. I mean, look –'

Dad said, 'So are you ill, or not?'

Zach's breathing was too fast. 'Please, let's go. I'll explain when we get home. Really. Please, Mum, *please*, just take me home. Now.'

Maybe it was the way he said *please*. But even so, Annis was surprised when Mum took the handbrake off and turned the car round. So was Dad; he made an outraged noise in the back of his throat, like he couldn't help himself.

Mum said, 'Edward, there's a bottle of water in the glove compartment. Will you give it to Zach, please?'

Dad passed the water over his shoulder to Zach without looking round, then gave Mum a big see-how-accommodating-I-am smile.

Oh God, Annis thought. *Zach had better be able to explain this convincingly, or it's going to be World War Three.* She glanced at him. He'd slumped back into the corner of the seat, eyes closed, his skin gleaming like white enamel. Annis could almost see his skull shining through. At least he *looked* ill . . .

They drove in silence until they got to the house. Annis got out of the car and waited for Mum to unlock the front door, wishing the journey had taken longer. Because now they were going to ask Zach what this was all about, and if he didn't have a decent excuse . . .

And right on cue . . . Dad said, 'OK, then. I've had enough of this. What's it all about? You're clearly *not* ill, so –'

Mum said, 'Let's go inside, shall we? And I'll make a pot of coffee, and we can sit down and talk like civilised adults.'

'Right. Why break the habit of a lifetime?' Dad muttered, but if Mum heard it she ignored it. She dropped her keys noisily on the worktop and filled the kettle without looking at him.

Zach sat down at the table, arms crossed tightly

over his chest like he was trying to hold himself together. Annis sat down opposite him. She wasn't sure whether Mum and Dad wanted her there, but that was tough. She wasn't going anywhere.

Dad stood at Mum's elbow until she'd made the coffee. Then he took the cafetière and slammed it down on the table. Brown liquid slopped out of the top. '*Right.* Now maybe you'd like to explain what the hell is going on. You make Annis tell us you're ill, you *demand* that we pick you up in the car, and then –'

'All right, Edward,' Mum said. She poured the coffee into four cups, added milk, then a spoonful of sugar to Annis's. She pushed a cup in Zach's direction. 'First things first. *Are* you ill?'

'Not . . .' Zach hooked a finger through the handle of the coffee cup and pulled it towards him, slowly. 'Not the way you . . . no. No, I'm not.'

Dad said, 'So – what? You wanted a *lift*? Do you have any idea how inconvenient it was to pick you up? Do you have any idea how worried your mother was? Do you have *any idea* –'

'Then what's going on, Zachary?' Mum took a sip of coffee, her eyes steady on Zach's face. Dad subsided, taking a gulp from his own cup.

Zach swallowed. Then he said, 'I need to go home. Back to England.'

There was a beat of silence. Then Dad spluttered, spitting his coffee out. Annis couldn't help noticing that it went neatly back into his cup. 'You *need* to go back to England? Why? A lucrative drug deal waiting for you, is there? Mafia thugs after you in St Jean-le-Grand?'

Mum said, 'Go back to *England*? Why? What's happened –'

'Oh, be *reasonable*, Helen, nothing's happened, the little brat's just bored, he's probably *cold turkey* or something –'

Annis said, 'That's *heroin*, Dad,' but no one heard.

'I wish you'd be quiet, Edward! Now, Zachary, will you kindly *explain* –'

'OK, *OK!*' Zach leant forward, his face so white and tense he could have been made of stone. 'I need to go home, because I'm being followed. There's someone –' Dad snorted, and Zach grimaced, hunching his shoulders – 'yes, Dad, I *know*, I know what it sounds like, OK? But there's someone trying to kill me. There *is*. I *swear*. I *have to get away* before he catches up with me. Please. I mean it. *Please* . . .'

Mum shot a glance at Dad. She took a very deliberate sip of coffee. 'Zach, darling –'

'Please, Mum, I *know*, I know, all right? This isn't a wind-up. It's not a joke. Take me back to England and I'll – I'll do anything you want. I'll stay in the house. I'll stay in my *room* if you want. I just have to get away from here.'

'All right,' Mum said, in a voice that didn't mean she was agreeing. 'Let's be sensible about this. Who is this person? How do you know he's trying to kill you? *Is* it something to do with drugs?'

'No – Mum, I promised I'd stop doing drugs, and I *have*. He's just – I just . . .' Zach took a deep breath. 'I just *know*. He's someone I – someone I met. When Annis and I went down to the ruins.'

'Who is he? What's his name? How old is he?'

96

'I – I don't know,' Zach said, stumbling over the words. He was lying. Annis wanted to shout, *Tell them the truth, for God's sake, Zach, don't you realise they'll think you're making it all up, don't you realise –?*

'You have seen him, I take it?' Mum said.

'Yeah – yes, of course, Mum, that's how I know he's –'

'So you must know how old he is. Roughly.'

'I don't . . . about my age, I guess,' Zach said, eyes flicking away.

'About your age . . .' Dad repeated, running one finger round the rim of his coffee cup. 'And how exactly has this seventeen-year-old assassin made his murderous intents clear?'

'He –' Zach rubbed his face with his hands, pushing his fingers through his hair. Then he looked up again, straight at Dad. 'Please. Dad. I know you think I'm lying. I promise I'm not. But please. Even if you don't believe me. Help me. *Please.*'

Silence. Dad looked back at him, his expression suddenly less resolute. For a second Annis saw the likeness between them. *And they used to be so close*, she thought, with an unexpected stab of sadness. *I used to be jealous. Dad used to treat Zach like his son and his best friend and his younger brother all rolled into one.*

Maybe he would have given in. Annis thought she saw him waver, open his mouth a fraction, take a deep breath. But Mum didn't give him time. She shook her head and stood up, striding over to the window as if she couldn't bear to stay sitting down any longer. She said, 'Zachary. We are not being unreasonable. You cannot possibly expect us to do what you ask without knowing all the facts.'

'Mum, *please*. I'm not stupid, I'm not mad, I'm not lying. I promise, *please* –'

'But . . .' Mum turned round, crossing her arms over her chest as if she was dealing with a difficult client. 'What *exactly* makes you think you're in danger, Zachary? Talk us through it.'

Zach stared back at her. Then, slowly, he hunched his shoulders, lowering his head to stare at his hands. He said, very quietly, 'I can't.'

'Because –?'

'Because you won't believe me.'

There was a silence. Annis looked from Mum to Dad and back again. *Come on*, she thought. *You're meant to say, 'Of course we will, darling, just tell us.' You're meant to say, 'All right, Zach, tell us everything and we'll sort it out.'*

Mum said, 'Zach, darling . . .' Her voice had gone funny. Annis couldn't work out what was wrong, until Mum said again, too gently, 'Darling . . . why don't you go to bed? Everything will be all right. I promise. No one's going to hurt you.'

Zach winced. 'I said I'm not mad, Mum! This isn't some kind of paranoia, it's *real*.'

Dad said, 'Your mother's right. Go to bed, sleep it off, and see how you feel later. You'll wake up and it'll feel like a dream.' He leant forward, trying to catch Zach's eye. 'You have to admit it's a bit far-fetched, matey. Come on. You're feeling a bit jumpy, that's all. You'll be right as rain in a few hours.'

Zach slammed his fists down on the table. He said, '*Right as rain?* You smug self-satisfied *idiots*, I'll *die*,

I'll be *dead*, and it'll be your fault, you –' He put his hands over his face, breathing in great hoarse sobs. Annis sat, frozen with horror, watching his shoulders jerk.

Mum and Dad swapped a look. Dad cleared his throat. 'Zach . . . if you could give us some *evidence* . . .'

Zach shook his head without taking his hands away from his face. He was still crying, the air catching in his throat.

Mum and Dad looked at each other again. In the end Dad shook his head, hunching his shoulders and curving his hands round his coffee cup as if he wanted something to hold on to. He said, 'Zach, matey . . .'

Annis thought, *This is unreal. This can't be happening. Zach's sitting there, scared for his life, and all Mum and Dad can do is . . . is* nothing. She clawed frantically at her mind for something to say. *I saw the boy too. He* is *trying to kill Zach. It's all true . . .* Yeah, and the *evidence* . . . ? They'd just think *she* was on drugs as well. But there had to be something she could do . . .

Zach dragged his fingers down his face, taking a long breath in, then lowered his hands. His face was wet. He stared at Mum and Dad for so long Dad started to shift uncomfortably in his chair. Then, suddenly, he leapt up, sprinted to the worktop and scooped up Mum's car keys before anyone else had time to move. He ran outside. The front door slammed after him.

Then Dad was on his feet, shouting, flinging himself at the door. A split second later, Mum was behind him, yelling at him to get out of the way. Annis saw the door open and Dad half fall, half throw himself through it; heard a solid stream of cursing, the car engine start up, more shouting, Dad, Mum, Zach shouting back. She stumbled to her feet and got to the door. Zach was trying to reverse the car. Mum was standing in front, banging her fists on the windscreen, incoherent with anger. Dad tugged at the passenger door, wrenching it open while Zach reached desperately for the locking mechanism. Mum shouted, 'Don't you *dare* – don't you *dare* –'

Dad collapsed sideways into the passenger seat. He made a grab for Zach's shoulder, pulling him away from the steering wheel. 'You little *fuck* –'

There was a flash, like someone taking a photo; a streak of white light leapt between Zach and Dad, so bright it left a black mark on Annis's retina. There was a bang, like the car had backfired; and Dad slumped down in the seat, clutching his hands together, his breath wheezing. Zach stared at him, mouth open. He said, 'Dad . . .'

Mum pulled the driver's door open. 'Get out of the car. *Now*. Or I will call the police and tell them you stole it.' She wasn't joking.

'Mum –'

'Get *out*.'

Zach bowed his head. He stayed there for a second, completely still, like he was praying. Then, with small, very precise movements, he turned the engine off, reached for the keys, and dropped them into Mum's waiting palm without touching her. He waited until she'd stepped back; then he got out of the car and walked into the house, head up, straight-backed, like someone going to the gallows.

*   *   *

Sooner or later there was going to be a storm. Annis could feel it building; the clouds had been growing for hours, like thick grey roots, sucking all the life out of the sky. Annis had been sitting on the front step for so long her legs had gone numb, but she couldn't move in case she made a noise and Mum and Dad realised she was there. Not that she was eavesdropping. She might have been eavesdropping to start with, when she'd sneaked back after lunch to see if they were still arguing, but they'd got louder since then. You couldn't eavesdrop on a conversation that was loud enough to hear without trying . . . If Mum and Dad *cared* whether she heard them, they wouldn't be shouting. Simple.

Dad said, 'I thought you *wanted* to go to this concert! You said you –'

'That was before Zach . . .' Mum's voice trailed off. 'I think we ought to stay at home, just in case he –'

'He's fine now, Helen. You saw how he was. Once we put our foot down he came to his senses.'

'But if he gets paranoid again, and there's only Annis here, and –'

'What's he going to do, Helen? We'll have the car.'

'I just think it's a bad idea, Eddie.' She sounded as tired as Annis felt. 'We don't know *what* he could do. Call a taxi or attack Annis or run away . . . We can't possibly leave them on their own. Not tonight.'

'So you're going to let our own children hold us to ransom?'

'That's not –'

'You do realise this is exactly what he wants? To control us? To make sure we don't do anything, anything at all, without his say-so? Come on, Helen. He's screwing us around. He *wants* us to be too scared to leave him.'

No, he's not! Annis narrowed her eyes and glared into the middle distance. *You don't get it, do you, Dad? He's the one who's scared. Because he's in danger. It's not a joke. And all you can do is row with each other . . .*

'Believe me, Helen, I was as worried as you were, this morning. But he's calmed down. And I think hanging around the house, letting him dictate our every move, is the worst possible thing we could do for him right now. Annis will be here. If there's any trouble, she can phone us. We'll only be a few miles away.'

There was a pause. Annis scraped the edge of her flip-flop along the edge of the step, back, forth, back . . .

Mum said, 'I am just so sick of worrying about him.'

'Of course you are, Helen.'

'All I want is . . . I want us to be OK again. I want to go back to how we were. I want this all to stop, Eddie.' She sounded about Annis's age.

'It's nothing serious. Really. He'll be fine. And we need to spend some time on our own, away from the kids. Annis is sensible; she can hold the fort. It's only a couple of hours, Helen. And we've already bought the tickets.'

Annis stood up and walked away. It was a foregone conclusion. Mum had gone squidgy, like a bar of soap that had been left in the sink. She'd agree to anything Dad said, because she was too exhausted to think for herself.

She leant against the wall, watching the swifts dart in and out of the barn. *And what am I supposed to do,* she thought, *when Dad's got his way, and they're at their concert in Limoges, and Zach tries to run away? Stop him? Phone Mum's mobile? Call the police?*

I ought to help him. Because he's telling the truth. Not the whole truth, maybe, but he's really scared. He's not making it up. That boy, in St Jean-le-Grand . . .

She carried on walking, round the corner of the house, along the terrace, past the side door, looking out at the fields, the valley, the walnut tree . . . *Patrolling,* she thought. *Like a sentry. Watching . . .* She hated it, going round in circles, over and over, like she was following her own footprints, but she couldn't sit still either. The uneasiness was sewing her stomach into a neat bundle, tighter and tighter. She could see the trails of dead grass circling the house, more of them, now, crossing and re-crossing as if there was an invisible barrier twenty metres away. She knew, deep in her gut, like a dull ache, that if she looked into the trees she'd see a shadow that wasn't cast by anything, a person-shaped blot on her retina. A boy in the dark, when the rest of the world was in sunshine. Just a figment of her imagination.

Except she knew now that it wasn't. *He* wasn't. Who – *what*ever he was . . .

And she knew that Zach was sitting at the window in their bedroom, staring out. She didn't even need to look up. He was there. Watching, like her; waiting.

She went round and round and round, until she got sick of tiny specks of stone catching between her flip-flops and the soles of her feet, and sick of the stinging nettles on the terrace, and the hot, heavy air making her sweat, and the way she seemed to see shadowy figures everywhere she looked. What was she supposed to *do*? There had to be something . . . She kept on walking, while the clouds built up and the light went faded and strange.

After hours and hours – or maybe only seconds, she'd lost track of time – Mum came out on to the terrace. 'Annis, darling –'

Annis almost carried on walking, but she made herself stop and turn to look. 'Yes?'

'We're going to go to this concert in an hour or so, after I've done my emails and got changed, but I just wanted to –'

Annis said again, 'Yes?'

'Darling . . . Zach will be fine, you know that, don't you? He's just a bit . . . muddled. He'll be fine.'

'So you keep saying.'

'Well . . .' Mum tugged one earring, pinching it between her finger and thumb. 'I wanted to say . . . anyway, if anything happens while we're out, you can phone my mobile, or Pascale in St Jean-de-la-Croix if it's an emergency, she speaks very good English, or . . . You shouldn't have any trouble, though, sweetheart, I think he's asleep.'

God, it was like Zach was a *baby*. Annis said, 'Whatever.'

'Your father's set his heart on going out, and . . . oh, I don't know, I'm not sure whether . . .' She spun her earring with her finger, twisting it until it creased her earlobe. 'Perhaps we should stay . . . do you . . . ?'

Stay here. So that you can tell Zach he's mad, Annis

thought. *So that you can stop him running away. So that if the boy comes and Zach's in danger he can't save himself.* She said, 'Mum. Go to the concert. Go.'

'Thank you, darling, that's sweet of –'

'I'm going for a swim. Before it rains.' Annis ran without looking back, skin tingling. Stupid, smug, blind, complacent, *selfish* . . . She fed the anger, keeping it simmering, because underneath it she was scared.

She didn't swim. She sat and stared at nothing, feeling the air thicken. She itched to go back to the house, carry on walking round and round, but she didn't want to see anyone else. *Maybe it's only the weather*, she thought. *Maybe Zach is imagining it.* But the thought was two-dimensional; it toppled over as soon as she looked at it.

She sat there for ages, but it still didn't rain.

Someone called, 'Annis! We're off!' Dad. In front of the house, waving at her. She didn't wave back, just watched them get into the car, put their seat belts on, drive off . . . Mum was wearing her blue silk shift, that showed her knees, and a long bead necklace. *She looks nice*, Annis thought – somehow, strangely, wishing she didn't.

The sound of the car receded. She got to her feet and went down to the house, expecting to see Zach at the fridge with his rucksack, rummaging for packets of cheese and Parma ham, squashing a loaf of bread into the front pocket . . . but the kitchen was still and empty. The silence hung in the air like a net. She called out, 'Zach?'

No one answered. She stared around for another few seconds, then ran up the stairs. Had he already gone? Sneaked out of the house? *Of course*, she thought. *That's what he'd do. He wouldn't let Mum and Dad stop him. He must have crept past Mum and Dad while they were arguing, called a taxi, got to Limoges airport . . . He's probably not even in the country any more. Good for you, Zach. Well done.* She pushed open the bedroom door. *Look. No Zach. See, I knew he'd –*

Then she saw him, huddled in a ball on the floor next to the window.

'Zach? Are you OK?'

He didn't move; didn't respond at all, so Annis wasn't even sure she'd said anything. She went over and crouched next to him, careful not to get too close. 'Zach!'

He raised his head. He looked awful.

'Mum and Dad have gone. Zach. They've *gone*.' She waited for him to leap to his feet, grab his rucksack, pelt down the stairs . . . He didn't move. 'I'll call you a taxi, OK? I've still got the fifteen euros Dad gave me. And you've got your bankcard, right? Have you got enough money in the account? Can you get a flight? Come *on*, Zach, you've got to *go*.'

He shook his head, and said something too quiet for her to hear.

'What? Zach, you've got to –'

'No.'

'But I thought –'

'It's too late.' He lowered his head, so it was resting on his knees, and spoke to the floor, without looking at her. 'I can't . . . I'm not strong enough . . . I can't keep him away any longer . . .'

'*What?*' She almost tugged at his arm, but she

106

caught herself just in time. 'What are you talking about?'

Zach met her gaze. His face was gleaming white, translucent. Even his irises were an odd colour. 'It's too late. I can't win. I tried and tried . . . honestly, Anz, I did *try*.' For a second he sounded like a little kid. 'But it's too late, I'm running out of strength, and he's strong, he's stronger than me, I can't do any more, it's too late –'

'Stop *saying* that! I don't know what you're on about. You're still alive, aren't you? How is it *too late*?'

'Because . . .' He exhaled, the breath hissing through his teeth. There was a fractional silence. He glanced at the window. Then, with a sudden, strange note in his voice, like a laugh, he said, 'Because he's *here*, Anz. He's outside.'

Seven

She almost thought Zach was joking, from the way he said it. *He's here* . . . but she stood up slowly, and looked out of the window, and every bone in her body already knew what she'd see.

He was there. Of course he was. On the terrace, looking up at the window. Somehow she could tell that, even though she couldn't see his eyes. In the weird gathering-storm light he looked almost solid. As she watched he dropped his gaze and began to walk along the side of the house, staring at the wall as if he was searching for a door. But it would be locked. Wouldn't it? Mum and Dad would've . . . He couldn't get in. Could he?

Her stomach lurched as if she was seasick. She turned away from the window, her T-shirt suddenly damp and sticking to her ribs. She wanted to close her eyes and huddle in a ball next to Zach. She said, 'What do we do?'

He'd hidden his face again. 'I don't know.' His voice was muffled.

'Well, *think*!' Annis wanted to shake him. *Come on, please* . . . He'd get to the other side of the house. He'd have found the front door by now. He'd be trying the handle . . . oh God, oh *God*. It wasn't locked. She'd used it herself, a few minutes ago. She dug her nails into her palm, refusing to panic. 'Right. OK. Let's call the police.'

Zach made a kind of sobbing sound that might have been a laugh. 'Great idea, Annis. Just give them a description of him, will you?'

'If he's really trying to kill you I don't think it really *matters* what he looks like –'

'Except that he's not – he's not a real person, Anz.' His voice was flat, like it had hit bedrock. 'You know he isn't.'

'But . . .' Annis bit her lip. No point arguing. She said carefully, 'So who is he, Zach? What does he want?'

'Me. He wants *me*.'

'But why, Zach? *Why* does he want you? Isn't there something you can do? Talk to him or something?'

'You don't understand. It's not like that. I can't . . .' He trailed off, hitting one knee with his fist. 'I've been keeping him away for ages . . . for days . . . and I can't do it any more, I'm too *tired*, he's getting stronger . . .'

'Zach, if you'd just tell me what's going on! Please, I could help, I know I could help –'

'Don't be stupid, Anz. You can't help. Believe me.'

A pause; like a door opening, the silence flooding in like water. She felt like she was sinking, full of a terrible inertia that weighed her down. She struggled. *Come on, come on* . . . Zach put his head between his hands, blocking his ears – although Annis knew that whatever he could hear, it was coming from inside – and curled into a ball. She stared at him, suddenly furious, because he was meant to be the clever one, the brave one, and he wasn't doing *anything* . . . She got to her feet. 'OK, if you won't talk to him, *I* will!'

'No – Annis –'

'If he wants *you*, he's not going to hurt me, is he?' She stomped down the stairs, not caring how much noise she made. *See? I'm not scared* . . . although she was. She heard Zach behind her, calling her name, but she ignored him. She'd had enough of this. She'd had about bloody *enough* . . .

The boy was inside the house, near the door. Waiting.

She fought the fear, the way the world swayed under her feet. She stood still, arms folded, at the bottom of the stairs, so that if the boy wanted to get to Zach he'd have to get past her first. She swallowed, trying not to feel sick. He was standing in the dark, only it wasn't dark . . . like a shadow, with no one to cast it . . . But there was something about him. There was something *familiar* . . . it was the same feeling she'd had before: the conviction that she was looking at something – someone – she ought to recognise, but she couldn't. Like her brain couldn't read what her eyes were trying to tell her. She heard herself say, 'Who *are* you?'

No answer. She hadn't really expected one. Behind her, Zach said, 'Annis . . .'

She ignored him. She could feel ripples of fatigue running up and down her backbone, settling in her stomach like a dead weight. She took a heavy, difficult step towards the boy, and felt the world reel. Ah. So it *was* him, giving out darkness like a fire gives out heat . . . She cleared her throat and said, 'Go away,' but her voice sounded very small and flat. 'Go *away*.'

Maybe he didn't understand. Maybe he was French. She fought for the word, trying desperately to stay lucid. '*Allez. Allez!*'

'Anz – there's no point –'

'*Vous n'êtes pas bienvenu.*' Was that right? He ought to get the gist, for God's sake! She added, helplessly, 'Fuck *off*.'

Zach gave a gulp of laughter. 'Don't bother, Anz. He's not French, for a start.'

She spun round. 'How do you *know*? Who is he, Zach? Why don't you just *tell* me, instead of laughing at me when I'm trying to help? At least I'm doing *something*, not like you, you've just *given in* –'

'Because I don't know what to do!' Zach's voice was hoarse, almost a whisper. 'I'm scared, Anz, OK? I'm fucking petrified. He's going to kill me, he's *here*, and I *don't know what to do*.' He was hunched against the banisters, staring down past Annis at the boy. Annis turned to follow his gaze. The boy hadn't moved, but as Annis watched, he took a small – almost hesitant – step forward. He was looking at Zach as if he couldn't see anything else. That tension again, between them: fear and something else, the *something* . . . Zach flinched. He was pulling at his hair, his fists clenched, his whole body shaking.

Annis said, 'Well . . . maybe he can't – I mean, *how* is he going to kill you? If he doesn't have a gun or anything –' Her voice was too high-pitched.

Zach made a gurgling noise that could have been another laugh. 'Trust me on this one, OK?'

She opened her mouth to argue and remembered the way she'd collapsed when the boy in black went past; and the feeling there'd been in the air – danger, a storm coming – when he looked at Zach. She said, instead, 'Can't *you* try talking to him?'

'We don't need to *speak*. Not – aloud.'

'Then –' Annis stopped, digging her nails into her palms. *Come on . . . This can't be happening*, she thought. *It can't be . . . if only I knew what was going on, if only Zach would . . . No. There isn't time for that. I have to do something.*

She glanced up at Zach. His face was gleaming through the gathering shadows, slick with wetness that could have been tears or sweat or both. His eyes were wide open, staring down at the boy. He looked frozen.

She didn't give herself time to think about anything else. She walked straight towards the boy, bracing herself against the waves of black tiredness as though she was wading into the sea. She felt the pull of the dark, as if she was breathing it in; the power, prickling on her skin, the same sense of danger that she'd felt in the ruins . . . There was a connection there, some-where, but she couldn't get hold of it. All she could do was cling to the words in her head, looping them round and round her mind like a rope. *I'll teach you to frighten Zach. You won't hurt him while I'm around. I'll teach you . . .*

Somewhere, distantly, she heard Zach say, 'Annis – *no* – please –'

She sank to her knees. She couldn't help it. But she felt the tiny flame of fury still blaze inside her, pushing her forward. *Don't you dare hurt Zach . . .* She lowered her head and started to crawl.

The boy had taken a few steps back. For the first time he was looking at her, not Zach, although he wasn't really *seeing* her. She couldn't meet his eyes – still couldn't see his face properly – but she felt his gaze. It sent a deep stab of cold right through her, down to her bones. But he'd stepped back . . . She said – whispered – 'Zach . . . I think . . .'

Zach breathed, '*No* – oh God – are you OK? Annis! *Are you OK?*'

She tried to nod, but her head was too heavy. She stared at her hands, spread flat on the floor in front of her, and took a deep breath. She'd say, 'Yes,' in a moment, when she was strong enough . . .

There were footsteps behind her, on the stairs. Then a pause, and Zach's voice, so hoarse and high it was hardly recognisable. 'Go away, go away, go *away go away go* –'

Annis knew from the silence that the boy hadn't moved. He hadn't moved towards Zach, but he hadn't moved back, either. She thought, *Zach has run out of energy. And as he gets weaker, the boy can get closer* . . . With a great effort of will, as if it was the last thing she'd ever do, she looked up.

She was still between Zach and the boy. She knew that from the way the boy was looking past her, his dark gaze direct as an arrow over her head. *I ought to stand up . . . ought to get in Zach's way . . . before he does something stupid, like try to shield me* . . . She pushed herself to her knees, bracing one hand on the floor. Zach was breathing so loudly it was almost sobbing, each breath catching in his throat, gasping out in something that wasn't quite a cry. He said, '*Anz* . . . I'm sorry . . .'

She struggled to one knee, as if she was about to propose, and for a crazy split second had time to feel a bubble of laughter surfacing in her throat. *Will you do me the honour of . . . ?* But there had to be something she could do. The boy was still, poised, watching and watching . . . tense, as if he was pushing an invisible wall . . . Slowly, very slowly, he took another step forward.

Annis thought, *No, no, Zach . . .* She glanced up, afraid, knowing Zach would leap to her defence, and something terrible would happen, something –

Zach spun away, and ran.

He was sprinting flat-out, skidding on the floor, towards the other side of the room, the French windows on to the terrace that – she remembered, in a flash of clarity – were locked. And as soon as he'd moved, the boy was running after him, mirroring his pace exactly, only a split second behind. Annis shouted, 'No – *locked!*' and Zach swerved, throwing himself into the corner of the kitchen, scrabbling helplessly at one of the drawers. What was he *doing*? And the boy was after him, hand stretched to catch him, reaching out for him in a parody of desire. Oh no, oh *no*. Annis took a few steps and then her knees collapsed again. *Oh God, help, please, someone, help.*

For a moment Zach and the boy stood eye to eye, at arm's length, poised like a – like – *something*, Annis thought, *there's something there, what are my eyes trying to tell me? I can't get hold of it . . .* There was an instant of silence, like between the flash and the thunder. Like peace . . . The boy held out his hand, slowly, almost gently. Annis thought, in confusion, *Wait, I know who he is – I think I know –*

Then Zach's hand came up. A flash of metal – a knife –

It flew through the air, straight as a die, at the boy's face.

Zach couldn't have missed at that range. No one could. The knife hardly had to leave his hand. And Zach was a good shot. He was aiming right for the boy's eyes. There was no way he could have missed.

Except that he did. He *did* miss. The boy didn't even recoil.

The knife fell to the floor. It made a sort of shallow clinking noise. Zach stood frozen, his hand still poised in front of him. The other boy was standing exactly where he had been, except that now both arms were by his sides.

Zach blinked. Then he lowered his hand. He was crying – not loudly, but Annis could hear the air stick in his throat, and there was water dripping off his jaw. She couldn't read the look on his face. It wasn't exactly fear, or not *just* fear . . . For a moment she felt an absurd rush of jealousy: the way they were looking at each other, as if no one else in the world existed. She wasn't there, it was just Zach and . . . Who was he? The flash of recognition had faded, like a dream.

Zach bowed his head and wiped his nose with the back of his hand. He'd lost.

Annis thought, *So . . . now. It's going to happen now – whatever it is . . .* She would have thrown herself into the space between them, shielding Zach with the last of her strength – dying for him if she had to – but she was too tired to get to her feet. The awful giggles started to resurface. *Maybe Zach's going to die*, she thought. *Again . . .*

The boy looked at Zach for what seemed like a very

long time; until Zach raised his head again to meet his gaze.

Then the boy turned away. He walked past Annis to the door and went out silently into the dim, cloudy light. He didn't look back.

Silence.

Annis thought, *What . . . ? He's gone . . . he's really gone . . . why did he . . . ?* She thought she saw Zach raise his head and take a couple of stumbling, urgent steps, as if he was going to call him back. She thought she saw him look lost, for a second, bereft, as if he'd been abandoned. She thought she saw his mouth move silently, shaping words that she didn't understand.

But she couldn't have done. She must have closed her eyes for a moment and dreamt it. Because, after that, she knew she *did* see the relief spread across his face, the tension dropping from his body so suddenly he almost fell over, the grin so wide it looked painful. And she heard him say, in a tone that was so joyous it could have been a prayer, 'Oh, thank fuck, thank fuck, thank *fuck* . . .'

She looked dizzily through the doorway. There was no one there, now. Only a trail of dim brown grass, leading away across the green. Nothing else. The door was still open, starting to swing in the wind.

She sank forward on to the floor and closed her eyes. *I don't understand*, she thought. *What happened . . . ?* Somewhere there was distant thunder, and the noise of the rain just beginning to patter against the windows, introducing itself, finally . . .

The door banged shut. Zach said, 'Annis?' but it blended with the sound of the rain, and she ignored it.

116

She felt the swell of sleep rising to claim her. She thought, *I wonder if the boy will get caught in the storm. I wonder where he'll go . . .*

That was the last thing she remembered.

There was something banging. She groaned and rolled over, squinting into the light. She was in bed, in her T-shirt and knickers. There was sunlight flooding in through the window. Bang-bang-bang . . .

It was Zach. He was kicking at the wall next to his bed, over and over again, until Annis started to wonder how come he hadn't bruised his foot. She said, 'Umph. Zach. Shut *up*.'

He whirled round. 'Thank God – how're you feeling? I was – I thought . . .' He tailed off and came over to the bed. 'Have a nice sleep, did we?'

She grimaced and closed her eyes again. Why did everything have to be so *bright*? 'I feel . . . urgh. What time is it?'

'Quarter past two.'

She sat up, too suddenly, so that the floor lurched sickeningly upwards, defying gravity. 'In the afternoon? Quarter past *two*?'

'So you've been out for . . . oh, about twenty hours. Completely. Dead to the world. I mean . . .' He stopped and shrugged. 'I was starting to get a bit worried.'

'*Starting* to get worried? Gee, thanks, Zach.'

'But you're OK now, right?' He peered at her.

'Er . . .' Annis took a deep breath, listening to her body. There didn't seem to be anything massively wrong. She was just a bit groggy. 'Yeah. I think so.' Something made her add, 'You?'

117

'I'm fine. I'm great. I'm fantastic.' And he looked it. He was still as pale as before – still that odd neon-white – but the tension in his face had gone. *Bright-eyed and bushy-tailed*, Annis thought. *That's what Mum would say. Bursting with energy and joie de vivre, like a recharged battery. Typical. I feel like death, and he's bouncing off the walls* . . . She turned over and shut her eyes again.

Zach said, 'Er . . . Anz . . .'

She grunted.

'I think you'd better get up. Or Mum and Dad will get . . . I mean, if you make an effort now it'll min-imise repercussions.'

She rolled over, reluctantly. '*Minimise repercussions?* What are you talking about?'

Zach gnawed his thumbnail, not meeting her eyes. 'Well . . . last night . . . I told them you were drunk.'

She sat bolt upright and stared at him. 'You did *what*?'

'I had to, Anz, you were out cold on the floor, and I couldn't move you, and . . . look, what was I sup-posed to say? It was all I could think of on the spur of the moment. If I'd said I didn't know what was wrong they'd have taken you to hospital, for God's sake.'

'And how did you know I shouldn't be in hospital?'

At least he had the grace to look sheepish. 'I thought you'd be fine. And you are fine, aren't you? Look, I'm sorry, I just didn't know what else to do.'

'Oh God. They'll kill me.'

'No they won't.' Zach met her gaze and gave her a frank guileless smile that made him look like a frog. She stared back at him until he gave up on it. 'Well . . . OK, they're a bit . . . miffed –'

'*Miffed?*'

'– but they'll be fine. Come on, Anz, you're their good little girl, they'll forgive you. You're under a lot of pressure, you didn't realise the *cassis* was that strong, it was partly my fault –'

'*Partly?*'

'– and – yes, *partly*, I wish you'd stop repeating everything I say – it would hardly be plausible if I said I'd forced the stuff down your throat, would it? Be reasonable, Anz. It was the best I could do. So I'm sorry if it tarnishes your halo temporarily, but desperate times and all that, and you're just going to have to live with it. And get up and get dressed and be especially sweet and penitent all day to make up for it.' He put on a sort of sympathetic bedside face.

Annis said, 'You think it's *funny.*'

'No, I don't.' He screwed his mouth to one side and stared at the ceiling. Then he caught her eye, and laughed. 'Yeah. OK. I do.'

'You bastard, Zach.' But the anger was slipping through her fingers. He was right. It *was* funny. 'You are unbelievable, you know that?'

'Yep. Come on. Shake a leg. I'll go and make you hot chocolate, if you want.'

She rolled her eyes and smiled in spite of herself. 'Oh, all right. But you owe me one, OK?'

'Yeah, yeah. Get out of bed, you lazy cow.' He shook his head in mock disgust. Annis snarled at him and dragged her pillow out from underneath her, but he darted through the door before she had time to throw it. For a second he stood in the doorway, hand poised on the handle in case he needed to duck behind the door. The grin faded from his face. He muttered,

'By the way . . . um . . . thanks.' Then he was gone.

Annis could have slept for another week, let alone another couple of hours, but she dragged herself out of bed, pulled on her jeans, and followed him downstairs. Zach was OK. That was the important thing. Whatever had happened . . . the danger had gone.

Zach met her on the stairs, coming back up with a croissant on a plate and a mug of hot chocolate. As soon as he saw her he jerked his head backwards and said in an undertone, 'Enraged father three metres north-north-west. To be avoided.'

'But –'

'Sssh. Listen.'

She stood still. Dad was talking French. At least, she thought it was French. You could tell he was pissed off because it was hard to tell. 'May – dezolay, Philippe, may voo mavay dee – we – we –'

Zach raised his eyebrows, like, *See what I mean?* and held out the plate and mug for her to take. 'I thought we could go outside. Then if they flip you can say you've been awake for hours.'

Annis couldn't help noticing how careful he was not to touch her fingers by mistake. So he still thought . . . For a second she stared at him, the night before coming back to her: the dark boy, the flash of the knife as Zach threw it, the storm breaking . . . Then she blinked and made herself concentrate. 'Right. Fine. OK.' She followed Zach as he tiptoed exaggeratedly back down the stairs and slunk out through the front door. She didn't bother being unobtrusive, because Dad had started shouting and wasn't going to notice anything at all for the next five seconds, which was when Philippe would probably hang up on him.

They sat against the wall of the barn, looking towards the swimming pool. The ground was still a bit damp, but the stone was warm against Annis's back. She sat back and closed her eyes. There was a silence so long she drifted in and out of sleep.

'You know, I feel great,' Zach said suddenly, like he was continuing a conversation. His voice was louder than it needed to be. 'I can't tell you how great I feel . . . I feel *wonderful*. God, I'm so *happy*. It's weird, it's like none of it is important any more. Dad, Mum, school . . . I don't *care*. I'm just – amazingly, totally – *happy*. Just sitting here. Isn't this *fantastic*? I feel like . . . it's *amazing*. Isn't it? Just to be *alive* . . .'

Annis would have rolled her eyes if she hadn't had to open them first. *Amazing* . . . He sounded like Penny. She said, 'I guess so. Given the alternatives.'

He laughed, like she'd said something really funny. 'No, seriously, Anz . . . I feel like . . . this total *euphoria*. Like I want to dance, or sing, or something . . . there's too much happiness, like it won't fit into my body. I've never felt like this – this *joy* – I'm just . . . so *happy*, I can't express it.'

This time she did open her eyes. She turned to look at him. 'Are you high on something?'

There was a flash of irritation on his face; then it dissolved into a grin that was so wide it made Annis uneasy. 'Jeez . . . why does everyone always think I'm stoned? No, I'm not on anything, Anz. This is *real*. And I feel great. It's better than drugs. It's amazing . . . Everything's *sharper*, you know? I guess I'm just high on *life*.'

Annis blinked. She said, 'Quite honestly, Zach, you don't sound your usual lucid self.'

121

'Not miserable, you mean? Not pissed off?'

'Not thinking very clearly.'

'God, you are so cynical. I'm telling you I feel wonderful – marvellous – *splendid*,' he said, throwing his arm out to one side and giggling, 'and all you can do is tell me I'm mad. Why can't you say –'

'I didn't say *mad*, I said –'

He ignored her. 'Why can't you just say, "That's brilliant, Zach, you feel happy for the first time in months, the best you've ever felt in your life, like something has finally fallen into place, hurrah for you"? I feel like I can *fly* –'

Annis sat bolt upright, panicking. 'You *can't* –'

'Jesus Christ, Anz! Metaphorically.'

She shouldn't have been pleased that he sounded annoyed with her, but she was. It made him sound more like himself. She said, 'Sorry. I didn't mean to be . . .' What? Cynical? That was rich, coming from *him* . . . She let the sentence trail off.

He shrugged and smiled, like a shutter had come down over his eyes. 'Never mind. Forget it.' He turned away, jabbing a hole in the grass with one finger. Then Annis saw the wide uncanny grin start to creep over his face again. 'I feel like I could *burst*, you know? With sheer . . . *joy* . . .'

Annis didn't want her croissant but she ate it anyway. It tasted of cardboard. Something was wrong. There was something wrong with him – still . . . *But the boy went away*, she thought, helplessly. *He went away of his own accord. So why* would *there be something wrong with Zach? I'm being paranoid. Maybe he* is *just happy. Would that be so terrible?* She swallowed a papery mouthful of croissant and said,

'Zach . . . about last night . . .'

'It's fine, Anz. All sorted. All over. Won't happen again.'

'But – what's going on – who *was* –'

'Don't worry about it. He will never come back – never never never –' He began to sing it, *never-never-never*, to a tune from one of Dad's awful Gilbert and Sullivan CDs.

'But –'

'Trust me, Anz, all over, nothing to worry about, he's gone, it's over, I'm happy, the lark's on the wing, snail's on the thorn, or possibly the other way round . . .' And suddenly he was on his feet and calling over his shoulder, halfway across the field, whirling in the sunshine like a dervish. Annis stared at him, screwing her eyes up against the light.

Something wrong, her mind said. *There's still something – missing . . .* But it was like an itch, just out of reach; something so obvious she couldn't see it . . . She watched Zach dance in the sunlight. He was holding his arms out to the side like a little kid, spinning in the light, stumbling in the long grass. She saw him lose his balance, his shoulders shaking with giggles, dropping to his knees. *Look*, she thought. *He's happy. It's over.*

Then he froze. Annis couldn't see what was wrong; he was just staring down into the grass, as if he'd seen something on the ground. He raised his head and turned to the side, staring towards the walnut tree. Then she realised what it was. He was kneeling on the trail of dead grass that surrounded the house: the loop the boy had made, circling and circling. She followed Zach's gaze, although she already knew what she'd see.

The tree was dead. The last tier of green leaves had gone; now they were entirely brown, falling and drifting in the breeze as if it was autumn. And the grass around the trunk was withered, too.

She couldn't see Zach's eyes. But she knew, somehow, that he was staring at the traces the dark boy had left behind him. And she saw the happiness ebbing away from him like water, leaving him stranded.

She thought: *The boy's gone. But it isn't over. It's not over.*

Eight

Mum said, 'Well, in that case, Edward, how do you explain the fact that all the plants on the terrace just *withered*? I know I asked you to sort out the weeds, but –'

Dad said, 'For once and for all, Helen, I did not *touch* the fucking weeds! I don't know, maybe one of the kids was trying to help –'

Annis averted her eyes and stared up at the towers of the chateau. It took up one side of the town square and cast two symmetrical spears of shade out over the cafe awnings and plane trees. Apparently it was of historical interest. Meaning, historically, there might have been an occasion when someone was interested in it.

'Oh, never mind . . .' Mum stalked past Annis, already digging in her handbag for the entrance fee, like she wanted to get this over and done with as quickly as possible. 'If you want to buy rosemary instead of just picking our own, who am I to gainsay you?'

'Jesus *Christ*,' Zach muttered, forcing the air out through his teeth. 'I could kill them both, I swear to you . . .'

Annis glanced at him, then away. She could feel the fury coming off him, like heat. It made her want to take a step backwards. She shrugged, trying to stay casual. 'Don't let it get to you.'

Zach didn't answer. After a few seconds she heard him take a deep breath. Then he followed Mum through the archway, walking just slightly too quickly. Annis stood still, watching him. She could feel herself relax as he got further away, as if she was *afraid* . . . That was stupid, of course. He was just Zach; she wasn't afraid of him . . . but he felt – dangerous. Wound up; like a spring, or a clock, ticking too fast . . . or a light bulb, about to smash – something with too much energy for its own good, something that could only take so much.

Dad said, 'Annis? Are you coming?'

'Yeah . . .' She hadn't slept properly. She kept waking up, and every time she opened her eyes Zach's bed had been empty. He hadn't slept in it for two whole nights. She told herself he had to be sleeping somewhere else – surely – but she was almost sure he wasn't sleeping, full stop. She'd heard his footsteps outside on the terrace, fading away then coming back, going round and round the house. She shook her head, trying to get rid of the worry, like it was water in her ears. She said determinedly, 'Yep. Sorry, Dad. So, this chateau, it's, like, eighteenth century, or something . . . ?' and followed him towards the entrance.

Mum had already paid for them. By the time they got through into the courtyard – Dad still saying, 'Of course, it's not like an *English* castle, the chateau is a very different entity,' waving his hands like he was on camera – the guide was waiting for them, smiling

126

round at her little herd of tourists. Everyone except Zach smiled back inanely.

The guide waved at Dad and started to talk. Annis stood at the back of the group, letting her attention wander. A cloud drifted over the sun, making her shiver in the sudden chill. The guide said, 'The statues near the roof are emblems. On the left is . . .' but Annis tuned out again. Zach wasn't listening either; he was scuffing at the ground with his flip-flop, tracing the edge of Mum's shadow with his toe. Annis stared at his foot, mesmerised, without knowing why. Maybe because it was just so *white*. Or . . . what *was* –?

'If you will move this way, please. Follow me.'

Annis moved obediently after the rest of the group, yawning. A kitchen, with lots of old pots and pans. Great. A staircase. Wonderful. Bedrooms . . . a long gallery . . . another staircase . . . More allegorical statues, a hall, another staircase, the view from the top of the tower – 'Look, darling, there's our house, just over there,' – down the stairs again, a cellar, more stairs – 'Thank you very much for your attention,' – another staircase . . . and then they were out in the courtyard again, in blazing sun and sudden heat.

Mum said, 'Annis? Have you seen Zach?'

'He's probably just –' Annis said automatically, then stopped. No. She hadn't. Not since the tour started.

Mum said, 'Edward? Have *you* seen Zach?'

'Oh, for heaven's sake! That boy is . . .'

That'll be a no, then, Annis thought. She turned to look at the staircase they'd come down, in case he was loitering behind everyone else. Nope. She rotated slowly on the spot, scanning the courtyard.

'. . . I can't *believe* he's wandered off on his own! He's a fucking liability.'

'He's been better these last few days, Edward, you know he's been getting better.'

'It's *OK*, Mum, Dad, relax, for goodness' sake, he's *there* . . .' Annis pointed. Then wished she hadn't.

He was at one of the tall windows on the other side of the courtyard. There was a kind of railing in front of it, and he was sitting on the railing, legs dangling over the two-storey drop, arms crossed over his chest. Annis felt the bottom fall out of her stomach. *Oh no*, she thought. *This is not good. This is not good at all* . . .

Mum said, 'Dear God . . . what is he *thinking*?'

Dad shouted, 'Zach! What the hell do you think you're doing?' Everyone in the courtyard turned to look. Zach uncrossed his arms and waved.

The guide looked up at him, then back at Mum. She said, 'Excuse me, Madame, but this is not . . . it is important that . . .' She paused for a second and then launched into a stream of impassioned French.

Mum said, '*Mais, oui, Madame, je comprends, bien sûr, je suis desolée, un moment, s'il vous plaît –* Edward, will you get him *down – mon mari va régler ça –*'

'Zach! You better bloody come down *now*!'

The other tourists swapped glances. One of the women – a young one in a short top – giggled, until she caught sight of Annis glaring at her.

Zach swayed from side to side; he had a weird, fierce grin on his face. He called down, 'What's the matter, Dad? Am I embarrassing you?'

Dad shot a swift look over his shoulder, then back at Zach. 'You come *down*! *Now!*'

'Why?'

'You get down here this *instant*, young man, or I will personally – I'll – you come down *now*.' It was like that was the only thing he could think of to say.

'Because I'm making a scene, and everyone's looking at you and thinking what a bad parent you are. Yeah? Not because you're worried about me. Not because you think I might fall and break my neck.' A fractional pause, as if he was waiting for Dad to disagree. But there was only silence, and the echo of his voice bouncing off the chateau walls. He rocked forward, clenching his hands on the railing. 'And you know what? You're right. You're absolutely right. Because even if I fell, I wouldn't hurt myself. I'd just –'

Mum said, 'Zachary, I'm warning you. You will be in *so much trouble* if you don't –'

But Dad got in first. He shouted, 'You little *brat*, shut up and come down here *right now*. If I have to come up there you will wish you'd never been *born*.'

Zach nodded to himself. Then he shrugged. 'OK. Whatever you say.' Then he leant forward, bracing himself with his arms.

And jumped.

Someone gasped. Annis didn't know who it was. One of the tourists, or Mum, or even Dad . . . a sharp intake of breath that said, *Oh my God, he'll break a leg at least . . .* She felt her own heartbeat falter, like someone missing their footing. She heard Dad say – *start* to say – '*Fuck . . .*'

Zach landed awkwardly, crunching on to the gravel

on his knees, one ankle twisting underneath him. There was a kind of dull crack, like someone dropping a plate. Then a pause. For an instant he was bent over, breathing in uneven sobs, like someone after they've been sick. Then he straightened up and got to his feet. He reeled, then regained his balance, holding out his hands and giving Dad that grin again. 'Ta-*dah* . . .'

Mum said, 'Zachary . . .'

Dad took a deep breath in. He had sweat running down his forehead. 'What the *hell* do you think you're –'

'Relax, Dad. I'm fine. Absolutely *fine* . . .' Zach's grin was a parody, now. 'I don't *get* hurt any more. I'm completely invulnerable.' He laughed, but it sounded like he was choking on something. 'Look – let me demonstrate . . .' He turned back to the wall, drew back his fist, and punched. His hand hit the wall with a kind of thud: the noise of bone hitting something immovable.

Someone murmured, 'Holy shit . . . the kid's flipped . . .'

Annis said, 'Zach –' She didn't mean to say anything; it just came out.

'See?' He raised his hand and wiggled the fingers. 'No pain. See? *See?* I'm invulnerable – I'm completely fucking *immortal*.' He looked round; everyone was staring, but no one spoke. He gave another laugh. At least, it might have been a laugh. Then he turned back to the wall and punched it again and again, putting his whole weight into it. There was silence, except for the sound of his hand thudding into the stone; as if no one in the whole world knew what to do. It was unreal. It couldn't be happening. Annis felt the dreadfulness of it rise up through her like bleach, wiping out everything else. *Please, someone, make him stop* . . .

Then – finally – Dad moved. He grabbed Zach roughly by the shoulders, pulling him away from the wall, swinging him round. 'OK, sonny Jim, that's *enough* –'

There was a bang, a flash of light so bright it was like the sun had flickered, and Dad staggered back, fell to his knees, and started to swear in a small, tight voice.

The tension dropped out of Zach's body, like someone had cut the strings. He took a few steps towards Dad, then stopped, biting his lip. 'I'm sorry, Dad.' His voice cracked. 'I didn't mean to – oh Christ, I'm really sorry.'

Mum said, 'Edward? Eddie? What's the matter? What –?'

Dad held his hands out to fend Mum off. Then, slowly, he stood up, and turned back to look at Zach. Annis felt her insides curl up. He was going to say something awful . . . something *terrible* . . . *Please, please, Dad, don't* . . .

There was a pause. Then he said, very, very gently, 'All right, Zach. Come on, there's a good chap. Don't worry about it. Let's just go home, shall we?'

Zach looked back at him, his face so blank he looked like he hadn't understood. The real Zach, the one Annis thought she knew, would have been sarcastic, if someone had talked to him like that – would have said, *I'm not a fucking child* . . . especially to Dad; especially now, when they were so angry with each other. But he didn't. He just nodded dumbly and let Dad escort him across the courtyard towards the archway.

Mum said, 'Annis! Stop looking gormless. Let's go,' and went after them, hoisting her handbag sharply on to her shoulder as she walked past the other tourists.

Annis clenched her teeth and didn't answer. She had a deep dark hole in her gut, like a whirlpool, dragging everything down. She thought, helplessly, *But I thought Zach was OK* . . . She trailed after Mum, too anxious even to give the tourists an evil look as she passed. She stared at Mum's shoes, crunching on the gravel. Left, right, left . . . Dad and Zach were in front, walking side by side, not touching. They went through the archway and came out into the sunshine on the other side. They looked . . . *Unsymmetrical*, Annis thought, frowning. Which was funny, somehow . . . Both the same height, but . . . Something wrong, something missing . . . She squinted into the sunlight, while the whirlpool sucked at her gut. What –?

She stopped dead, blinking, feeling suddenly queasy.

Dad's shadow tagged at his heels like a stumpy black figure.

Zach's shadow wasn't there.

The rest of the day went past in a hot, prickly kind of dream. It wasn't until after dinner, when Annis was sitting outside, eavesdropping again, that reality switched itself back on, suddenly, like an electric current. She sat up straight and paid attention.

Mum's voice murmured, 'We shouldn't really . . . oh, all right, darling, but go for the cheap one . . .'

Then there was the sound of a cork coming out of a bottle, and the fat glug-glug-glug of the first glass being poured. Then four seconds of silence, while Annis watched the bats swooping and diving through the dusk, her hands clasped round her knees.

Finally Dad said, 'I was wrong, Helen. I'm sorry. I reacted badly. I should have seen he needed help.'

'We were both wrong. We both thought he'd be fine, once he was away from all that . . . we didn't realise how bad it was . . .' Something that might have been a bottle clinking against a glass and another brief glug. Then Mum laughed shakily. 'God, I'm half cut already. This must be where he gets it from.'

'Nonsense. Whatever mess he's in, it's his own bloody fault. He has to – yes, I *know*, Helen, but he has to take responsibility.'

'He's a child, Eddie. He's just a child . . .'

'I know. Don't be silly, Helen, I didn't mean we shouldn't look after him. I just meant . . . Never mind. Whatever foolish things he's done to end up like this, he needs our help.'

There was a tiny red spark moving through the darkness, getting brighter. Annis sat up straight, bracing herself against the wall. Then she saw it was Zach, walking towards her, with a cigarette in his hand. She gestured at him not to say anything, and turned her head again to listen. Mum said, ' . . . I just don't know what we're meant to –'

Zach said, 'Stop eavesdropping, Anz.' It wasn't very loud, but it wasn't like he was whispering, either.

Annis made a face and flapped a hand at him, like, *Shut up, I'm trying to listen while they discuss what to do with you . . .*

133

'Anz. *Anz*. Come for a walk with me.'

She looked up at him, meeting his eyes in the half-light. His face was so pale it was almost blue. She said, 'But don't you want to know what they're saying about you?'

'Annis, *please*.' A beat. The bats flitted past, weaving up and down. Zach reached out a hand, but he didn't touch her. He swallowed. 'I don't want to be on my own.'

She stared at him, trying to make out his expression through the gathering dark. *I don't want to be on my own* . . . She stood up. As soon as she moved he turned and walked back the way he'd come, so that she had to follow the glow of his cigarette, until he flicked it away into the grass. Then she had to do a detour to make sure it had gone out, grinding it into the ground with her toe, just in case.

By the time she caught up he was sitting against the wall next to the swimming pool, lighting up again. It was like he was trying to pretend he didn't really want her there, that he hadn't said *please* . . . She sat down a little way away and waited.

He smoked the new cigarette. She heard his breathing, the tiny crackle of the paper burning down, the subtle creak of the grass when he shifted his weight. It was only after he'd finished it – stubbing it out against the wall before he tossed it away – that he spoke. He didn't turn to look at her.

'Do *you* think I'm mad?' It sounded casual; almost.

'Only if I'm mad, too.'

He laughed, in a tight, involuntary way that made Annis think of a sneeze. 'Thank God for that . . . I thought – I wasn't sure . . .'

'I don't think you're mad.' She took a breath. 'But I'd quite like to know what's going on.'

She could just about see enough of him to know that he was nodding; over and over again, like it didn't mean *yes* but something else. He said quietly, 'I don't know if you'll –'

'Believe you? Zach, for God's sake!' She only just managed not to grab his shoulder and shake him. 'I saw that wall collapse on you, remember? I saw you with a broken neck – I saw you *dying*!'

Zach said, 'Oh. Yes. So you did.' There was a split-second pause.

And then they were both laughing, so hard it hurt. Annis bent over, clutching her waist, feeling herself convulse with giggles. And Zach was hunched over too, shaking, croaking and sobbing and gasping with mirth. She started to surface, but as soon as she looked at him she went under again, flailing helplessly, giggling until she thought she would never be able to stop. *I saw you dying* . . . Oh dear oh dear . . .

Slowly she managed to get a grip on herself. *OK, Anz, not that funny, really not that funny* . . . She braced herself and turned to look at Zach. He was coughing up the last dregs of laughter, shaking his head as if he was exhausted. She heard him heave a few deep breaths, and felt her own breathing slow in sympathy. She could still see the outline of his temple, the skin of his forehead gleaming under his hair.

There was silence, and the last of the laughter fell away. And in the space that it left, she thought, with a strange unshaken certainty, *He is giving off light. I'm not imagining it. I never was.*

And suddenly that same steady clarity made it easy

for her. She didn't feel anything. She was in control. She drew in another long breath and said softly, 'Tell me who that boy is, Zach.'

There was a pause, but she knew he was going to answer. He raised his head a little, to stare towards the swimming pool and the last remnants of daylight in the sky beyond. He said, 'I think . . . he's me.'

Silence. She waited, marvelling at her own icy patience.

'He's part of me, anyway. He's my shadow. Only not just my shadow. He's . . . Without him I can't sleep or feel pain or die. I wasn't joking, today. I think I *am* immortal, now.' He stopped, as if he was giving the words time to breathe.

Annis thought: *immortal*. And the sure, quiet part of her mind added: *yes*.

When Zach started speaking again it was as if he was explaining something academic, like when he used to help Annis with her homework. 'He's my . . .' He bit his lip. 'The darkness, you know? Like night and day, or yin and yang or . . . the opposite of what I am now, only . . .'

'He's your death.'

He turned to look at her, then. 'Yes. I think so.'

'That's why –' Annis felt her voice crack, and swallowed. 'That's why you didn't die, when that rock hit you, when the wall collapsed. You should have done . . . but you didn't, because he wasn't there. Is that right? And that's why you were so scared, when he followed you, because –'

'Yes.'

'And now he's gone away, so . . .'

But Zach didn't answer.

It felt like there were more words hovering at arm's length, circling in the air like midges, but Annis had no idea how she was supposed to get them into her mouth. She blinked and braced her tongue against her teeth, ready to speak, but nothing came out. And in the end the new tranquil voice said, *Don't bother. The silence will ask your questions for you.*

Zach said, 'I thought it was over. But it isn't, is it?'

She still didn't say anything. She'd never known she had this kind of strength: the strength to stay quiet, all this time, just waiting for the answers.

'It was my own fault. I mean – it was an accident, I didn't mean to – but . . .' He trailed off. 'I was . . . oh, shit, I can't explain . . . you wouldn't understand.'

'Try me.' Her voice sounded as if it was coming from a long way away.

He looked at her. She thought, *That is the first time he's ever looked at me like that; like we're the same age.*

He said, 'Are you sure? I mean –'

'Tell me.'

He held her gaze, until he had to look away.

Then he told her.

He's out there, somewhere. Somewhere he's walking across grass, and it's withering under his feet. Or he's brushing past people on a pavement, and they're glancing at him as he goes past and then reeling, staggering, blacking out, without even having time to wonder what's happened. Or he's walking down a deserted street past boarded-up houses and all the small nocturnal animals are crawling out of their lairs to die in his wake.

And it's my fault. Somewhere, he's me.

Do you remember the day we arrived at the house in France? 'Course you do. Mum and Dad too exhausted to argue, and you all moody, the way you always are after a long journey, and me . . . I was so fed up I was going crazy. And the talk they gave us, before we even got in the front door: Do not go down to the ruins, children, they are VERY DANGEROUS. And as soon as I heard it I knew I'd go down there, the first chance I got. And when I did, that evening, when it was getting dark . . . It felt like . . . you know when Mum uses a

138

sponge to wipe everything up, and after a while it gets soggy and grimy and disgusting? It felt like that. Like the ruins had been soaking up all the misery and anger, from Mum and Dad, and the people who lived there before, and before that, for years and years – and any moment now it would start to ooze back out. The whole place was like that, storing all the emotions you wouldn't want to have, building up power like a generator. It was so strong you could smell it.

The weird thing was, I felt like I'd been there before. I *recognised* it. Not the building, I mean, but the feeling. I fitted into it, like a key in a lock.

And I felt so fucking wretched I started to like being down there, because it felt the same way I did. The more time I spent there, the more I liked it. Like when you're so dirty you'd rather be filthy all over than get clean again. I wanted to stay there for ever. I was addicted to the misery. It felt right. I thought I deserved it.

So I kept going back, spending whole days down there. It wasn't like there was anything else to do. And it made me feel better, I guess, in a bleak, dark way that kept everything at a distance. It was my place. Mine. And it was an escape. From you, from Mum and Dad, and from myself. Like a drug.

Until the day the wall collapsed on me.

That row with Dad, when I ripped up his book. Well . . . you were there. You saw it. You know what happened. What you don't know is that I went to the ruins and down into the cellar and cried my eyes out, because I knew then that we'd never forgive each other. I've never felt the way I did then. It was like my body had turned itself inside out, so even my skin hurt. And I couldn't see or hear or feel anything except how much I hated Dad, and how much I hated me. And I would have done anything to make it stop. Anything.

And maybe . . . I'm not sure. Maybe I said that, aloud.

There was a moment like the last gulp of air before you go under.

It was like I'd asked a question. Something answered me. Something activated itself, like I'd flipped a switch. And I knew – somehow I *knew*, suddenly, that the walls weren't there any more. It was still dark, still quiet, but I was somewhere else. The real world had gone and there was just a kind of void, an aching, appalling, *insane* emptiness. And –

Something changed.

Christ, that's so lame. *Something changed*. But it did, and I don't have words for it. Like the world split in two – only it was me, splitting apart from myself. I was raw and new and gasping for air. I didn't know if it hurt or not. I mean, it was so weird I couldn't tell. I think – maybe – I think it *did* hurt. But I loved it, you know? I was free, I was weightless. I'd slipped the chains. There was this moment, when it was all mixed up, the pain and the ecstasy and . . . It was so good, and so horrible. I can't tell you. It was like . . . dying.

No. It was like *living*.

And when I came back to myself, it *didn't* hurt. Nothing did. I was back where I thought I was, in the cellar, and there was this strange hazy light everywhere and silence like my ears ringing after an explosion and I wasn't unhappy any more.

And I was sitting opposite myself, and I was the most beautiful person I'd ever seen.

I can see him now, if I close my eyes. My shadow. Myself, only made out of darkness, not quite solid. Such a deep, infinite black, like a night sky, so thick it could cast its own shadow. Darkness that shines the way light does . . . And his eyes – the look on his face . . . All I wanted to do was stare and stare. Yes, I realise this sounds a tad narcissistic. But it wasn't like that. I didn't *fancy* him. It was just . . . like meeting my soul.

And the best thing . . . the best thing of all was that he'd taken all the pain away. I don't know how I knew, but I did. When we split apart . . . all the misery – he'd taken it with him. So now . . . I couldn't feel it any more. It was the best feeling in the world. All the shit . . . and I don't just mean all the big stuff, the stuff with Mum and Dad – I mean all of it. Not just wishing I was dead, but all the tiny things, the stuff you don't even notice, the stuff you accumulate all the time, like tarnish. The little scratches and stains that you get just from being human, that you wouldn't even notice until someone wiped them away. It was like my wish had been granted. Like my whole fucking life had been anaesthetised.

So I got up and went outside. Everything dazzled me. Everything, even shadows. Imagine being dazzled by *shadows*. I was all shaky. I was trying to pretend that nothing had happened, so I got out a cigarette, but I couldn't light it. My coordination had gone funny. It was like I'd lost something. Not like a limb, or anything like that. More like – something inside me. Like my balance had gone. Does that make sense? And he was there, all the time, watching me. I knew exactly where he was. He was the only important thing in the world. It felt ridiculous, standing there with my cigarette lighter, as if I cared whether I got a flame or not. But I felt so good – high . . . It was amazing, when I'd felt wretched for so long. Like some amazing drug. I wanted to laugh, or shout, or throw my arms round my shadow and thank him over and over again.

There was a bit of me that knew it was all wrong. Part of me knew, even then. I knew I'd done something terrible. I knew I'd have to go back to being my old, whole, miserable self. That was why he looked so beautiful, I think. It wasn't desire, it was *need*. I needed him, and I knew it.

But I ignored that. I mean, you would, wouldn't you?

Then, when you turned up . . . I'd finally managed to get a light. I looked up and you were there. And I suddenly realised I'd have to pretend nothing had happened. But it was like someone had switched the light on and I had to act like I was still in the dark. Impossible. And I couldn't make myself care, not really. It was all so funny, and so wonderful, and so weird. And when I fell . . . do you remember me falling over, when I tried to climb the fence? I lay there and realised that I should have been hurting, and I wasn't. I think it hit me then. I wouldn't ever feel pain again, not if I didn't want to. I just lay there, giggling. And you got more and more pissed off and I didn't give a damn. I was in freefall. When you climbed back over the fence I was glad you were going. I remember staring at everything, just marvelling, drinking it all in. I sat down against the wall and told my shadow to keep away, just for a little while. I wanted to make the most of it.

I did mean to take him back. I was going to . . .

I remember seeing that little bit of stone fall at my feet. I think it was a bit of mortar, actually. I remember laughing at it.

And I remember looking up at the wall, like an overhanging gut. Thinking, Yeah, actually, it does look pretty fragile . . . and then only having time to think, Maybe I *should* get out of the –

And then the wall . . . well, I know it collapsed. But it wasn't like that. It was like I was falling, upwards, head first. Looking up at the stones and they were bigger. Not closer, *bigger*. Just for a split second. Hanging there – *I* was hanging there – and then the stones jumped apart. And the one I was looking at *grew*, in this awful speeded-up way like a video, grew and grew until it was the size of a planet. And something picked me up and threw me.

People say you see your life flash in front of your eyes, but it's bollocks. I'm glad I didn't see mine. I had enough hassle while I was living it; I don't want an action replay, thanks very much. What I saw instead was just what was in front of my face. Like when someone's making a movie on a camcorder and their hands are shaky: grass and trees and people's clothes sliding in and out of the frame, too close up to understand. I saw rough grey stone and flecks of mortar and sunlight round the edges. My own hands spread out against nothing. The ground bearing down on me like a ceiling. Sky. Then there was a wet dull thud, an impact that went through me like a gunshot, and the taste of hot iron.

And I felt – nothing.

143

*   *   *

I knew it was all wrong. When I landed. I knew something horrible had happened to me. The shape of my skull had changed. When I breathed, the air took a longer path to my lungs. I had to think about it, or it wouldn't work. And the ground was too close; it was part of me. When I opened my eyes, I was looking at the grass from the wrong angle. But I didn't *feel* anything. Pain, I mean. I wasn't numb. I wasn't paralysed. I wasn't in shock. I just knew my body was wrecked. I started shaking. Every time I breathed in it was harder to make the air get to the right places. My legs were twisted. There was a sort of hollow bit in my throat where there was warmth spreading out like nausea, a gap where there should have been something holding me together. But it didn't *hurt*. I couldn't believe it. I waited for the pain. I was sure it was going to swamp me, all at once, drowning me. It *should* have come. I knew that. It was all wrong. It should have hurt so much it killed me. But it didn't.

I don't know how long I was like that. Not long. You came and looked at me. I knew that because the light changed, and I could feel the vibration in the earth when you walked. I wondered if I ought to say something. Then you went away again and it didn't seem important.

And then . . .

My shadow came closer. I don't know where he'd been. I think maybe he felt like I did, at first: sort of amazed at everything, wanting to be on his own . . . but when you'd gone he came towards me. And it was like . . . the pain started to come back, too. Like a current changing direction. It wasn't flowing away from

144

me any more. He was bringing it back.

The funny thing was, I wanted him so much. I wanted him to put his arms round me. I thought if he could just put his arms round me I'd be OK. I thought he could put me back together. But the closer he got, the more pain there was, stronger and stronger, like a sick black wave. I couldn't keep it away. It didn't come from him. It came from the places in my body where things had changed, surging and flooding inside me until I was helpless on top, struggling against the tide. But I knew it was because of him. Somehow. The closer he got . . . all I wanted was to go to sleep in his arms. But the pain got worse and worse and I couldn't hold on to what I wanted. He knelt down beside me and . . . I wanted him. He was the only person in the world. It was like love, or almost . . . But the pain was blotting me out. I couldn't see or hear. And I thought, I remember thinking: If he touches me I'll die. I can't bear it. I'll die.

I didn't say anything aloud. I don't think I could speak. But there was enough, just enough of me left to think, Go away. It took almost as much effort as saying it. I imagined looking into his eyes and thought, Leave me alone. Go away. The words were so clear they could have been written on the inside of my skull. They were so clear they left a scar. My mouth didn't move. I didn't make any noise. But he understood.

He understood. I saw him understand.

Leave me alone. He stood up, still staring into my eyes, and took a few paces back. As he moved away the pain ran off me like water. It was so good. I was back on solid ground, like the blackness had spat me out. I wasn't dying any more. I didn't care about the look in his eyes. I didn't care that just a second ago I'd wanted him to touch me more than anything in the world. It was enough that my body wasn't hurting. It was fantastic. I stayed where I was, savouring it. So my body was fucked. Who cared? The pain had gone.

I lay there smiling. It was all I'd ever want. For nothing to hurt ever again. He was standing a couple of metres away. Every nerve in my body was telling me where he was. I could feel the distance between us, stretched taut, like wire. But I knew that if he came back to me, so would the pain.

I sat up. He stepped towards me. And I – with my mind, I *pushed* him. Slammed a wall up in my head, hard enough to smash him backwards. No. NO. I'm not yours, I thought, I'm mine. Only mine. And I won't let you hurt me. I don't want you back. NO.

It was silent already. But the silence hollowed itself out until we were sitting inside it. And –

Christ, I know what this sounds like. But it's true. You know it's true.

My body started to heal.

It felt like there was something inside me, forcing the bones into place, sucking out the dents in my temple. I couldn't move. I felt my neck wrench and stretch, mending itself, squirming down under my skin as if it didn't belong to me. The ground rocked and jolted and spun. Pebbles pressed up into my knees. The warmth in my stomach soaked away and the air seemed to be taking a shortcut to my lungs. I heard my blood pounding in my ears. My face dragged itself back to where it normally was. My ears popped.

The euphoria had faded. I wasn't high any more. The

146

real-life, everyday stuff was growing back, like mould. Being fed up, being pissed off . . . Oh Jesus, who am I trying to kid? *Pissed off?* I was *terrified*.

But I still couldn't feel any pain. And that scared me even more.

I stood up. The world held me carefully, like a hand. I took a few steps, dropped to my knees in the grass, and threw up. I puked until nothing came out except bile and long strands of spit.

When I looked round, he wasn't there.

I knew where he'd gone. I could feel him. There was a bond between us, like there was this compass needle in my head, always pointing at him. I knew where he was, how far away, and if I closed my eyes and concentrated I could get a kind of blurry picture of what he could see. He was still me. It was just that I was keeping him away. If I concentrated I could keep us apart. My will was stronger than his – just. But it got harder and harder, and every time my concentration went he'd get a bit closer. In the end it was like trying to keep a sieve afloat, trying to press the water out with my hands. Until I was watching from our window and he was outside.

It was love, though. Even though I knew he'd kill me. That was why I couldn't stop the leak.

But I was so scared. I was so scared it filled me up and there wasn't room to think or feel anything else. So scared I would have done anything.

So scared that I threw that knife at him.

I was trying to kill him. I really *wanted* to kill him. And he knew that.

And – the bond snapped. As if there was too much anger between us, too much strain on the wire. As if it could only take so much.

He's still part of me. But I don't know where he is. I can't call him back. He's not listening any more. He'll never forgive me.

And I don't *want* him back. Because if he comes back to me, I'll die.

Nine

It was properly dark now. There was a faint breath of wind, warm on Annis's right cheekbone, and she could hear the water in the pool slapping softly against the sides. She sat very still, as if she was holding something fragile.

Zach said, 'That's all.' He drew a long breath, looking at her as if he expected an answer.

Then he started to cry.

Annis felt her skin prickling all over with wave after wave of goose pimples of shame and blank helpless pity. *Oh God, Zach's crying, oh God* . . . She wanted to look at him, but she kept her neck rigid, facing away into the dark, as if that would make him stop. She couldn't bear it. *Stop, please, please stop* . . . Every nerve in her body was tugging at her – *pat his shoulder, throw your arms round him, anything* – but she sat still. *If I touch him*, she thought, *I'll get an electric shock. It won't help. It will hurt.*

And it was as if he was on his own, anyway. The *way* he was crying: noisily, his whole body shuddering, in such abandoned, unself-conscious misery that it felt wrong to watch. And it was Zach . . . Zach, who hadn't cried in front of her for years, not since he was a kid, Zach who despised anyone who cried. Annis didn't want to remind him she was there. She thought, *He'll be furious, he'll hate me for having seen this. He'll never forgive me.* She kept her face turned away, as if he was getting undressed, but she knew from the noise that he was choking and spluttering and digging his fists into his eyes like a baby. She didn't need to look. A sharp ache started in her throat, like someone jabbing a knuckle into her larynx. God, he sounded so *miserable* . . . She should do something . . . *Come on, Annis, do something* . . .

But there was nothing she could do. She felt the humiliation of it. Absolutely nothing she could do. Only sit and wait for him to stop.

So she sat and waited for him to stop.

And in the end, he did. His sobs got quieter and quieter until they were almost silent. He wiped his face with his hands, still shuddering, but calmer, taking deep breaths. It wasn't like he'd got to the end of anything, only that he was too tired to carry on. He sniffed with a big wet squelching noise. Then, in a small, hoarse voice, he said, 'Sorry.'

Annis shook her head, even though she knew he couldn't see her. She said, 'No problem.'

They sat in silence. Annis felt everything she wanted to say well up and then drain away again immediately. She thought, *I may never speak again.*

'Anz?'

It took an effort to say, 'Yes?'

'Aren't you going to say something?'

It was like trying to read from a book with blank pages. She said, 'Like what?'

Zach sniffed again. Then he cleared his throat, leant away from her and spat into the grass. 'Well . . . I don't know. I thought, "You stupid arse, Zach," might be a good one. And, "What do we do now?" seemed like a definite candidate.'

'There's not much point, is there? Unless you've got a good answer for either of those.'

A pause. 'No, not really.'

'Well, then.'

He swallowed. 'I'm in trouble, aren't I?' When she didn't answer he made a noise that was a bit like a cough. 'Anz . . . I can't sleep. I can't think straight. I can't even touch anyone without giving off electricity.'

'Maybe,' she said, not feeling anything, 'maybe it'll just sort itself out.'

'Oh . . .' He buried his head in his hands. 'Come on, Anz. Next you'll be telling me I've imagined the whole thing.'

'And have you?' Her voice was very cool and calm, so that she heard it and thought, *I never knew I could talk to Zach like that.*

'Jesus, Annis! Of course I . . . There has to be something we can do – because otherwise I don't know what'll happen to me, we *have* to –'

'*We?*' Her voice seemed to come from somewhere behind her.

He took a breath in, and started to say something. Then he got it.

She watched his face change. She felt detached, curious to see how he'd react; she didn't *care*. 'Because I don't see where *I* come into it, Zach.'

'Because . . .' He closed his eyes for a second. 'Anz . . . please. I can't tell anyone else. And I – I'm so scared, I don't know what to do.'

'You'll think of something.' She got up, although she didn't know where she was going.

'Anz. Don't leave me – you can't leave me, you *can't* –'

'Can't I?' As if her blood had turned to water: freezing, crystal clear.

He was staring up at her now, his face gleaming through the dark. Annis thought, *He's come back from the dead, and he's looking at me like* this *has come as a shock* . . .

Zach said, 'Annis? What did I say? Look, I – don't be stupid – this isn't about you, this is *serious* –'

'*What?*' But she couldn't have said anything else, even if she'd had the words for what she wanted to say. She was made of ice, and ice didn't think. It didn't care why it was cold; it just *was* . . . She took a long breath in, savouring the silence. Then she hawked the phlegm into her mouth, the way he'd done, a moment ago – the way he'd taught her, when she was small – and spat, very deliberately, at his feet. She turned her back, and walked away.

She heard him call after her, then she started to run.

She lay on her back in the field, staring up at the stars. She counted twenty-seven, carefully, before the iciness started to thaw. Then she dug her fingers into the grass and shouted until she was hoarse. The anger was so big she couldn't find any words that actually *meant* anything. In the end she sat up, wiping the water off her face, trying to pull herself together.

The first proper thought she had was: *I am* not *going to help him.*

She knew she should have been surprised at herself. She knew, in a sort of academic way, that it didn't make sense. It was out of character. For God's sake – if he'd asked her for help a month ago, a week ago, she'd have jumped at the chance . . . and now he really needed it, and suddenly this weird fury had kicked in from nowhere, forbidding her to lift a finger.

She thought: *It's his own fault. Everything that's happened to him is his own fault. Everything from telling on Dad to getting expelled, and now this. It's like he's been trying to screw things up. And why should I help? He doesn't give a shit about me. He only cares about himself – and his fucking shadow, his beautiful shadow . . . He said his shadow was the only person in the world. I don't even figure.*

She thought: *He thinks he's so special. But he's just a coward. All he ever wanted was to get away from us all. Like Dad, deciding he didn't have to live by the rules like everyone else, deciding he could just ditch everything that made him feel bad. It's like the drugs. Zach wanted to escape. And it's gone wrong, and it's his own fault. He was asking for it. Whatever happens, it serves him right.*

I've been so worried and scared and sorry. And he doesn't even care . . . It was like a dam bursting. *He doesn't give a shit about me.*

She thought: *I hate you, I hate you, I hate you.*

She couldn't even cry as well as he could. She couldn't muster the same abandoned, heartfelt tone; she wasn't *trying* to cry, but even so she felt self-conscious, like she didn't have any right. She could feel the muscles in her mouth stretching as she sobbed, and the stickiness of tears on her hands. It was like being in front of a mirror, watching herself, knowing that she was only faking. It wasn't *real* unhappiness, because that was what Zach had. She thought, *Even this is second best.*

And it wasn't fair, it really wasn't *fair* . . . She thought: *How come everything always happens to him?* But it wasn't a real question, because she knew the answer. Everything happened to Zach because he was the sort of person everything happened to. He was, and she wasn't.

She shut her eyes, and she could see him, the way he'd lain there in the ruins, dying. She thought, *He was dying. By rights, he should be dead now. The stupid, selfish shit* . . .

After a long time she stood up and walked back to the house, letting the swish of the long grass calm her down. She felt flattened, like a field after a storm. When she got to the terrace she stood still, looking at the plants where a sliver of pale light spilt out of the windows. Yes, they were dead. She closed her eyes and wished she was somewhere else. *Anywhere*, she thought, *anywhere where this hasn't happened, and life is going on as normal* . . . She tried to picture it, conjuring up the details, the daylight. For some reason she could see Kensington Gardens; not the way it would be now, in summer, but how it had been the last time she was there. The trees had been bare, and the low winter light had bleached everything out. There'd been kids, a family playing football . . . and she'd been with Zach, because he'd been recovering from a hangover and needed some fresh air . . . She could remember the smells, grass and trees and water overlaying the traffic fumes. *That's normal life*, she thought. *Kensington Gardens on a winter Sunday afternoon. It's just as real as this is.*

The image was so strong that when she opened her eyes she half expected it to be daylight, and the darkness came as a shock. But she remembered, now. *I do love Zach. I do.* It was a relief, like being back on solid ground.

She blinked, letting her eyes adjust. Even the thin slice of light that had been shining through the window had gone, like someone had turned the lamp off inside. She opened the French windows, turning the handle as quietly as she could.

She could hear someone moving. And when she peered through the murk, she could see a faint luminescence, more like moonlight than the light from a light bulb. Something white moved, glowing dimly, leaving trails on her retina. Then there was a muffled thud, and a scuffle, like someone had knocked something over but managed to stop it before it fell. She said, 'Zach? Why are you in the dark?'

He looked round. 'I've blown the light bulb in the lamp. I touched it by mistake, and there was this spark, and I don't want to chance the main light as well.'

She took a few steps to her left, ran her hand over the wall till she found the light switch, and turned it on. The room jumped into focus, dazzling her. She said, 'What are you doing?'

He looked at her, holding her gaze for slightly too long. Then he shook his head, running his hand through his hair. 'Falling over things, mainly . . . You'd think all this – *brightness*, in my head, you'd think it would mean I could see in the dark, but I can't see anything . . .' A pause. 'Anz . . . look, I don't know what I –'

'I'm sorry, Zach.'

He glanced at her again. He stared at her for a long time, as if he was memorising her face, then he nodded, and something in his expression relaxed. He took a deep breath and said, 'I was just trying to plug the cable in, for the Internet, but it's hard, when you can't actually see the phone socket . . . I thought, well, I thought maybe if I had a bit more information –'

'You think there'll be information on the Internet? What are you going to search?' She went over to the kettle and turned it on. 'Shadow loss? How to get your shadow back? "Help, I've unintentionally become immortal"?'

He clenched his jaw and gave a tight, brittle shrug. 'Do you have any better ideas?' When she didn't answer he sat down at the end of the table, watching her. 'What're you doing, anyway?'

'I'm helping. I'm making coffee.'

'Oh, fantastic. Exactly what good will –'

'And it sounds like *I*'d better go on Mum's computer, if you're sending out sparks.' She turned round and smiled at him, showing her teeth. 'You can go through the bookshelves.'

He rubbed his nose wearily. 'The bookshelves? Right, because, obviously, there'll be lots of useful information –'

'There might be something. Look in anything the Maines left us when they sold the house. See if they say anything about the previous owners, or the ruins. Come on, Zach. You're right, we need more information.' She thought, *Where have I heard that tone before? Oh yes. Zach talking me through my maths homework.*

Maybe he recognised it, too. He smiled, reluctantly, as if he couldn't help himself. He said, 'Aye, aye, Captain.'

She made the coffee, then brought two mugs over to the table and sat down at Mum's computer. Zach took his coffee without a word and knelt down at the bookshelves, pulling out books and flipping through, rattling the pages.

It was past midnight. She hadn't realised she was so tired, until she saw the time on the screen. She had to scrunch her eyes up and concentrate, to stop herself falling asleep. She could feel a headache starting to collect behind her skull like a patch of damp on a wall. Lucky Zach, never having to sleep again . . . never feeling pain . . . she envied him, she really did . . . and immortality . . . lucky Zach . . .

She woke up with a jerk and looked round. She didn't know how long she'd been asleep, but Zach was still on his knees, staring at a book, so it couldn't have been very long. She hit her forehead with the palm of her hand, trying to clear her head. Come on . . .

The Internet didn't have anything useful. She tried everything she could come up with, but it was useless. She scrolled down the page, followed a link 'about your shadow – seeing your shadow side', which turned out to be some kind of psychological thing – yes, all very well, but no bloody use – and checked the next couple of pages. Then she tried again. *Disconnected shadows. Shadow death. Shadow immortality. Shadow* – er . . . oh, for God's sake! She

157

took a gulp of coffee, trying to keep herself alert, but it had gone cold. She said, 'Zach, have you got any ideas about what I should put into the search engine . . . ?' He didn't answer. She stood up to make some more coffee. 'Zach?'

He said, very slowly, 'Ye-es?'

She stopped where she was, holding the cafetière, and peered across to see what he was reading. He'd dragged a box out from under the bookshelf, and was kneeling over a pile of papers, his hair falling over his face. She wished she could see his expression. She said, 'Have you found something?'

'Not . . . exactly . . .'

'What?' She went over and crouched a little way away. 'Zach? What've you found?'

'It's Mum's paperwork . . . I think these are the deeds for the house, but there's all this stuff from the estate agent, about the outbuildings and stuff . . .' He passed a sheet to her without looking up.

She read: *historic outbuildings . . . minor structural problems with the old farmhouse, now uninhabited . . . however, great opportunity for further development . . . achieved planning permission in 1983, although in fact he sold the house before . . . several changes of ownership due to circumstances unconnected with the house . . . the Maine family are anxious for a quick sale . . . hence the – very advantageous – price . . .*

She said automatically, '*Minor* structural problems? Like walls collapsing, for example. God, Dad's right about estate agents, isn't he?'

Zach shrugged, still not looking at her. 'Several changes of ownership. No one wanted to stay here.'

'No.' Annis didn't blame them. She'd felt it too,

even before anything happened – the ruins sitting like a blot on the landscape, waiting . . .

Silence. Zach carried on riffling through the papers. After a while he paused, and made a movement as if he was about to give her the bit of paper he was reading, but in the end he kept hold of it, spreading it flat on the floor as if he wanted to stop it getting away.

Annis leant forward, careful not to brush against him by mistake, and read over his shoulder.

'It's a letter from Monsieur Maine.' Zach watched her as she read.

I'm afraid I can't tell you very much about the house's history, as my wife and I have only lived here for a year or so, and the family from whom we bought it had owned it only for a few months. They, I understand, had bought it from a couple who had inherited it from the previous owner, a young man who spent most of his time in Paris. Of course, I may be misremembering even these details. I believe the old farmhouse – now, unfortunately, unsafe – has not been lived in for some time.

We decided to leave as my wife and I feel that the property is too large for us, especially as our grandchildren are at the age when they need constant attention! Having spent many happy years in London, I am glad that the house has been bought by an English family. Perhaps it will be a new, auspicious start for the place!

When she looked sideways Zach was still watching her. She said, 'What?'

'Why did he bother to say *why* they decided to leave? We'd already bought it by then. It's like he's trying to convince himself . . . Why did he think it needs a *new, auspicious start*? Why did everyone keep leaving?'

'Not everyone left,' Annis said, trying to be logical. 'If that couple inherited it –'

'Oh yes. The young man who lived in Paris *died*. That's OK, then.' He shook his head. 'They knew there was something wrong. Everyone who comes here realises, sooner or later.'

'Yes, but . . .' She clung to the maths-homework, let's-be-scientific-about-this feeling. 'We already know all this. He doesn't say anything about shadows, does he? Or even about the ruins, except that they're unsafe.'

'So –'

'So keep looking,' she said, and got up. She put the kettle on and watched the steam billowing, breathing in the smell of hot plastic, trying to think. The Internet was no good. There wasn't anyone to ask. And if Zach didn't find anything in Mum's papers . . .

Zach said, 'Shit, shit, *shit* . . .'

She spun round. 'You've found something?'

He smacked his hand down on the bookshelf, so hard the books shuffled together towards the edge, like they were suicidal. 'No, I haven't. I haven't. There's nothing here.' He added, 'There's fucking *nothing*,' as if he wasn't sure she'd understood, the first time.

'You've looked through everything?'

'Yeah, it's all legal stuff and plans and – oh, *shit*. I thought . . . this is crazy, there must be something we can do, some way of finding out . . .'

She stood still, looking past him to where her reflection looked back at her from the French windows. Nothing. No answers. Which meant . . .

She said, 'No.'

'What?'

'No. Zach, we've got this wrong. There may not be anything written down – it may not have happened to anyone else – but if we just try to *think* –'

'Really, Anz, I'm touched by your belief in the power of logic, but –'

'Shut up and sit down.' She made the coffee, deliberately keeping her back to him, and when she turned round he'd sat down.

'Go on, then,' he said. 'Think.'

She refused to get irritated. She took a gulp of coffee and pushed her hair away from her face, trying to concentrate. 'All right,' she said. 'What do we know about your shadow, already?'

'What is this, a criminal investigation?'

'Do you want me to help you or don't you?'

There must have been something in her voice, because Zach blinked and nodded. He said slowly, 'He's . . . he takes all my pain away. Every time I hurt myself it sort of – slides away, to him. And I heal.' He swallowed. 'He's my death. Without him I can't sleep. I used to know where he was but now I don't . . . Jeez, Anz, is this really –'

'He makes other people fall asleep,' Annis said. 'And when you touch people there's electricity –'

'Maybe not electricity, just *light* – or energy, or –'

'And when he touches them they collapse and – so you give out light, and he gives out dark. That makes sense. Or you give out life and –'

They both said together, 'He gives out death,' and looked at each other, frozen.

Silence. Annis said, 'I mean . . .'

'Yes. He does. All those plants. He killed the walnut tree.'

Another pause. Annis felt a sudden ache in her back, the muscles protesting at being up so late at night. She said, being careful with the words, 'I've got close to him three times. The third time was the worst.'

Zach frowned at her, not understanding.

She said, 'And the shocks, when you touched people. They've been getting stronger. Haven't they?'

She didn't say anything else. She watched him realise what she meant.

He said, 'Oh Lord. You think . . .' He rubbed his eyes, screwing up his face so he looked about twelve. 'You think it's all getting worse. You think the longer it goes on –'

'I didn't say that.' She didn't look at him. 'What do you think?'

'I think . . . you're right. The longer it goes on the worse it gets,' he said. His voice was very quiet. 'After he came into the house you slept for twenty hours. I thought you might die.' A pause. 'Do you think someone . . . *might* . . . die . . . ?'

Annis took another sip of coffee. She'd made it stronger than normal, but she still couldn't taste it.

Zach said, 'Oh Jesus. We have to do something.'

Annis said, 'We have to find him.'

'I can't – I told you, I don't know where he is any more.'

'We have to stop him. We have to destroy him.'

'How? I threw a knife at him, and that didn't work – so *how*?'

'I don't know! But you said, we have to do something – we can't just let – Zach, there must be a way –'

'*How?* How, how, *how*?' He squeezed his eyes shut and shook his head. A tiny fleck of water landed on Annis's face. 'I can't call him back, because he won't listen to me, he wouldn't come back – and he'll get stronger, and I'll get weaker, and I tried to kill him and it didn't work – and if he's death, you can't kill death – and it's no good you saying *there must be a way* because I don't think there is, I can't see how there could be.'

Annis pressed the heels of her hands into her temples until she felt sick. 'Zach – stop it, we have to think rationally.'

'Fuck it. *Fuck it.*' He scrambled to his feet and stumbled away, throwing the French windows open. He stood there for a moment, braced in the doorway, his skin white against the outdoor dark. Then he ran, without looking back.

The French windows swayed, swinging almost shut. Annis took a deep breath. She downed the rest of her coffee and waited for the caffeine to kick in.

She closed her eyes. *If only there was someone we could ask,* she thought. *Someone who might know where Zach's shadow has gone, or how to find him. But there's no one.* She thought determinedly, *Maybe we're wrong. Maybe the shadow will just die, if it's on its own long enough. Maybe it can't survive, without Zach.* But she didn't believe it. The shadow was giving out more and more dark; and Zach was giving out more and more light . . .

She thought: *But there has to be something we can do. If only we knew more.* She wrapped her arms round herself, pretending someone was hugging her. If only . . . She was nearly asleep. She blinked, trying to clear her head. She could hear the tentative footsteps of an idea, as if it was creeping up on her. She didn't turn to meet it, in case she frightened it away, only sat still and let it approach her, stealthily, like a hunter moving in on its prey.

She stared through the French windows at her reflection in the glass, deliberately keeping her mind empty. *Maybe I can – no, shut up,* she thought. *Wait for it. It's coming up behind me. It might be good.*

She sat there for a long time, watching the idea walk into her head, blurry-edged, and then take shape slowly. She didn't dare say it aloud to herself, because even looking at it made her heart pound and her palms go sweaty. *No,* she thought. *I can't. Can I?*

Maybe not. But I can try.

She swallowed and tugged sharply at her hair, pulling it back into a business-like ponytail. Then she went out into the dark, shutting the door behind her, pretending to herself that she didn't know where she was going.

Ten

She'd been scared, before. But not like this.

The moon had risen, so it wasn't all that dark; hardly dark at all, in fact. She thought, dreamily, *I always thought moonlight was a bit of a myth – you know, all that bright-as-day stuff . . .* But it was so strong it made the ruins look like a stage-set. *If I were a camera*, she thought, *this would be a great photo. If I could blink and – there! – a study in silver and black, the first photograph in pen-and-ink . . . Yes. It's beautiful, the way Zach's shadow is beautiful. It's only because I'm here – only because my heart's going so fast I feel like I might faint, and my skin's prickling all over, and the corners of my vision have gone black . . .* She had to brace herself against the fear, the animal instinct that said, *Run, run.*

I am not going to run. I am going to go through with this. For Zach.

She clung to the wire, steadying herself for the moment when she'd have to start climbing. Wave after wave of cold ran up her backbone. Even standing still was the hardest thing she'd ever done. Only her will power kept her there. She clenched her eyes shut and saw Zach, how he'd been a few hours ago,

165

crying into his hands. She clung to the image until it eclipsed the fear. Then, not giving herself time to think about it, she pulled herself up the fence as fast as she could, clambering blindly until she dropped down the other side and felt the ground under her feet. *OK. Good girl. Hardest part's over . . . Ha ha.*

The funny thing was, she could think quite clearly, so that part of her mind was saying, *God, creepy doesn't even come close – unless it's just me, knowing what I'm going to do, and not really the place at all . . .* as if she wasn't shaking and trying to swallow the acid taste in her mouth. She thought: *I'm going to ignore the fear. Just because I'm a coward doesn't mean I have to pay attention to it. Zach would despise me if he saw me like this . . .*

She took a long, last breath of fresh air. She could have sworn she could taste the moonlight: clean and clear, like water. Then she went up the steps, through the front doorway, and into the dark.

There was a kind of jolt. As if, for a second, the earth had juddered on its axis. Only for a second, and then it was steady again; but she hadn't imagined it. She almost reached out, to get her balance, but she didn't want to touch anything. She stood still, instead, and let her eyes adjust to the blackness.

There was enough light from the doorway to see a few paces in front of her, but that was all. Everywhere else there were shadows so thick they might have been solid, so impenetrable she couldn't see where the walls were. Something moved in the nearest block of dark, taking shape, reaching towards her. *Oh God, run,* run . . . She made herself blink, over and over again. *Stop it. There's nothing there. There's nothing. How babyish, to be scared of the dark* . . . She looked away, the back of her neck tingling. If only she could see properly . . .

I should have brought a torch. I should have thought this through more carefully.

She started to make a list of everything she'd done wrong. Every time she came up with something new she made herself take another step into the room. By the time she got to *in fact I should never have got out of bed this morning* she was surrounded by dense black emptiness; she could tell it was the middle of the room because of the way her footsteps were dull and flat, as if the air was cushioning the sound. She was calmer, now. The fear was still there, like broken glass under her feet, but if she walked lightly she could ignore the worst of it. She took a long breath, imagining inky air flooding into her lungs. *So. I'm here.*

Now what do I do?

What had Zach done? She racked her brains, trying to remember what he'd said, but it was hard to concentrate, because of the blackness pressing on her mind, the blank unrelenting weight of the place. It made her ache with tension. *Come* on. *I've decided to do this, so* – uncertainty flickered like a candle, *and why* am *I doing this?* but she ignored it – *so I'm bloody well going to do it. This is the only thing I can think of to help Zach. So think. What did he do?*

What had he said? About . . . She couldn't remember much. He'd been in the cellar, hadn't he? Oh God. She tried to tell herself that probably wasn't important, there was no reason why *she* had to go down to the cellar, but it was no use. She looked round, staring into the dark until she could make out a jagged edge of black in one corner. Then, very carefully, she made her way towards it, convinced she was going to feel the floorboards collapse under her feet at any moment. She slid one foot forward until she felt the first step down, then put one hand on the wall to steady herself.

I can't believe I'm doing this. I can't believe I'm going to –

She couldn't just stand there for ever. She had to move.

She felt her way down the stairs, until she could feel that she was in a big, damp space, full of blackness that pressed on her eyes like felt. She stood still, smelling the age of the stone, and something else, like sour milk.

There wasn't a door on her right. So she had to go left. Slowly, holding her hands out in front, she stumbled towards the wall. There'd be a doorway here somewhere. She couldn't see it, but if she ran her hands along the wall, she'd find it eventually. On this side of the room the darkness seemed a little less black, the fear a little further away. *Just find the door, and go . . . Wait.* She paused, her fingertips dragging along the damp rough surface of the wall. Something nagged at her. Something inside her. What . . . ?

How do I know, she thought, *that there isn't a door on the other side? I can't bloody see anything, can I? I'm not thinking straight . . .*

She turned, and as soon as she walked back she felt the current of terror intensify. The blackness thickened again, until it was as complete as a blindfold. Deliberately – with a strange thrill of defiance – she carried on walking. *The fear goes in one direction,* she thought, *like gravity. It's pushing me away.* She held her hand out in front of her, her palm buzzing with anticipation. Her steps had slowed – she couldn't help that – but she could feel the wall getting closer, smell moisture and old stone, smell darkness itself . . . A strange, distant voice in her head said, *So Zach walked into the dark. Into the dark, and the fear, just because he wanted to . . .*

There was a doorway. A door that felt oddly smooth, like grease, dry and slippery and warm, as if it wasn't part of the same building. The touch of the – wood, was it? – whatever it was under her hands made her gasp, the sound coming from her throat so unexpectedly it made her jump. She couldn't find a handle. The door was as immovable as the wall. She kept running her hands over it, searching for a lock, a keyhole, anything, but there was nothing. And the surface of the wood made her think, for no reason, of butter – something slick, something rotting – so that in the end she couldn't bear to touch it any longer.

She thought: *It's no good. Whatever's behind this door, I can't get to it. I should give up and go home.*

The thought left her weak with shameful, irresist-ible relief. The fear sucked at her like the backwash of a wave and then receded; so she was shaky – crumbling at the edges – but intact. The shadows were only shadows. The darkness was only darkness. She slumped down, half sitting, half crouching against the wall. That was it, then. She didn't have to try any more – didn't have to go through that door – didn't have to face the fear . . .

I've failed, she thought. *I can't open that door, and whatever I'm looking for is behind it. I tried to help*

Zach, and I couldn't. I wasn't brave enough, or strong enough. And now terrible things will happen to him, and it'll be my fault.

The darkness was so total, so featureless, that it was like a screen. She could see herself and Zach projected on to it. And he was so white . . . She saw the gleam in his eyes grow into something else, the energy taking hold like a fire, burning him up. She saw his face start to shine and shine, until he was too bright to look at, until there was nothing left of him, and you couldn't see anything in his eyes but a terrible cold bleakness. While somewhere a long way away the shadow walked, and everywhere it went people died, withering like grass or falling asleep on their feet and never waking up. *That's how it'll be*, she thought. *Light so bright it hurts your eyes, and darkness that takes you with it. Nothing in between. Zach won't be Zach any more.*

And I can't help him. I've failed. I'm too scared . . .

She put her hands over her face and felt tears collect under her fingers, pooling against her skin before they trickled down and dripped off her chin. *Oh, Zach, Zach . . . I can't do it*, she thought. *If anything happens to him I want to die too. This is all the wrong way round. He's the clever one, the brave one, the one that everyone thinks is brilliant – and I don't blame them, I do too, if he dies, if something awful happens, then everyone will say it should have been me, and they'd be right, for heaven's sake, they'd be completely right . . .*

She smiled painfully into her hands. *Remember when he came back from Morocco, all thin and brown, and sat on my bed and told me everything* he'd done, whispering the worst bits in case Mum heard? Or when Mum and Dad made us go to that awful black-and-white film at the National Film Theatre and it was so dull, all about people falling in love and being too virtuous to do anything about it, and Zach stood up halfway through and shouted, 'This is obscene! It's disgusting! I refuse to watch this sort of filth!' and grabbed me and we walked out and had hysterics in the cafe . . . ? Or when I didn't manage to finish Romeo and Juliet before I had to give my talk in English, and he told me that in the end Juliet woke up just in time and they both lived happily ever after? Or the way I didn't speak to him for a week after that, and in the end he borrowed fifty quid off Dad and took me for tea at the Ritz, to make up? Remember?

Remember when I failed my piano exam, and I sat and cried at the kitchen table, and Mum fussed and told me it would be OK next time if I only practised, and Dad kept saying, 'It's only an exam, Annis, and you weren't planning to be a concert pianist anyway, were you?' And Zach just paused, on his way out, and casually, uncharacteristically, kissed the top of my head, without saying anything . . .

Yes. She remembered. Of course she remembered. But . . .

She said to herself: No. No buts. Do you remember, or don't you?

She stood up again, wiping her face, and turned to stare into the blackness where the door was. She reached out her hand and pressed her palm hard against the silky surface, not letting herself flinch.

Zach asked, she thought. He wanted something to

171

change, and it did. It was the asking that did it. Being here isn't enough. I have to ask.

She thought: *I am not afraid. And I need* this door *to open.*

It didn't open.

Not exactly, anyway. That wasn't the word. It didn't *open.* It simply wasn't there any more. The feeling on her skin didn't change: only now, somehow, she knew it was only air. The sensation of warmth and greasy wood was just her imagination, the touch of emptiness when she was expecting something else. As if the door had never been there, as if she'd been pushing against nothing at all.

She almost laughed into the darkness. *Why aren't I scared?* she thought. *I feel like I'll never be scared again. But it's still there – whatever it is – through the doorway . . .* The power was pulsing through her, so close now it made her teeth vibrate. She thought, *Here goes. For Zach.*

She stepped through the doorway, into the heart of the dark.

And –

The shadows glittered and roared and spat her out.

She was sitting – was she? Yes, sitting – against a wall. There was a pale five-legged, almost-familiar thing curled up on the floor, which twitched as she watched. The floor was black. Only – black . . . she thought, *How come I never realised that black isn't really* black? *It's more like grey . . . only grey is more like white, and white is like . . . white is unspeakable,* she thought, *like that thing on the floor, too bright to*

172

look at . . . like I was wearing sunglasses before and someone's taken them away . . . She closed her eyes, trying to remember what darkness looked like. *Come on*, she thought. *Black. What was it like? Black, black . . .*

Everything swirled up round her like a whirlpool, picking her up and dumping her, hard, on the ground, so she was facing the other way. And – yes – now it *was* dark, so dark that the air had started to separate into coarse, muzzy grains. The girl opposite her was shining, lit from inside . . . *like an angel*, she thought, *like a rotting angel, giving off marsh gas . . .* But she couldn't see her properly, because there were too many shadows. And her whole body hurt, aching with cold and fatigue. It hurt so much she fought, instinctively, screwing her eyes shut again and –

And she was back where she'd been before, where the world was all numb and dazzling and . . . What had happened? She couldn't think straight. *What's going on? Something I had to do*, she thought. *Something important.* She sifted through the brightness in her head, searching for a memory she recognised.

Hang on. She couldn't remember *anything. This can't be right*, she thought. *I should have some memories, shouldn't I? Not just this brightness everywhere I look, dazzling me. I'm sure there's something I'm supposed to be doing. Something I was trying to do. Because . . .*

She sat up straighter, trying to look around her. It didn't quite work; she knew she was supposed to move her head, but her muscles weren't functioning the way she was expecting them to. The five-legged animal on the floor curled up into a ball, four of its limbs folding into a row, and she felt her fingernails dig into the palm of her hand. Oh. *So that thing there is my hand*, she thought. *God, it's a very weird colour. Why is it so white? I wonder if the rest of me is like that. Bother, I was trying to get a tan. Come on, concentrate! Raise your head and look around. It's not hard. Come on, Annis –*

I'm Annis. Bloody hell, of course I am – oh God, yes, I remember now –

The world flickered and came into focus.

She was slumped against the doorway, her head cold where it rested on the stone, one foot twisted underneath her. She felt odd. She couldn't put her finger on what it was, but she definitely felt – *odd* . . . She closed her eyes because the shadows were starting to make her eyes water, as though she was staring at the sun, but even with her eyes closed the world seemed too bright. And too *loud*, come to think of it. The breeze in the trees outside, her heartbeat thumping . . . She thought, *I have no idea how I got here.* She had a vague impression of vivid dreams – coloured darkness, lightning, something bright and wonderful and awful – but nothing that she could get hold of. It was like waking up after being ill.

She stood up, too quickly, so that her head reeled. She felt too light, too strong. She leant against the wall and breathed in the musty scent of the stone, because at least everything *smelt* right. She closed her eyes and tried to pretend she felt fine. *I'm Annis. I remember now. I came here to help Zach, who is . . . who is my brother, of course . . . because something bad has happened to him, so I thought I'd do the same thing to myself, because* . . . There was a gap in the logic somewhere, but she couldn't plug it. She let the rest of her argument swirl round and drain away. Anyway . . . *I think I must have managed it, because I feel all wrong. So all I have to do is remember why I thought this was a good idea, and then* . . .

She gave up on trying to stand, and slid down the wall, feeling the skin scrape off her hands with the friction. Normally that would hurt, wouldn't it . . . ? But it didn't. In fact it was almost pleasant, feeling the not-pain. Mmm. She brought her hand to her face and watched blood ooze down the side of her wrist. Then it stopped. Her skin tingled, creeping and fizzing as if it was being stretched from inside. When she wiped the blood away there was nothing, only the familiar lines on her palm. She thought: *Oh. I think I ought to be more surprised.*

Don't. Please, don't. It hurts.

She had no idea where the words had come from. They arrived in her head as if she'd thought them herself. *But I didn't think them*, she thought. *And it doesn't hurt.* She peered into the shadows, listening, trying to work out if there was someone there. She thought, *Where are you? Who are you?*

Here.

Where?

Here. *Here.*

And the world flipped over like a coin, the way it had before. The brightness went dark. The pain came back – only now there was the new rawness on her hands, and the dull weight of fear under her ribs. She looked back at the pale girl's eyes, thinking, ***Please, I can't bear it. What's happening? This is all wrong.***

175

No – no . . . She recoiled, willing herself back into her own body, away from the pain. *I am Annis. I am here.* She felt sick. She sat back, taking deep breaths, trying to ride the dizziness. *What's happening? This is all wrong, this isn't how Zach said it would be* . . . She clenched her fist until the not-pain blossomed again, like an anchor, keeping her in her own body. She thought, *She's there. Whoever I was, just now . . . sitting opposite me, watching* . . . She squinted through the silvery murk.

And stared. Stared and stared. For longer than her whole life so far. Stared until her whole body seemed to evaporate and she was only her eyes. Stared and stared, because she was – the shadow – she was just so – so –

Falling in love, she thought. *This is it. And I never thought it would be like this. I want to look at her for ever . . .*

Her shadow said, **Yes.**

Annis could feel herself smiling. *Like a present*, she thought, *like the best present in the world, only she's something I've always had . . . And whatever happens now, it's worth it, just to have seen her, to know she exists . . . God, yes, and she's me, only she's not, not quite . . . As if I'm looking at myself in a mirror made out of polished iron, so that the colours are darker than they should be . . . no, no colours at all, only solid shadow, a reflection made out of dark . . . but she's not blurred, the way Zach's shadow is, my brain doesn't lock her out, I can see her perfectly, she's really there* . . . She let her gaze travel down over the shadow's face, her body – and felt a pulse of warmth and longing and something else –

176

Love. Yes.

And then Annis looked away quickly, because it was almost, God, almost like she was checking her out . . . *which is just weird, because for one thing she's a girl, and for another she looks exactly like me . . .* And she was scared, too, because the longer she looked the harder it was to stay herself. She could feel the balance between them, like a see-saw; if she didn't concentrate it would tip, and she'd be the shadow again, with all that pain . . .

It's all right.

Yes, it was. Everything was all right. Which surprised her, rather, because a moment ago it hadn't been, had it? She stared into the darkness, trying to remember. *I was scared, wasn't I? Scared for Zach, as well as for me – there was something wrong, something I had to put right . . .*

Don't worry. I'm looking after you.

Oh, Annis thought. *I see. She's taken all the fear with her – and the hurt, the jealousy, all the dark nasty stuff . . . All the pain. No wonder I feel so peaceful.* She looked into the shadow's eyes, still smiling, and felt the shadow smile back.

Come back to me. The shadow held out a hand, inviting. Annis got to her feet and took a tiny step towards her. The skin on her palm started to itch, where it had healed over. **We shouldn't be apart. Just take my hand.**

Annis thought, *She's right. I want us to be together again. I want her back with me, even if she brings the pain back, too . . . No – what am I doing? Wait . . .* She turned away, because she couldn't think straight while she was looking at the shadow. She thought,

What am I doing here? There's a reason for all this. Zach. I was trying to help Zach . . .

But it's no good, she thought. *I wanted to talk to my shadow – make her tell me, explain everything I didn't know . . . but she's not like that. It would be like asking myself. I understand more, now. She's part of me – or I'm part of her. She's my shadow, and I'm her soul . . . And we need each other. Once we're apart, we don't balance any more. Zach's shadow* will *kill people, because he can't go back to Zach; and Zach* will *burn away, because he can't go back to his shadow . . .*

She blinked, and realised she was staring into her own – no, the shadow's – eyes. *But that means . . .*

She thought, *I wanted to find out how to find Zach's shadow, and how to stop him, before . . . Maybe*, she thought, *maybe if the shadow can feel pain, that means he can just be killed, the way you can kill a person. So all we need to do is find him before he – before anyone gets too close to him, before he gets too strong . . . If only we can find him.*

Where would he have gone? She imagined him wandering randomly, criss-crossing the countryside, trying to keep away from people. She thought she knew, now, that he wouldn't *try* to hurt anyone; it would just – happen . . . She shuddered suddenly, because she could imagine what it would be like: that veil of darkness getting thicker and thicker, and the pain getting worse and worse . . . the loneliness, and the anger, because Zach had sent him away; and maybe he *would* start to hate people, because he was so miserable. And all the time the blackness growing inside him, spilling out wherever he went, until at last

178

it was so strong it could kill someone. Annis thought, *How could Zach have done that? What a horrible, horrible thing to do . . . And his shadow is himself, doesn't he understand . . . ?*

And his poor shadow . . . where would he go? She shut her eyes and tried to visualise it. *Where would I go*, she thought, *if I were . . . ?*

Yes? If you were . . . ?

She blinked. *Of course! My shadow will know*, she thought. *Or she might be able to guess – my shadow –*

The floor rocked and the walls spun, but this time the transition was easier. She opened her eyes and the room was full of blackness. Although it wasn't exactly *darker*; it was more like she could just see the darkness better. The pain was back, too, filling her, like water in a flannel, about to drip, but she was ready for it. She relaxed into it, like an ice-cold bath, and it eased a little. Her hands were the worst, where she'd dragged them down the wall – or where her other self had dragged her other hands down the wall . . . She pushed her palms flat against each other, feeling the oddness in her skin. She thought, *I'm not real. I'm a shadow. Other people can't even see me properly . . . I'm a kind of ghost.*

She felt the panic rise, and almost pulled back, away into her real self, just to get away from it. But instead she let it flood and ebb again. She thought, ***Where would I go, if my other self had sent me away?*** Even the idea of it made her uneasy; the images she'd had before resurfaced, but sharper now, more solid. She thought, ***It's like I feel everything more deeply this way, when I'm the shadow and not myself.*** She had to concentrate to think at all, riding the surge of emotion. *Where would I go?*

Her other was watching her, her eyes shining. *Yes, where would you go? Think. Maybe this way we can help Zach – if we can only find his shadow, we can destroy it before anything bad happens . . .*

Annis stared back, not sure whether she was desperate for the brightness itself or the thicker darkness behind it. She wanted to stand up and go to her other, hold out her hand . . . But she tried to think. There was the world outside the ruins, like a map in the dark. *Somewhere*, she thought, *is the place where I'd end up. Somewhere there's –*

Zach's shadow.

She knew where he was. She couldn't explain it, but she knew where he was. Like a denser shape in the darkness, a long, long way away. She could – *hear* him, almost, or feel him . . .

Her other leant forward, her whole face gleaming. *Where?*

I don't know. But – somewhere. In that direction . . . It was like a magnet inside her, a very faint movement that could have been attraction or repulsion. But it was unmistakable. She could feel the knot of darkness where he was, like a blip on a radar screen, but it was more than that. She recognised him, now, the same way she would have recognised Zach. It gave her such a rush of elation that for a second the darkness seemed to fade, as if she was whole again.

Not for long, though, and when it came back she couldn't bear it. She made the odd, dislocating gesture in her head that brought her back to herself, and crouched down, breathing deeply. The numbness was a relief. She didn't want to look at her shadow, because now she knew what it felt like to be her. Or – she was her, still, but she could choose not to be . . .

She thought, *So you can find him.*

Annis . . . It was her own voice, but it wasn't. **Please. You know it's wrong for us to be apart. It's dangerous. The longer it goes on – the stronger we get –**

But you can find him. You can find Zach's shadow.

Yes, I think so. But –

Then we don't have any choice. Please. We can help him. And once you've found him, Zach can destroy him, and it'll all be OK. And I won't let us stay apart too long. I won't let anyone hurt you. I promise. She felt an uncomfortable voice say, *But you're hurting her already,* but it wasn't her shadow, and she ignored it.

You'll send me away? For Zach?

Yes.

If it had been a real conversation, with a real person, Annis thought that would have been the moment when she would have looked away. But she couldn't. She just waited, feeling the silence ring in her ears.

All right. The shadow smiled; if that was the word for a look so direct and painful, a look that made Annis want to cry.

Thank you. She felt the relief, and then the dread, straight on its heels, but not as strongly as she expected. *Even now,* she thought, *she's taking my feelings away. She's protecting me. I suppose I should be grateful.*

I'll take them for as long as you need me to, the

181

shadow said, as if she'd heard the thought. **I've got your pain, and I'll take your feelings too, if you want.**

Annis bit her lip. Zach hadn't said anything about feelings . . . the physical pain, yes, but he still felt fear, and hurt, didn't he . . . ? But she said, *Thank you.*

Then – goodbye. The shadow walked towards the blank grey wall of darkness, her outline going fuzzy. She paused for a moment, before she reached the deepest shadows, and looked back. **Promise me you'll follow. Promise you'll call me back, as soon as you can. Don't leave it too long . . .**

Annis nodded, speechless. *My self*, she thought. *I'm sending my self away . . .*

The shadow turned and was gone, disappearing into blackness so quickly Annis gasped at the way she felt the distance between them growing. It tugged at her gut, like something unravelling inside her. She felt the shadow move further and further away, until she was breathless and nauseous and coldly sweaty.

She leant shakily against the wall for a moment. Then she went weak at the knees. She sank to the floor and waited, until the tension faded to a steady pull, constant enough to ignore. *I can still change my mind*, she thought. *At any moment. I can run after her – reach out my hand – get her back . . . And any moment I can see what she's seeing, feel what she's feeling . . .*

She stood up again, stumbled up the stairs and outside. She breathed deeply, letting her eyes adjust to the moonlight that filled her head like icy water. There was a kind of joy in the way her lungs expanded and closed again, like wings. *Zach was right*, she thought. *It* is *like a drug.* She knew that for everything she couldn't feel, her shadow felt something worse; but all the same she couldn't resist digging her fingernails into her hands, savouring the tiny spikes of not-pain, grinding until she felt the skin break and heal again, instantly. There was a kind of sick excitement in her stomach.

She had her back to the ruins, but it didn't even occur to her to be scared.

Eleven

Her eyes didn't adjust to the light. When the sun rose it was like going blind, looking at everything through a wash of acid. But it was wonderful; it didn't hurt.

She was sitting against the pile of rubble that had been a wall, staring into the mesh of sunlight shining through the trees. When she lifted her hand against the sun her fingers looked too long and narrow, as if the brightness was eating them away, but they didn't seem to block out as much of the light as normal. Even with the blaze of the sunrise as a background, they were very white. They weren't as solid as they should have been, either. Not that it worried her, much.

She knew that if she closed her eyes and concentrated she could flip the world over and be her shadow. But she didn't want to, somehow. She liked the dazzle and the ringing in her ears, the strange euphoria. And she didn't want the pain. When she thought about her shadow she felt a nudge of unease, like something refusing to let go. It wasn't as bad as it had been, because every time she felt it – or fear, or worry for Zach, or any of that stuff – she could push it back, along the bond between them, so that her shadow took it away. She knew the shadow was only really keeping it for later, but it felt good. She felt sorry for Zach, not being able to get rid of his feelings like that. But it meant that she didn't want to swap minds with the shadow. She didn't want any of it back.

And this was so *lovely* . . . the dawn, the whole world glowing like a slide with the light behind it . . . even the ruins weren't creepy any more. They were like a flat battery; the power had gone. She'd been here for hours, but she didn't want to move; and anyway the time had gone like a flash. She thought, dreamily, *I wonder if time is something else that my shadow has taken with her* . . .

She thought she felt someone looking at her. *Don't be silly*, she thought, *I'd have heard them coming* . . . but maybe she wouldn't have, with the ringing in her ears, a high piercing note like the sunlight . . . She looked round.

Zach was there, his face so white it was like a fingernail jabbed into her eyeball, making her flinch and look away. He dropped down the last couple of metres of wire fence and ran towards her, starting to shout even before his mouth had moved. 'You stupid – what the hell have you *done*? What were you *thinking*?'

'Relax – Zach, it's fine.' She wanted to laugh; then she thought, *This is exactly how it was before, only I'm him, and he's me* . . . and she couldn't help herself. She bit her lip and stared at the ground.

'For fuck's sake – please tell me you didn't – you haven't –'

And I understand now, she thought. *He was right*

to laugh at me, when I was so angry. This is the most wonderful feeling in the world, and he's standing there squawking as if I should be worried . . .

'Annis. Look at me.'

She raised her head to look at him, lost in a whirl of sunlight. She couldn't even see his face clearly; all that extra light, coming from nowhere, she couldn't bear to look . . . Except for his pupils. She stared at the two small dots of black – real *black*, the only things in this whole new world that were really black. She said, 'I can't see properly. Is that what it's like for you? Everything's all blotted out . . .'

A pause which rang and rushed in her ears, like she was ill.

'You did,' Zach said, at last. 'You *stupid*, stupid little girl.'

'I only . . .' She didn't mean to look away, but her head moved of its own accord, so she was gazing down at her shoes. 'Zach – I only did it because – my shadow, my other – she can help –'

'Your –? Where – can I see –?' For a second there was an odd note in his voice: eager, *hungry*, almost. Then he turned on his heels and said, without looking round, 'Christ, I should've known you'd do something like this. You have to do everything I do, right? You can't just let me –'

She said, '*Zach*. Will you *listen*? Please.' Then silence, again, that resonated in her head like a bell. 'Zach – I know what you're thinking, but I had to, OK? My other – my shadow – can find yours, she's gone to look for him, and then –'

'She can find him?'

'Yes. I went inside her head, and she can feel where

he is. So it'll be OK. She's on her way to him now – and I can keep track of where she's going, so we can follow . . . It'll be all right, I promise, Zach.'

His face didn't give anything away. 'And then, when she's found him, I can kill him.'

'Yes.' She didn't like the way he said it, but she ignored that. 'Zach – can't you see this is a good thing? We can get to your shadow before anyone dies.'

'If we've got that long.'

'Yes,' she said. 'If we've got that long. So we'd better get going.'

He was still expressionless. 'OK.'

'It'll be all right, Zach.'

'So you keep saying.' He smiled, then, as if he was too tired to keep a straight face. 'Anz . . . are you sure it's – safe? For you? I mean, you'll be careful – if your shadow gets too strong, you'll call her back?'

'Yes, I'm sure. Besides, you're in more danger than I am. You've been apart from your shadow for – what, four days? I've only just sent mine away.'

'Yes . . .' He turned away, shading his face with one hand. 'As long as it works like that. We don't know, do we? Like how fast a disease develops. It might not be the same for everyone.'

She rolled her eyes, feeling the tingle of not-pain in her fingertip where she was biting it absent-mindedly. 'Well, I don't think we can worry too much, at this point. Do you?'

'I just don't like the idea of you being in danger.'

'No, Zach. You don't like the idea of needing my help.' She said it automatically; it took her a few seconds to realise it was true.

'That's not fair.'

''Course it is.' She felt an echo of the anger she'd felt the night before, and stepped away from it, slipping it sideways to her shadow. 'I don't mind. I know you don't really care about anyone except yourself. I'm used to it.'

He stared at her. 'You really think that?'

'Yes.' She could hardly believe she'd said it. It was this new, harsh light, filling her head; there wasn't room for emotion. 'Don't worry. I'm not angry about it.'

When he opened his mouth she thought he was going to argue. But he didn't; he only frowned and looked at her closely. Then he turned away. In a flat, empty voice, he said, 'Yes. You're probably right.'

For a second she felt bad. Then that went sideways too, to her shadow, sliding away into the dark, until there was only a trace of it left. She thought, *I'm glad I can do this. It makes life so much easier.*

They walked towards the fence without a word. Annis watched Zach climb, screwing the toe of her shoe into the ground. She should have been feeling hopeful, triumphant . . . because she was helping him, she was going to stop his shadow stealing his strength, and killing people . . . but she couldn't summon the energy. She stood, waiting for him to drop down the other side, and wondered where her shadow had gone. It could be anywhere. She hadn't even noticed the direction she'd taken. For the first time, she thought: *Oh my God. What if Zach's shadow has gone to – oh, I don't know – Mongolia? What will we do? I don't have any warm clothes with me . . . and we'll have to get a flight, and . . .* She was at the top of the fence, trying not to overbalance, poking her fingers through the wire. *OK, so we'll need Mum's credit card . . .*

Zach didn't wait for her. He was already striding up the hill towards the house, face turned away from the sun. She dropped down, ignoring a cracking sound in her ankle, and jogged after him. Normally she'd have been irritated, because here she was, running after Zach, as usual . . . but now she didn't care.

He didn't look at her until they were standing outside the French windows. Then he stopped dead and spun round, so that she expected him to say something more significant than, 'So what do I need to pack?'

'How should I know?'

'Don't you know where she's going? I thought that was the plan, Anz. We're supposed to follow her, right?'

'Yes. I just meant –' Annis said, crossing her arms over her chest, and then couldn't finish her sentence. 'I know the direction, but she's gone so fast, she's already too far away to – I mean, I don't know *exactly* . . .' She thought, *What's the matter with me? Just because we're too far apart for me to know exactly where she is, just like that . . . I can find out where she's going. It'll be easy. Just flip that switch in my head and look through her eyes – no, be her – and I'll know where she is . . .* But she didn't want to. It was like deciding to jump into an icy pond.

Zach had narrowed his eyes. He said, 'What's the problem?'

'Nothing. There isn't one. I know the direction, vaguely, just not . . . She's further away from me than your shadow ever was, OK? That's probably why.'

'But –'

'But *yes*, I *know*, I can still find her, it just takes a bit more effort, OK?'

'I don't like this.' Zach rolled his shoulders uncomfortably. 'How do you know she's – safe?'

'I just do.'

He didn't look convinced, but he nodded slowly. 'So what do we take with us?'

'Everything we'll need.' She started to push past him; then pulled sharply away, in case there was a spark. But there was nothing. She thought, *Fine, in that case* . . . and pushed harder. But there was something blocking her way; not Zach, but an unyielding, slippery wall in front of him, like a shield.

He frowned at her; then seemed to realise what she was doing. He said, 'What the . . . ?' and raised his hand. He flattened it in front of his face, staring. Annis saw the skin go even whiter, and the tendons start to stick out, as if he was pressing it against something flat. 'God . . . that's weird.'

'What is it?'

He shook his head. 'I don't know. A kind of barrier, I guess. Like . . .'

She put her hands up, mirroring his, and felt resistance. Her hand slid smoothly, frictionlessly, away, curving around Zach's body. It was like the hemisphere of resistance between two magnets. It made her feel queasy. She said, 'We can't touch each other.'

'We couldn't before, anyway, because of the electricity. But this is – this is something else . . .' He bounced his fist off thin air. Annis felt the vibration on her face; it should have made a sound, like someone knocking on glass, but it didn't. 'Like force fields, meeting.'

Annis tried to laugh. 'Right. Very sci-fi.'

'Makes sense, though.' He sounded interested. 'And it might be why your shadow can find mine – if there's some kind of repulsion . . . if they're negative energy, and we're positive . . . and normal people are neutral, because –'

'I don't like it.'

'Why not? Did you need to hold my hand? Poor baby . . .' He stopped, grinning, waiting for her to tell him to shut up, until it was obvious she wasn't going to. Then his face went serious. 'Oh, come on, Anz, it's the least of our problems.'

She tried to smile. 'I know. It's just that . . . I don't know why it freaks me out. But it does. It's like we're trapped in these invisible cells.'

He shrugged. 'You'll get used to it. It's not much of an inconvenience, is it? If it means I can get my shadow back –' His voice was impatient, like she was making a fuss for no reason.

'Oh, right, so you're grateful now?' She felt the smile on her face get broader, but now it wasn't affectionate. '*If it means you can get your shadow back –* you mean, thanks, Annis, for putting yourself through all this, purely for my sake?'

He shot her a look. 'Yes, all right, Anz. You've made your point.'

If he'd only said it like he meant it. She said, 'So you *are* grateful? You accept my help, then? You'll let me bail you out, even though it offends your pride?' Her brain was cool and clear, completely emotion-free. 'You admit that you need me?'

'Of course I need you – for goodness' sake, Anz –'
There was a funny expression on his face, like he was studying her.

She felt a cool rush of anger, like adrenalin, and this time she hung on to it, enjoying the energy it gave her. 'Then say *thank you*! Or I'll call my shadow back right now, and you can go to hell. Say, yes, Annis, I am a stupid tosser who got himself into this mess and needs you to rescue him. Say, I'm pathetic. Say –'

'Thank you. I'm a stupid tosser who got himself into this mess and needs you to rescue him. And I'm pathetic.' His voice was flat, like it was something he'd learnt by heart.

She stared at him. He clenched his jaw. Then he went indoors, without looking back at her.

She thought, *What on earth made me do that? And – I – enjoyed – it* . . . There was a sudden flood of guilt inside her, but she caught it almost before she had time to feel it, letting it drain across to her shadow. There wasn't any point feeling bad.

She thought, *Right. First things first. I need to pack a bag.*

As it happened, she didn't really need to know where they were going, because there wasn't much scope for decisions about what to take. She shoved a couple of tops and a spare pair of jeans and a jumper into a bag, and even if they'd been going to Antarctica it wasn't like she had anything more suitable. She didn't say anything to Zach, but she saw him doing the same, just grabbing whatever was clean and within easy reach. They had to be quick, anyway, because it was only a matter of time before Mum and Dad woke up.

Then they went downstairs again. Annis found Mum's handbag, and took two credit cards and all her cash. It wasn't much, but she thought maybe she would have felt bad, before . . . Now she was just pleased she could be so efficient. She thought, *It makes life very easy, when you don't have to feel anything you don't want to feel* . . . Zach was watching her, his face as neutral as a mask. She told him to get some food and he didn't even answer, just filled a carrier bag with bread and cheese and fruit and bottles of water like a servant. That was odd; it would have made her old self feel uneasy. Now she didn't care.

Then they'd packed everything they could think of. Annis looked round, in case there was anything they'd forgotten, but if there was, she couldn't think of it.

Zach said, 'So are you going to reveal the destination of our magical mystery tour? Because we should get going.'

'Just a sec . . .' She moved her lips, silently, mouthing words like *food, soap, clothes, water,* the way Mum did at the supermarket. She felt strange . . . uncomfortable . . . she was going to have to make contact with her shadow, and she didn't want to. She told herself it was stupid, because after all she *was* her shadow, it was just a different way of looking at things . . . but when she tried to imagine the swollen darkness in the air, and the pain, she flinched away automatically. *No wonder Zach tried to keep his shadow away,* she thought. *When I call mine back for good it'll be like biting down on a toothache.*

'Annis? Come on. What's up?'

'Nothing.' She screwed up her face, and concentrated. And –

There was a kind of peace in her head, like silence late at night, but her whole body ached, and her hands stung. Anxiety and sadness were weighing her down, like bricks, so she had to struggle to stay afloat. *Come on . . .* She was somewhere familiar. That was strange, in itself, but she had to relax into the pain and the dark before she could make out what she was looking at. It was a round-cornered square of wrinkled grey, with a lurid tinge that she realised belatedly was the sun shining off it . . . There was a deep noise, nothing like the ringing not-noise that had been in her head, and that was familiar, too. She knew where she was, nearly, if only she could see past the shadows that clung to everything like moisture. *I've been here before. Lots of times.*

Then it was so obvious she laughed. Someone a few seats away from her craned round, uneasily, but his gaze skipped over her face. He couldn't see her properly. She laughed again. *Of course. I'm in a plane. That's the sea . . .*

But . . . where am I going? She took a deep breath, surrendering completely to the dark, *being* the shadow as hard as she could.

Remember. I remember.

Yes. The airport . . . slipping past people, half excited, half horrified at the way she could go anywhere without being challenged, the way people's faces went confused, then blank, as she passed . . . and the little kids that looked up, meeting her eyes – *seeing* her – before they yawned and collapsed gently sideways on to their parents, out for the count . . . She remembered walking past a florist, just to find out . . . and hearing, thirty seconds later, the gentle rain of petals, the sudden horrified exclamation as the woman came out from behind the counter and saw . . . That had been fun, almost. She'd felt a tiny relief from the pain, in spite of the way it built up again immediately. And it was the same, when she'd looked at a moth, beating against the glass, and seen it flutter to a sudden halt and drop like a bit of fabric: a fractional space, before the blackness welled up again like oil. She had to find ways to let the darkness out. It wasn't like walking through the fields, where it seeped out as she went, soaked up by the grass; here there wasn't enough life to absorb it. It had started to collect inside her. She had to concentrate to keep it there.

But that wasn't what she was trying to remember. *Where am I going?*

She felt around in her head for the nub of resistance that marked Zach's shadow. He was closer now, much closer. And she could feel how quickly the plane was travelling, the miles reeling in like a fishing-line. *Sooner or later*, she thought, *I won't be able to get any nearer to him. But for now . . .*

She remembered standing in the middle of the airport lounge, listening; then she'd gone to the nearest bookshop for an atlas. She'd walked out with it, and the man at the desk had looked round when the alarm went off, and squinted at her, but he'd shaken his head and rubbed his eyes under his glasses and turned back to his computer. She'd held the atlas open on the right page, facing in the right direction. Then she'd smiled and looked on the departure board for the next flight. It was so obvious.

London. He'd gone *home*.

Yes. That was all she needed to know. She dragged

herself away, back to herself, and gasped at the numbness flooding through her, the brightness, even though her eyes were closed. For a second it was almost uncomfortable; then she felt the relief, the gratitude that she was free of that awful painful heaviness, the toxic stuff gathering inside her . . . God. That was horrible . . .

Zach said, 'Anz? *Anz?* What the fuck –?'

She had her hands over her face. She took a second to drag a fingernail down the side of her cheek, letting the not-pain reassure her. *It's OK. I'm me, I'm not her* . . . Then she said, through her fingers, 'Yes, I'm here.'

'You're back.' She heard him hiss through his teeth. 'What the hell happened? You had this look on your face, and I recognised you, but you weren't – you weren't *you* . . . what were you –'

'I was being my shadow. To find out where she's –'

'What are you talking about?'

'I – did that thing, we *swapped*, so she was here and I was there, so it must have been her, looking through my eyes –' She stopped, because of the way Zach was looking at her. 'What?'

'You swapped places with her?'

'Yes. You know, you concentrate and think of the dark, and things sort of switch . . . I feel what she's feeling, and vice versa . . . I can't explain, but you know what I'm talking about –'

'No.' Zach turned away. He said, 'I didn't know you could do that.'

'Didn't you ever –?' But she remembered now: he'd never said anything about being his shadow. Only about the pain going away. She thought, with an odd, secret flare of pride, *I can do something Zach can't.*

'I suppose it never occurred to me to try.' His voice was flat. 'I didn't really care how he felt.'

She could have said, *And she loves me. She's taking everything bad away, to protect me – not just pain, but all my feelings too* . . . but she didn't. She just said, 'Don't you want to know where we're going?'

Zach swallowed, but he still didn't look at her. 'Yes, of course.'

'Guess.' She said it casually, trying to lighten the mood.

'Don't be such a fucking cow. You know I don't know.' He didn't shout it, but all the same she drew back, shocked.

She said, 'He's gone home. To London. I just meant . . . I thought it was funny, that's all. We've been racking our brains, and he goes *home* . . .'

'Hilarious.' He turned away, shouldering his rucksack. 'Let's go, then. At least we won't have to find hundreds of pounds for the flight.'

'Yes.' She picked up her bag and walked to the door.

'Wait. We should leave a note, or something.'

'Why?' She looked round, imagining Mum and Dad discovering they'd gone. She could see it quite clearly – the initial panic, the anger, the crippling worry, and then the arguments, until it wasn't even about *them* any more . . . But she couldn't muster any kind of sympathy. *It'll serve them right*, she thought. 'Anyway, it's safer not to tell them.'

That look again, on Zach's face, the one she couldn't identify. 'Safer?'

'Otherwise they might come after us.' She sighed heavily. 'Oh, all right, just don't tell them where we're going. Say we're going to . . . Mongolia.'

'Mongolia. Right.' He ripped the top page off Mum's notebook and scribbled something. 'Anz . . . they'll worry . . . If we say we've gone home, they'll be livid, but at least they won't *worry* . . . They won't call the police or anything. They might not even come after us. But they think I'm off my head, remember? If we say we've gone somewhere else –'

'Whatever.' She flapped her hands at him, as if he was an insect. 'Zach, I don't care, OK? If you're feeling scrupulous, fine. I don't care what you do. Just don't blame me if it backfires.'

He held her look, then scribbled something else. She thought about leaning over to read it, but she couldn't be bothered. Zach put the pen down and looked up. 'Anz . . . You do still – you do love them, right?'

She grimaced, raising her eyes to the ceiling. 'That's great, coming from *you*.'

'No, I wasn't – it was a real question. Do you?'

'Yes, of course I do. But they've been shitty to both of us, and frankly I think they deserve a few days of tenterhooks and general parental angst. It's not like we owe them anything. Now can we go?'

He nodded, biting his lip. Then he reached down and put the note on the table, picking up one of the dirty coffee mugs as if he was going to use it as a paperweight, but he carried on holding it, staring down at what he'd written.

Annis said, 'Zach? Shall we go, then?'

He nodded again, without looking up. 'I guess

it's too early for a taxi, so if we walk to St Jean-le-Grand . . . then we can get a train to the airport . . .' But he sounded distant, preoccupied.

She put her arms through the straps of her rucksack and stood in the doorway, waiting.

He said, 'Do you really think that Mum and Dad have been shitty?'

She wasn't sure why it made her laugh, but it did. 'Yes. Don't you?'

He did look round, then. And for a second . . . if his face hadn't been so white, he would have looked the way he used to. He was grinning, suddenly. 'Thank God for that. I thought it was just me.'

She grinned back. 'No.'

'You wouldn't believe how good it is, to hear you say that.' He started to laugh. 'Oh God . . . I've been beating myself up about it all. I thought they were really good parents, and it was me, fucking everything up . . . Thanks, Annis, thank you so much for saying that . . .' He pushed his hair back with one hand and breathed out so deeply Annis saw his shoulder blades move. He raised his other hand, too, and then looked at it as if he'd realised he was still holding the coffee mug. 'What am I doing with this?'

She was still giggling. 'I don't know.'

'No, me neither.' He made a face at her, and held the mug up as if he was toasting her. 'Cheers.'

She said, 'Zach . . . it's OK, none of it was your fault, not the stuff with Cecilia. You did the right thing.'

'Yes.' He smiled back at her: an open, grateful smile. Then he wrinkled his nose, and took a mock swig from the empty mug. 'To dysfunctional families.

And all who sail in them.'

Annis picked up the other mug. 'All who sail in them.'

'And screw Mum and Dad.' He held her gaze for a second, and he wasn't joking any more.

Then he threw the mug at the French windows.

The smash wasn't as loud as she expected, but it was beautiful, like an explosion of splinters catching the light. Then the door gaped at them, jaggedly, like something had taken it by surprise. The mug landed on the terrace, the handle flipping off into the bed of dead herbs.

Annis said, 'Screw Mum and Dad,' and threw hers.

And then, somehow, they were both grabbing for everything they could reach, ripping things off the shelves, throwing whatever came to hand . . . Zach was skimming books at the pictures on the walls, leaving broken webs in the glass, and Annis was hurling cutlery and fruit and bread, putting her whole weight into each missile. Once she ran out of fruit she threw the bowl, and it made a proper, hefty smash, blasting itself into shards. The top came off a tin of coffee and spewed black dust along the floor. A dish-cloth landed on Zach's shoulder and he picked it off between his finger and thumb, looking so fastidious Annis collapsed in helpless giggles. He looked round and picked up a pile of CDs to throw back, and she had to duck to one side of the fridge while he spun them at her. Then she couldn't resist; she opened the fridge and threw everything, until there were broken jars of olives and pools of milk and a block of butter skidding across the floor. They were both gasping with laughter, and a kind of triumph, because, after all, Mum and Dad had been asking for it . . . She paused, trying to get her breath back. Zach lifted a chair above his head and smashed it down across the kitchen table. There was a crash, and the noise of wood breaking. She saw the struts fly into pieces round his head. He jerked his face away, and wiped a fleck of blood out of his eye, but he was still laughing, and his skin healed before she had time to see what had happened. And then there was a sudden silence, and she realised how much noise they'd been making. *Oh, bugger.*

She could hear Mum's voice; muffled by the walls, but she was awake, she must have heard – surely . . .

Zach said, 'Oh, shit. We've woken them up . . . Come on. We've got to go *now*.'

She didn't even stop to reply; just turned and ran out of the front door, thankful that she hadn't bothered to take her rucksack off. Zach was a little way behind; she could hear him breathing as they sprinted through the field down towards the road. He was still spluttering a bit, and she could hear the mad laughter trying to resurface. *Oh my God*, she thought, *we trashed the kitchen, we completely* trashed *it . . .* but she was still grinning, she couldn't help it. *Yes. They deserved it.*

Zach was shaking his head, now, grimacing as if he couldn't quite believe what they'd done. He said hoarsely, 'Anz . . . what were we *doing*?'

She didn't answer. She kept on running, because she knew he'd wanted to do it as much as she did – more, probably. And it wasn't a joke.

'Anz? Why didn't you tell me to stop?' He was overtaking her, now. 'You should have told me to stop. It's not like you . . .'

She ignored him. She put on a determined spurt of speed, and – amazed – felt her feet get faster, felt her body obey without any protest.

She thought, *This is brilliant. I can do anything. I can do anything.*

When did I first realise there was something wrong?

With you, I mean. When did I first realise there was something wrong with *you*?

The first time I saw your shadow in your eyes? When you stood there and you weren't *you*, any more? Or when you oh-so-casually dropped the bombshell that you and your shadow could swap places, just like that, when I'd never realised that was possible, even before I sent my shadow away? But . . . No. When you said that, it was *me* I cared about. When I realised that you and your shadow had something . . . different. Something special. I never wondered how my shadow was feeling – or even what he was, except a handy way of wiping out everything that had been making me feel bad – until it was too late.

You told me I'd never given a damn for anyone else in my whole life. And you know what? You were right. I don't think it had ever even occurred to me, to care about anyone else . . . I mean, in reality. I didn't even realise that I didn't care. I thought I was normal. If you'd asked me, I'd have told you I was a warm, affectionate sort of person, and I wouldn't have known I was lying. It wasn't until you said . . . and I started to defend myself, because, hey, of course I care about people, like my mates, and you and Mum and Dad . . . and then I actually thought about it, for the first time. And I knew you were right.

The thing is, if you feel bad about someone, it's easy to think it's because you love them. Like when I made Dad tell Mum about Cecilia (may she rot in hell). I thought I felt shitty because I loved them both, and I didn't want either of them hurt . . . but it wasn't that. I was pissed off because from now on my life was going to be so much less comfortable. Sure, I felt bad that they felt bad . . . but it wasn't because of them. I didn't like the way it affected *me*, *my* life. I missed all the stupid things, like Dad winking at me when Mum went off on one about something, and Mum deciding for no particular reason that I could choose what takeaway to get, and everyone making the same joke at exactly the same time. Those were the things that got to me. I wouldn't have cared how unhappy Mum and Dad were, if they'd been a bit better at hiding it. But I knew it was my fault, and I resented them for making me feel guilty. And that wasn't love. It wasn't even close.

Even that day . . . ages ago, the morning last winter . . . it was a Sunday, one of those nothing-y days when the sky is white but everything else is in shades of brown, freezing cold, the kind of day when you wish you'd stayed in bed. I can't even remember what I was doing, except that for some reason I needed something from the shed. White spirit or something. And I push the door open and Dad's there, on his mobile, propped up on the lawnmower. He doesn't look round. I'm about to say, Is the white spirit in here? only it's like he's read my mind, because he sighs and says, No, I'm sorry, darling . . . And I'm about to turn round and go away again, when I wonder why he called me *darling*. It's not his style.

He says, I know, darling, I feel the same way, but I *can't* . . .

And I think, Oh . . . Mum. Why doesn't he just go inside and talk to her face to face? She's in the kitchen, she's just made a pot of coffee and everything . . .

I can't believe I was so slow. But it takes me thirty seconds to get it. And then it's because he says, I can't get away this evening, but I'll see you tomorrow, all right? Oh, and that meeting – I know he's a fucking arsehole, but I do need that report to give him . . . Good. Yes, I love you too . . .

I think, Jesus Christ. And I try to get out of the door without him hearing me, but I trip over Mum's bike and he looks round.

That's the worst bit. We look at each other, and he knows I've heard, and he knows he's shafted, and we both know that nothing will ever be the same again.

But even then . . . I was furious, of course I was . . . and I told myself – I really *believed* – that I was angry on Mum's behalf. But really it was because I knew he'd ruined all our lives, for at least the next six months . . . Like I could see the atmosphere in the house going sour there and then, clogging into bits, like milk. And I didn't

205

see why suddenly *I* had to deal with it. I remember thinking it was like he'd dumped his little bastard straight into my arms, smelling of shit and vomit, and all I could do was pass it on to someone else, and then it would all be *my* fault . . . And really, *really* I was just so outraged that MY DAD had done something so sordid, that MY DAD wasn't bothered enough about us to behave well, that MY DAD – that I loved, more or less – was having an affair with his patronising, rude, *thick* secretary. I mean . . . it's stupid. For God's sake, it's not like *I'm* married to Dad. If it wasn't for Mum, I wouldn't care who he shags. But it felt like he was being unfaithful to us as well. To *me*.

The only person I've ever cared about – properly, I mean, not out of self-interest – is you. You, Annis. You should be flattered.

God . . . don't you think that's amazing? That I can pinpoint the first moment in my whole life when I suddenly gave a damn about another person? Yep . . . And what makes it even better is that it was only a few days ago. Seventeen-and-a-bit years of complete egotism finally gave way to a tiny flicker of common humanity. I hope you're proud of me. It took me by surprise, I can tell you. I looked at you and *cared*. For no logical reason. Just . . . love, I guess. This wave of – yes, of guilt and selfish worry and anger, all that as well, but – absolute *terror*, that something was wrong with you. Something irrevocable. And for a second all the stuff I'm scared of for myself was nothing. I would have done anything, anything at all, to make you OK.

* * *

And you're still asleep, and I'm starting to think you won't wake up.

It was on the plane. I mean, I think I'd wondered, before that . . . the way you talked about Mum and Dad, the way you helped me trash the kitchen . . . That was perfectly normal behaviour for me, but highly out of character for you. You seemed . . . not cruel, that's too strong, but . . . I dunno. Heartless. Like nothing was quite getting through. But I thought, Well, the worm's got to turn eventually, she's earned a bit of a rebellion . . .

And at the airport, we were both kind of high. I was dreading it, to be honest. I thought there'd be all sorts of problems about booking the tickets, what with only having cash or Mum's credit card, and both of us being under eighteen . . . And I was kind of scared that one of us would touch someone by mistake, or give off a spark and wipe out a metal detector, or . . . oh, hell, I don't know. Anything could have happened. But when we were there, and you were marching about like you knew exactly what to do . . . It went so smoothly. And the weird thing was, suddenly that didn't surprise me. I felt so safe. Ridiculous, isn't it? I felt like *I* was the kid, trailing around after my older sister. I felt like you were in charge. For the first time in ages, someone was looking after me. You were more grown-up, then, than Mum and Dad had been for *months*. I believed that you could get me out of this mess. It was all going to be OK.

Our flight was about midday, I think. And it was all normal. At least . . . *almost* normal, as if the whole thing was an elaborate stage-set, made of something slightly too flimsy, so the daylight shone through the walls. But I knew that was just me. And I kept telling myself that nothing was going to go wrong. I was nervous because I'd blown that light – you remember? – and I didn't want to think about what would happen if we started to blow the electrics on the plane, but I ignored that. And every time I glanced at you, you were striding along like the world was your oyster, which amused me because I thought that walk was strictly my speciality.

No. It was later. On the plane.

A tiny thing. It was such a tiny thing.

You had a window seat. I was next to you, crammed in so close I could feel that sheet of resistance between us, which was uncomfortable but better than being worried about touching someone by mistake. You were staring down at the clouds sailing past us like massive shining icebergs. They'd given us lunch and you were fiddling with the plastic knife. I kept checking my watch neurotically, trying to work out how long I'd been apart from my shadow. It was better than trying to think about what I was going to do, once we'd found him. I kept listening for him in my head, the way you keep testing a sore tooth to see if it's got any better, but he was never there. It was like a section of my mind was curtained off, inside. Like when I had tantrums when I was small and shut myself in the wardrobe. My shadow had closed me out. And I didn't blame him. I deserved it, after all. I'd tried to kill him, hadn't I?

I remembered what you'd said, about concentrating and thinking of the dark, but it didn't do anything. It was horrible, not to know. And if I was feeling like that . . . Jesus, how was *he* feeling?

And then . . . I see you holding the plastic knife like a pen. And you jab down into your wrist and draw it down the whole length of your forearm, to the elbow. It breaks the skin. The tip goes . . . I don't know, maybe a few centimetres into your arm. The blood wells up round it and runs sideways on to your jeans. And this is a *plastic* knife. It's the bluntest thing in the world. In real life – well, I suppose it must be possible, just, to cut your arm open with it. But it would hurt like mad. And it would be really *difficult*, to put enough pressure on the blade, getting the angle right, so it wouldn't bend or break. No one would bother. They'd just use a razor.

I don't say anything. I don't know what to say.

I keep watching you, using my peripheral vision so you don't notice. Not that you'd notice me, anyway, because you're looking down at your arm, totally absorbed, with this expression on your face that makes me feel weird, like I'm watching something private. You take the knife away and put it neatly back on the flip-down table in front of you. You use the napkin to wipe the blood off. And – of course – there's no mark on your skin.

I think, What is she *doing*? But I know. I know, from the look on your face, that you feel the way I did, before the wall fell on me. Before I started to understand . . .

And I think: When she calls her shadow back, that'll come back, too. If she keeps doing that – if she's not careful . . . When she calls her shadow back – if –

If she calls her shadow back . . .

I catch myself saying it in my head and I look away, because I can't think straight. I tell myself I'm being stupid. You're the sensible one. Of course you'll call your shadow back, just as soon as you've helped me find mine.

I want to lean over and say something casual, just to let you know I've seen. I want to say something perfect, so you realise it's a dense thing to do but you don't resent me for pointing it out. But I can't. All I can think of to say is, Don't do that. Please don't do that. You're hurting yourself. And I've ignored enough drugs lectures in my time to know that's worse than useless.

That's when I feel the terror, creeping up on me. I want you to be all right. That's all I want. And I know – already, even then – I know you're not going to be. I know something's gone wrong.

And I was right. Look at you now.

Twelve

It was all so beautiful. Annis couldn't concentrate on anything. She was buzzing with a kind of high-pitched tension like electricity, which was almost unbearable, sometimes, and sometimes . . . On the plane it had been great, like being so excited she couldn't breathe, loving the height and the speed, and she'd started to see white flecks in the corner of her eyes, like swirling silver sand or a snowfall of light, like bad reception on TV but beautiful, really, really beautiful . . . She'd thought it was because they were so high up, looking down at the sunlit clouds, like Antarctica, so bright she could hardly bear it, like seeing God, but it didn't go away, at Heathrow, in the taxi, on the street, even when she was looking at their front door. Peeling faded red paint and grimy stained glass and it was all so wonderful, blazing, so filled with daylight . . . It was ridiculous, really, to expect her to do ordinary human things like finding her front-door keys and picking up the post from the doormat so she didn't slip over on the junk mail. She couldn't help giggling. It was like when she was small, and she played games like Going to the Shops or Making a Cake . . . She dumped her rucksack at the bottom of the stairs and thought, *Why am I bothering? I mean, honestly . . .*

'Where is he? Is he here?' Zach, behind her.

She paused, letting the strap of her rucksack slide through her fingers, and listened.

Zach said, 'You said he was coming home. So? Is he here?'

'I don't know.' She looked up the stairs, towards the square of light coming through the window. 'It's my shadow who can feel him, not me.'

Zach cleared his throat, and took a step past her. She felt the space between them twang, like a piece of elastic. 'So . . . he might be here . . .'

She walked away, down the hall into the kitchen. There was sunlight falling across the floor, making the tiles glow red like an abstract painting. *Oh, so beautiful*, she thought. And the windows themselves: the glass, blurred with a kind of shining haze, as if there was a sheet of gauze across it; the garden, the overgrown green of the lawn blazing; the coloured panes of the back door, the bottom square broken like a yawn, showing its teeth . . .

Oh – *shit* . . .

The handle of the door was just under the broken pane of stained glass. It was one of the locks you could open from the inside. So someone had broken in. *Yeah, right, someone*, she thought. *As if I didn't know exactly who would break in like that, neatly, not trying to cause any unnecessary damage . . .* She yelled, 'Zach! *Zach!*'

She felt fear suddenly running down her back, like an ice cube melting. Somewhere, she knew, her shadow was even more scared than she was, but there wasn't time to think about it. She was already grabbing a kitchen knife from the block on the worktop, running upstairs, her heart pounding. '*Zach!*'

She could see it, in her mind's eye: how it had been, that night . . . Zach and his shadow face to face, the tension between them like a wire, and how she'd knelt on the floor, waiting for Zach to lose . . . And it was worse, now, because she knew exactly what would happen, if he did. She started to shout again, but she was too breathless. She swung herself round the newel post on the landing. Zach's bedroom door was open.

It was so silent. She wanted to run, but her feet slowed down in spite of her, as if they were scared someone would hear.

'Anz? Is that you?'

Her whole body sagged, like someone had cut all her tendons. She flopped into Zach's room like a jelly-fish, trying to breathe deeply. He was standing there, looking down at the mess on the floor. She said, 'Are you OK?'

'He's been here. He's gone now. But you were right. He was here.' Zach's voice sounded funny, like a metronome that hadn't been wound up properly.

'Yes, he broke one of the panes in the back door. Dad'll be furious, stained glass is really hard to replace, at least it wasn't the whole thing . . .' She was babbling with relief. She swallowed and looked round. Zach's room looked like it had been ran-sacked, but then, it always did. 'Anyway . . . how did *you* know he'd been here?'

Zach nudged at the pile of clothes next to his foot. It looked like there was a family of mugs breeding underneath a manky pair of boxers. He said, without looking up, 'Have you seen the living room?'

'Why? What . . . ?' She took a few steps backwards on to the landing, and peered round into the living room. It looked ordinary, from here. Apart from being fairly tidy, of course . . . 'What's he done?'

'Go and look.'

She went and looked; and as soon as she got through the door she saw what he meant. Mum's plants were dead. There were piles of leaves on the floor, like it was autumn, and all the branches were brown and bare. Even the cactus on the mantelpiece was just a small furry *thing*, like a shrivelled head. It gave her the chills, because everything else was so normal. Nothing was out of place. There weren't even any books on the coffee table, or . . . She saw a couple of little black beads on the carpet, like raisins with legs. Flies. And a tangle of dark thread that was a spider.

She felt sick. He'd been here. And if he came back . . . She thought, *He wouldn't be able to hurt me, not now.* But that wasn't the point.

'He's been in here, too.' Zach was still standing where she'd left him, staring at the floor. 'Maybe he's been *living* here. If that's the word I'm after.'

There weren't any plants in Zach's room. Annis looked round, feeling a kind of dread ooze up from her gut. What had he found? She said, trying to sound casual, 'I don't see how you can tell. Or has he tidied up a bit?'

Zach nearly smiled. 'Sort of.' He picked up one of the festering mugs and held it out to her. She took an automatic step backwards, feeling something wrap itself round her ankle. 'No, Anz. Look.'

She shook whatever it was off her shoe, and looked

214

gingerly into the mug. There was a film of brown across the bottom. She said, 'Yuck. But I don't see –'

'Mould. He killed the mould.' It *was* a smile, now. 'Anything alive, you see? We could rent him out to hospitals, to kill germs . . . except that he might kill the patients too, of course –'

He was joking. Obviously. And it wasn't like she was upset about *mould*, for heaven's sake. It was nothing, compared to the plants; killing mould was a good thing, surely . . .

So she had no idea why it hit her, suddenly. But it did. She had to run to the loo before she threw up.

It was funny, how she could still feel sick, when she couldn't feel pain. Odd. As if it was the emotion making her sick . . . She rested the side of her face on the toilet seat and stared into the white porcelain-coloured water, taking stock. *I'm scared, and disgusted, and miserable, and I feel guilty about Mum and Dad* . . . She knew it wasn't anything like as bad as what her shadow felt, but all the same . . . She concentrated, and felt it fade away, soaked up by the shadow. That was better; now she was cold and clear again. *Like I've flushed my mind*, she thought, wanting to laugh. *I've reset everything, like a computer. I have memory but no emotion.*

She levered herself up, washed her mouth out, and went downstairs again.

Zach was sitting on a chair in the hall, hugging his rucksack. He looked so tired . . . no, not tired, exactly, but thinner, as if he was transparent, less solid than he ought to have been . . . And there was a strange, blind look in his eyes. When Annis was at the bottom of the stairs he glanced up, but it was like he was following the movement without actually focusing on *her*. He said, 'Anz? What's wrong?'

'Nothing. I feel fine.'

He nodded a couple of times. 'We were so close,' he said, turning to stare at the wall. 'He was *here*, just a little while ago . . . maybe, if we'd only been a bit quicker . . .' He trailed off. Then he leant forward, suddenly, squinting at the answering machine. 'Oh, hell. Look.'

The light was flashing. Ten new messages. Annis rolled her eyes – they were probably all from Mum and Dad – and pressed the *play* button. There was a hiccup, a little burp of white noise, and then silence. The light went out.

Zach hissed through his teeth. 'What did you do?'

'Nothing. Electric things don't like us, that's all.' She walked backwards; after a few steps the light came back on. No new messages. Oh, great. She said, 'Well, at least we don't have to listen to them now.'

'Check your mobile.'

She did. It wouldn't turn on. Zach watched her with narrowed eyes, then checked his own phone and swore under his breath.

She said, 'What's the big deal, anyway? It's not like we need to talk to anyone.'

'Yeah. It's just me and you, right?' There was a flat note in his voice.

She shot a glance at him, but she didn't answer.

'So what do we do now, Anz? Where's your shadow? More to the point, where's mine?'

It shouldn't have knocked her off balance, but it did. She'd almost *forgotten* . . . She was going to have to swap minds with her shadow, any minute now.

And the more light there was welling up inside her now – filling her mouth and eyes and ears, like mucus – the more dark there'd be, when she did . . . And all those little things, the damage she'd done to herself, secretly, to feel the not-pain – that meant . . .

She said, 'I'm going for a shower.'

'Anz –'

'It's fine, Zach, I've got time for a shower, it's not *that* urgent. Relax.'

She saw him decide not to argue. She thought, for no reason: *He'll lose touch with reality, as the light gets stronger. Maybe this is how it starts.*

It should have made her want to find her shadow, this second, because time was of the essence. But it didn't.

She said, 'Right. See you in a bit. Don't touch any switches.'

She stood in the shower, letting the water run down over her face. It wasn't that she was scared of being in her shadow's head . . . just that she didn't much fancy the idea. She thought, *Zach doesn't know what it's like . . . all that darkness, just waiting for me . . . It's OK for him, he can't swap minds with his shadow even if he wants to. And he'll destroy his shadow as soon as he finds him. But as for me, oh well, boring old Annis will call her shadow back to her, of course, she won't mind not being immortal . . . Mind you, there's no reason why I should. I could destroy my shadow, too, and then Zach and I would both live for ever, in this wonderful dazzling fog, never feeling pain . . .*

She shook her head until the water splattered on the

217

shower curtain. No. What was she thinking? *Shut up, Annis. Zach can't call his shadow back, because he'd die . . . And of course I want my shadow back eventually. Just – not yet . . .*

She tried to keep her mind blank, scrubbing at her hair and nails and ears until she was sure all the grime from the flight was washed away. Then she turned the water to freezing and stood in the jet for as long as she could bear.

After about thirty seconds she turned the water off, wrapped herself in a towel and sat down on the bath mat. She knew the door was locked but she checked anyway.

Then she gritted her teeth, thought, *For Zach . . .* and threw her mind off balance, waiting for her shadow to catch her.

She was in a space without walls, a blur of daylight filtering through layers of darkness like veils. There was something above her – a pillar, a frozen fountain . . . no. It was something alive: a tree . . . She knew that, because she could feel it absorbing the darkness from inside her, breathing it in. It was a relief, like someone draining pus out of an abscess. She blinked, trying to see more clearly. There was a noise like something scratching behind a wall, and she realised it was the sound of the leaves curling and dropping as the tree died. She thought, *I didn't mean to, I don't want it to die . . .* but there was nothing she could do. *Oh God, I'm so sorry . . .*

Where was she? *I've been here before,* we've *been here before.* Suddenly the pain hit her, catching her off guard, pulling her apart with its fingers. She made a noise like an animal, whimpering with the shock. There was the long line, glowing red-hot down her forearm, the little burning crescents where she'd dug her fingernails into her skin . . . *on purpose*, she thought, incredulous, *I did that to myself on purpose* . . . She didn't understand. She couldn't remember why she'd wanted to do it. And . . . she thought, *Oh no, poor Mum, poor Dad, they'll be frantic, how could we have done that? How could I –?* The guilt rose up like a wave, swamping the words.

She knew, now, there wasn't any point fighting it. She took long breaths, trying to let the hurt go through her, like light through glass. She didn't know how long it took, but eventually she could ignore it, and look round, frowning into the shadows. Flatness . . . a circle of something around her that had been alive, but wasn't now – grass . . . and the hump of a hill . . . more trees, the nearest one drinking a trickle of dark that seeped from her fingers . . . and people. *People –*

No. It was all right. They were a long way away; and they were closed to the darkness, shielded by buzzing fields of energy that filtered most of it out. Before, in the airport, she'd had to be nearby, or to make eye contact, before the blackness even touched them. Now it was stronger, but it was still OK. Wasn't it? No one was close enough to feel it . . . or at least, only as a tendril of grey, brushing against them: a headache, a yawn, a toddler stumbling and sitting down suddenly on the grass . . . She stood still, as far away from the people as possible, and tried to keep the darkness inside.

Where am I?

Somewhere familiar . . . Of course – the park! Kensington Gardens. It had to be. She recognised it – like seeing a study in charcoal – but as well as that, it made sense. She thought, *Yes, because we're the same person, that's where I'd go . . .* Not her favourite spot, near the statue of Peter Pan – but that made sense too, because there'd be more people there. For a moment she felt strangely, ridiculously *glad*, as if she'd caught her other's eye across the distance, and they'd smiled at each other. She could almost see her: wrapped in a towel in the bathroom, surrounded by the blaze of light, free of pain, safe . . . *Yes*, she thought. *Yes. I love you. It's all right.*

But it was like a shaft of sunlight, dying away as soon as it had come. She was left in the dark again, starting to shiver. She had to concentrate. She knew where she was – that was a start – but where was Zach's shadow? Shouldn't she be able to sense him?

Oh God. I've lost him. All this, and I've lost him . . .

Where was the other epicentre of the dark? That was how it was, before – a little bump of denser blackness, behind the veils of grey . . . like a swelling under the skin. Or as if there were ripples spreading out from her, and they met his, somewhere, and echoed back to her . . . She couldn't describe it, but she didn't need to. She could tell what she was looking for. A pulse of darkness that wasn't her . . .

Nothing.

No. That was stupid. He had to be there, some-where . . . *I could feel him, before, from* miles *away . . . and if he was in our house, he can't have got that far* . . . She cast her mind out like a net, dragging the depths of the dark. Where was he? Something felt different – wrong . . .

She thought: *he's been destroyed. Somehow, without us knowing – oh, thank goodness, oh, thank you, he's gone –*

There was a flicker of deeper black, in and out of sight as swiftly as a fish.

The relief went out, like a flame in water. She fixed her gaze on the trace of darkness in her head, trying to follow its progress. It was elusive, much harder to pinpoint than before . . . *Which is stupid*, she thought, *because he's closer, he ought to be* easier *to find* . . . but it flashed here and there, dim and blurred, as if there was an extra layer of shadow over her eyes. *What's wrong?* she thought. *What's changed?*

At least she knew the direction. It was hard to find, like following a compass needle that kept swinging, but she turned until she was facing towards him, and started to walk. She was glad it took her across the park, so she didn't have to get close to anyone. She felt the grass withering underfoot and was glad about that, too, because it meant the darkness wasn't building up inside her as quickly, ready to surge when she walked past someone . . .

She stopped. She didn't mean to. But she couldn't go any further.

It wasn't quite like the barrier between her and Zach had been. It wasn't elastic, or slippery, like magnets repelling each other. It was more like a fog, but solid, so you could only get a few paces in before you had to stop. It didn't feel like a law of physics; it felt like the world was holding her back, like an adult stopping a child from crossing the road. It said, *No. Not a good idea.* And Annis knew it was right. ***All that darkness***, she thought, ***me and him together, who knows what would happen*** . . . But it was frustrating, too; because she needed to find him, she *needed* to find him! And the world wasn't going to give in. It wasn't even listening.

She tried to walk forward, pushing until she felt tears of exertion on her face. No good. And it was so big. You couldn't tell where it ended. She thought it had to be circular, with Zach's shadow in the middle, but there wasn't any curve, that she could see. It could be a mile across . . . And as she stood there, breathing the smell of sunlight and dying grass, it seemed to push her backwards, very slightly, as if it was growing . . . She thought, *It can't be, **not** that fast* . . . but she wasn't sure.

I can't get any closer. She could have tried harder, but she knew there wasn't any point. She saw things more clearly, when she was the shadow; she understood the way the darkness worked. But if she couldn't get any closer, that meant . . .

It meant she'd failed. Because it wasn't any use, was it? *Your shadow's over there somewhere, Zach. Anywhere between here and Bayswater.* **Oh God, oh God** . . . She'd done everything she could, but Zach would still –

She almost flipped away, back to her other, because she couldn't bear it. Zach would fade away, eaten by the light until there was nothing left of him . . . that blank, blind look on his face – that was how he'd be, for ever, only a ghost; like a lens, focusing light until it sparked, caught fire . . . She could see it. The way his skin would go from neon to sunlight to floodlight . . . and he'd disappear, what made Zach *Zach* would disappear.

She reeled. But she clung on, because there was still something here she didn't understand. She braced herself as the pain rose and drained away again, as if it had remembered her. *Not long*, she thought. *Hold on. Just for a little bit longer, and then I'll go back to my other* . . .

A dribble of darkness slid sideways, away from her, towards the nearest bush. Oh, well. At least it wasn't a tree. She turned and walked back in the direction she'd come, blindly, threading her way through the thick shadows. The strange thing was, she could feel the sunlight on her skin, uncomfortably warm. Why was Zach's shadow so hard to find? There was something . . .

Then it came to her, clearly.

Zach's shadow was hard to see because there was so much *more* darkness than before. That was all it was. Before, he'd been like a beacon of dark, in a grey world; now her world was so murky it was harder to see him. She breathed out, relieved, because that was only to be expected, wasn't it? She'd known there'd be more darkness, as time went on. When she was her other, there'd been more light – so it made sense. It was a question of balance. Of course she would give out more and more darkness . . .

She thought: *but – I was giving out more darkness than he was.*

That barrier . . . it was pushing me back because my *darkness was growing. Not his. He wasn't very different from how he was before. It was* me.

That was impossible. No, it was . . . she was imagining it. She had to be . . . *Because he's been apart from Zach for* ages. *How* could *I be stronger than him? It doesn't make sense.*

Except . . . what had Zach said? *We don't know, do we? Like how fast a disease develops.* But that was stupid. She was worrying too much. Surely . . .

And my other – she thought – *yes, she gives all those feelings away. What if that speeds everything up? She's feeling less and less and I'm feeling more, and I can't keep it all inside me . . .*

No. Oh no . . . She'd failed. She couldn't find Zach's shadow for him, after all – she couldn't get close enough, the shadow could be anywhere – and now everything was going wrong, too quickly . . . Fear swept over her like a sandstorm, biting into her skin. *I can't help him; I should stop trying . . .*

No. No, she couldn't bear it, she wasn't *going* to bear it –

She took hold of herself, dragging her mind away, twisting out of her shadow, back into her body. And she found herself sobbing, the tears running down her neck and soaking into the towel, as if she'd been crying all the time. But it was easy to stop, because she'd left all the pain behind. She felt fine. It was like getting into a hot bath when she'd been frozen stiff: she knew she'd been cold, but she couldn't imagine what it had felt like. She looked at the patch of moisture on the edge of the towel and smiled, shaking her head. God, what was she *like*?

And . . . she remembered it all, perfectly: *my shadow can't help Zach, she's getting too strong . . .*

But she couldn't have been thinking straight. It was stupid to panic, just because of a vague, illogical feeling. The sensible thing was to wait and see – it wasn't like her shadow was going to *kill* anyone, not imminently . . .

She stood up, rubbing her head vigorously with the towel, and then scuttled into her bedroom and got dressed. When she came out, savouring the luxury of a clean T-shirt on her skin, Zach was still sitting where he'd been before, on the chair in the hall.

He looked up sharply. 'Anz? Where is he? We should go now – follow him – I mean . . .' He clenched his hands on the straps of his rucksack. 'I got some stuff, like the kitchen knife you had, and . . . where's he gone? Did you . . . ?' He trailed off, watching her face like a camera.

'She's finding him. But it'll take a while.'

'Is everything – I mean . . . It's OK, right? Nothing's happened?'

'No, of course not.' She'd put her jeans back on, because all her good clothes were still in France, and she could feel rough edges of mud round her ankles. 'Everything's fine. She's almost found him. But it's hard, you know, she's still fine-tuning . . .'

A frown slid over his face like a shadow. 'Anz . . . you look like –'

'I'm *fine*. Jesus Christ, Zach! I'm helping you, OK? So stop giving me the third degree!'

He nodded; not as if he agreed, but as if he couldn't think of anything else to do. Annis thought, *What am I doing? I'm lying to him . . . I should tell him the truth, and then . . .*

Yes. *And then? Then he'll know there's nothing*

225

anyone can do. At least this way there's hope.

She said, 'I'm going out. For a walk. I just want some time to think.'

'Right.' He nodded again. 'When will you be back?'

'Soon.'

She ran down the stairs and out of the front door, hearing it slam behind her with an odd ringing note, the glass buzzing with the resonance. She'd meant to walk and think and get her head round everything, but she couldn't concentrate, because there was all this daylight billowing round her like a curtain, sliding itself over her hands like silk. It was so wonderful . . . How could she even think about calling her shadow back, when there was all *this*? She thought, *It's stupid, to worry too much . . . and Zach will be fine, it'll all be fine, it'll sort itself out . . .*

She started to run. The world jumped in front of her eyes, green and gold, blinding her with its beauty. She felt her muscles tire, the tingle in her throat that ought to have been a burn, the sensation building in her legs as the acid built up. She kept on going, thinking: *yes. I can live for ever. I can run for ever. I never want to stop . . . never, never . . . God, this is wonderful, why would I want her back when I'm so happy, I'm so, so happy . . .*

The day went past her like a high-speed train. She was running down a high street somewhere, past familiar logos and swinging pub signs, hearing the beep of pedestrian crossings ringing in her head. A man stepped out in front of her, in her way, and she reached out her hand easily and felt the spark leap from her skin to his. It felt good – like energy releasing itself – even though he went white and dropped to

226

his knees, swearing, and she ran round him, grinning at the other people who turned and stared as she passed . . . She met someone else's gaze and saw her blink and frown, like she'd seen something she didn't understand, but by then Annis was gone again, running easily, revelling in the breeze on her skin, the heat of the sun, the specks that danced like snow across her vision. She knew she should have been worrying about Zach, but there wasn't any room left inside her. She was like a harbour that had got silted up; there just wasn't enough *depth* . . . and that was good, wasn't it? *Yes*, she answered herself. *Yes, it's good*.

Until it was dusk, and she was lying on some more grass somewhere, staring up at the shocking lambent blue of the sky, wondering when time had got so slippery. *I'm speeding*, she thought, and giggled to herself. Then she felt tears running down her face, because it was all so beautiful, so perfectly painfully beautiful . . .

She only realised she was thirsty because she licked the salt off her lips, but it hit her in a rush, like she was coming back to herself. *Of course I'm thirsty*, she thought, *I've been running all day and I haven't drunk anything and it's hot. God, I'm hungry too. I should be getting home. What's the time? What am I doing?* She sat up. *Where am I?*

She looked at her watch. It had stopped. Because of the electricity, maybe; not that it mattered . . . There was a church tower behind her. Eight-thirty.

Eight-thirty? But it was – *Oh God, I was supposed to – I meant to go straight home . . . I only . . . what happened . . . ?* She stared, blinking, waiting for the

227

hands to swing back to where they should be, but they didn't. Eight-thirty. It was getting dark.

She looked round, working out where she was. For a second it was almost like being her shadow: trees and grass and everything seen through something nearly opaque, only this time it was light, not dark . . . but she screwed her eyes up and concentrated. Oh, yes. Not Kensington Gardens, this time. She was only a few streets away from home. She got to her feet and walked, very carefully, keeping an eye on her watch, even though it wasn't working.

She got to the end of their street. She walked past number five, seven, nine, then turned to walk up the steps to their house . . . She heard a door slam and looked round. Next door. She looked away again, frowning while she dug in her pocket for her key.

'Annis! Annis, just a sec –'

Pete, from next door. He leant over the wall, waving to attract her attention.

She should have ignored him. But it was *Pete*; and she knew, in the same factual, detached way that she knew his name, that she liked him. She'd fancied him, in fact, for a few months last summer, when he'd put on a bit of weight. She turned to look at him, trying to remember how to be polite. 'Hello, Pete.'

'Hey . . . is Zach in? I've been trying to phone all day. I need to – well, I . . .' He rubbed his head with the flat of his hand until the hair stood up vertically. 'It's good to see you . . . can I just pop in for a few minutes and say hi to Zach? He's not answering his phone.'

'He's not here.' It came out before she'd even decided to lie.

Pete blinked. 'Oh. I thought . . . I mean . . .' He bit his lip. 'I saw him . . . earlier . . . and I wanted to have a word, because your mum –'

'*Mum?* What about Mum?'

'Well – she's been phoning my mum, asking if we'd seen you and were you OK, and I didn't want to say you were here in case it was a secret, but I couldn't work out what was going on and I wanted to check with Zach.' He'd said it all in one breath. 'I mean . . . yesterday, it was pretty obvious Zach didn't want to talk, but if there was anything he wanted me to say to my mum, to tell her to tell your mum, if you see what I mean, well, I just thought –'

Yesterday? Annis narrowed her eyes and stared at him, until he quailed and gave her a helpless kind of smile. She said, 'You'd better come in.'

She was careful not to touch him by accident, but when she flattened herself against the wall to let him go past he wilted a bit, like she'd insulted him. He was tall and lanky, with pale ginger hair and a sort of flat face; beautiful, because everything was beautiful, but not because of the way he looked, only because he was behind that sparkling veil of light. She realised she was staring, and said, 'Please, go through. Oh, by the way, would you mind putting the kettle on? I can't – it's a long story . . .'

He bobbed his head, beaming, like he was honoured by the request. As he went into the kitchen Annis heard him say, 'Hey, Zach! How's it going? Look, I'm sorry about yesterday, I didn't mean to scare you away . . .'

She followed him, slowly, not bothering to listen to Zach's reply. Yesterday. Yesterday they'd been in

229

France. It seemed such a long time ago – before she went down to the ruins, before she'd sent her shadow away – but it wasn't really. Their flight had got in to Heathrow that afternoon. So . . .

Zach was at the kitchen table, leaning forward, his chin on his hands. He glanced up when Annis came in, but then he looked straight back at Pete.

'It was . . . yesterday, I . . .' Pete looked from Zach to Annis and back again, smiling and frowning at the same time. 'Mum was at work, so I had to water the plants and – oh, shit, by the way, I don't know what happened to your plants –'

'It's OK. We know. Go on.'

'Right. Well. I let myself in, and I heard the back door slam, and . . . well, you were there, weren't you? I mean . . .' He fluttered his fingers, like he was playing an imaginary keyboard. 'I saw you sprinting across the lawn.'

Annis looked at Zach, but he was still staring at Pete. She said, 'Are you sure it was Zach?' although she already knew it couldn't have been. It was the shadow.

Pete turned to her, raising his shoulders to his ears. 'Yes. Why . . . ? It was getting dark, but it was definitely . . . going hell for leather, really, like . . . look, it doesn't matter, I don't mind, I just wanted to check what we were supposed to tell your mum, if she phones again.'

Going hell for leather . . . Annis thought, *Why would he run away? It's not like Pete could hurt him* . . .

No. She remembered being her shadow, desperate not to get too close to anyone . . . Zach's shadow was scared *he*'d hurt *Pete*. He hadn't minded about getting too close to Annis, before, but now something had changed – now –

She should have been afraid, then; because if her own shadow was stronger than Zach's . . . but she wasn't. She was cool and calm and she didn't care.

Pete was biting his fingernails, so fiercely it made a kind of ripping noise. He said, 'And – Christ, this is stupid, but – your back garden – it was OK the day before, and now it's all brown and – and the plants in the living room, we've been watering them, honest, it's like you killed them on purpose . . .' A pause. 'Look, mate, it's none of my business, it's just a bit weird, and I thought, you know, I wondered what you were playing at. I mean, your mum's really worried –'

Zach sighed, blowing the air out of the side of his mouth so his hair quivered. 'Pete, mate . . . it's a long story.'

'Well, I think you should sort it out, whatever it is.' He held Zach's look for a second, then turned away, grimacing apologetically. 'No, I'm sorry, forget I said anything –'

'You really want to know?'

'I –' He stopped. 'Only if you want to tell me. If there's something I can do.'

Annis said, 'Zach. You can't. You *can't* tell him.'

Zach said, 'Sorry, Pete. Annis is not entirely herself at the moment, for reasons which I'm about to explain.'

'Oh yeah, 'cause he's going to *believe* you! Zach, this is stupid, you can't seriously think he can help – we don't need any help, anyway, we've got it sorted, *I*'ve got it sorted –' For the first time in ages, she felt

231

a lump swelling in her throat. 'Why do you need him? You've got *me*!' She smacked her hand down on the dresser behind her, so hard it *had* to hurt – surely – but it didn't.

Pete tore at his thumbnail with his teeth. 'Look – Zach, no pressure –'

Zach drew a line in the air with his finger; it said, very clearly, *Shut up*. He said, 'Anz. You can sit down and help me explain to Pete, or you can piss off. Either is fine by me.'

She shrugged, trying to be casual, and suddenly she *was* casual. 'I'm not sure you've thought it through, that's all. He's already scared your shadow away – you do realise, if he hadn't done that, the shadow would still have been here? It'd all be over by now, if he hadn't been such a stupid, useless *prat* . . . And now you want to – what? Let him *help*, somehow? We don't need him, Zach.'

'*I* need him.' Zach turned to face her, breathing heavily. 'Do you understand that, Anz? I need him.'

'Why? Why on earth would you need –'

'Because he isn't *you*!'

Because he isn't you. Zach clenched his jaw, but he didn't move. Pete knotted his fingers into a pale, freckled ball. Silence.

And it was like a part of her minded – a very small, quiet part – but the rest of the hurt was at a distance. It tugged at her, like a fish on a line, telling her it was there, but it didn't matter, exactly. *My shadow*, she thought. *My shadow minds much more than I do* . . . She said, 'All right.'

'Anz – I didn't mean –'

'No, it's *all right*. I understand. You can explain to

him if you want to. It's fine, really.' She turned to look out of the kitchen window, at the beautiful, beautiful world. 'I know. How about you start by explaining *this*?'

She smashed her fist through the window.

Thirteen

The not-pain shot down her arm, like icy water on a hot day. She was wearing it like a glove, marvelling at the strength of it. There were flecks of blood on her skin, but the tiny wounds had closed already and the splinters of glass were dropping harmlessly away. The jagged gap in front of her face smelt of dry earth and plants, summer night, next-door's barbecue. She closed her eyes and savoured the would-have-been-bruising on her knuckles. *I enjoyed that*, she thought. *I wonder how many windows the house actually has . . .*

There was a pause.

Pete said, 'Er . . . yeah, I think I *would* like an explanation of that. Please.'

Zach said, 'Anz . . .' For a second his voice held something she didn't understand: concern, maybe, or fear. Then there was the noise of a chair creaking. He cleared his throat. 'Listen, Pete, it's a long story. And it's . . . you'll think I'm winding you up. But I trust you, OK, you have to believe me.'

Annis brushed the last glittering shards of glass off her hand and ran one finger along the broken edge of the window. *It's like* playing *at pain*, she thought.

Pete said, 'Er . . . Annis? Are you . . .' He tailed off. 'Zach, shouldn't she – um, like, disinfect that, or something?'

'I'm fine.' She turned and waggled her hand at him, smiling, so that he shifted from foot to foot, chewing his lip. 'Look. No marks.'

Zach gritted his teeth. 'Annis, you're not helping.'

'That's OK, Zach, you don't need my help any more, do you? Not now you've got *Pete*.'

Pete rubbed his nose with the palm of his hand, over and over again. 'Annis – look, honestly, I don't want to be a nuisance –'

'He'll be really useful, I'm sure, even though he probably won't even believe what's happened to you. Because at least he isn't *me*.'

Zach just met her gaze, silently: like, *What do you want me to say?*

'Have a good time.' She picked up a tiny blade of broken glass from the floor and squeezed it between her finger and thumb, like a talisman, feeling it bite. 'I'm going out. See you in the morning.'

'Wait . . .' For a moment she thought she'd won, but Zach bit his lip, staring at her, still with that odd look on his face, and she knew he wasn't going to change his mind. 'Anz . . . when will you know, about my –' He shot a look at Pete. 'We need to find him, soon. You'll tell me, won't you, as soon as –'

She looked at him levelly, enjoying the power. 'Yes, I'll tell you. Probably.'

Poor Zach, she thought. *He has to rely on me, and he hates it. No wonder he needs someone else around.* She almost said it, feeling the sarcasm all ready to go, but in the end she couldn't be bothered. Zach couldn't touch her; no one could.

And why should I care, anyway? she thought. *Zach doesn't care about me, or want me, or need me . . . Let's see how far he gets, with Pete to help him.*

She smiled at him, then at Pete. She knew the smile wasn't quite right, but it was another one of the things that had started to go, along with sleep and pain and caring what people said to her. Like being human was a kind of language, and she hadn't spoken it for a while . . .

She said, 'See you later. Sweet dreams. Well – Pete, anyway . . .' She looked at Zach and felt the smile widen into a kind of off-balance grimace. 'Have a nice night, boys.'

She went out of the front door, into the street, and raised her face to the summer stars. She could still see them, just about, through the blazing dust that swirled across her vision like snow. Her head spun with the dazzle of it, the blinding, deafening, unbear-ableness of it . . . *This is everything*, she thought. *This is what I want. Zach doesn't matter. My shadow doesn't matter – I don't matter, compared to this – so huge, so bright, so infinite . . .* Time started to slip through her fingers, harder and harder to hold on to, lifting and spinning. She loosened her grasp and let it slide.

She came home because she was hungry. Not that she *needed* to eat – being hungry didn't hurt, any more than anything else did – but she could sense that somewhere her shadow was feeling it, and it brought her back to herself. It was morning. She tried to focus, but she was all shaky, buzzing and full of energy, and

236

everything she looked at was covered with a sort of glittering membrane. She concentrated. *I should go home. I should* . . . There was something she was supposed to do . . . wasn't there? Something she couldn't quite remember . . . She kept shaking her head, trying to clear it. Of course she loved the swirling filter of light in her eyes, the just-too-quiet almost-music in her ears, but they made it harder to find her way home. Home . . . *I am Annis Randall*, she said to herself, *and I live at number eleven Maxted Road* . . . *I am* . . . *I live* . . . *Zach*. His name was the only thing that stayed steady, like a word in dark ink, something to focus on. *Yes. I have to get back to Zach.*

Oh bother, she thought. *I didn't tell him about his shadow – that my shadow can't get close enough to find him* . . . *maybe I should have told him the direction, at least*. She squashed the thought, easily, and ran. She was thankful it was so early and there wasn't anyone around. She had some odd memories, like dreams, of people brushing past her in the dark, her own hands, gleaming, reaching out, the crack of electricity . . .

She thought, *Stop it. I'm just remembering that man the other day. The one I touched by mistake. That's all.*

It was lovely, running easily along her street, everything shining like platinum. She loitered for a few minutes in front of a garden, looking at the white roses that blazed like tiny bombs. But she knew as soon as she got through the front door that something was wrong.

She didn't know *how* she knew, exactly. She couldn't see very clearly, and the soft, singing silence in her ears muffled the voices in the kitchen. Maybe it was the smell; which was stupid, but there was a hint of something in the air, like black coffee and alcohol and too many cigarettes . . . She took a deep breath, tasting the unease on her tongue. A distant part of her brain said, *You know, this is the only sense that still works properly* . . . but she wasn't listening. She walked down the hall, trying not to make too much noise. What was wrong? It smelt like – like the night Zach was in that climbing accident, and Dad sat there chain-smoking, before Mum rang from the hospital to say he'd be fine.

When she opened the door Zach stood up. He looked at her for five seconds, silently. Then he sat down again. Pete was sitting opposite him, slumped across the table, his head pillowed on his arms. Someone had pinned brown paper over the broken window. The table was covered with dirty glasses and mugs. There was an empty cafetière and a full ashtray. The room stank of smoke.

She stood where she was. Either she was swaying or the floor was rocking gently, like a ship on a calm sea. She wanted to drift into a dream. She forced herself to say, 'Good morning.'

Pete made a grunting noise, like an animal. He raised his head and looked at Zach. He had a red crease down one cheek where it had been resting on his sleeve. 'Where . . . What the – oh. Shit. Zach. Hello.' He turned to follow Zach's gaze, and his eyes widened. 'Annis! God, Annis, where've you *been*? We were worried about you.'

'Out. I said I was going, didn't I? Does it matter?'

'Er . . .' Pete shot a look at Zach, but he wasn't

238

looking back. 'Not exactly, I mean, er . . . just, we were worried. And Zach – he told me everything, by the way, I hope you don't mind. Zach said he needed you to get his shadow back. That's all.'

'Oh – yeah.' She went over to the kettle and stared at the plug on the wall, wondering if it would explode if she tried to make a cup of tea. 'Yeah, he does, but . . . my shadow's still working on it, and –'

Zach said, '*Still?*'

She looked over her shoulder at Pete. 'Can you make a pot of tea? Thanks. Yes, Zach, *still*, what do you expect, a fucking miracle?'

'What's taking so long?'

'It's just – oh for goodness' *sake*! It takes a while, OK?' She heard her own voice and thought, *That's pretty good, I wouldn't know I was lying.*

But he did, somehow. He shook his head, not looking at her. 'So talk me through the process, then.'

'Don't be stupid, it's not a *process* –'

Zach dipped his finger into the ashtray and looked at the grey smear on his fingertip. 'But you needed to go AWOL for two days to figure it out? Me, I'd call that a process. Unless you've got a better word for it.'

'It isn't me at all, anyway, it's my shadow. *I* don't have anything to do with –' She stopped, hearing what he'd said. 'What do you mean, *two days?*'

Pete was waiting for her to move away from the kettle so he could reach it. He said, 'Well, not really two *days* . . . two nights and a day –'

'But –' She turned round and stared at him, then at Zach, waiting for one of them to laugh. 'I was only gone for . . . it was eight or nine when I left, and now it's –' she looked at the clock on the wall – 'ten past five, and that's only eight hours –'

Pete blinked. He took the kettle over to the sink and ran water into it, carefully, not spilling any. 'Er . . . Annis, I think you'll find that was the day before yesterday. That's why we were so worried, you see. Zach thought something really bad might have happened, like –'

Zach said, 'Shut up, Pete.'

She took a deep breath. They were lying. Winding her up. They had to be . . . Any second now Zach would start to choke with laughter, say, 'Jeez, Anz, how can you fall for it *every time*?' She waited, but she knew he wasn't joking. *The day before yesterday.* No. She couldn't have been out that long. It was only one night – hardly even that, just a few hours, really, just a quick euphoric haze. It *couldn't* have been that long –

She looked at Pete. He was watching her, but when she caught his eye he turned away. Either he was a very good actor, or Zach was right. Two nights. Not one: *two*.

She said, 'I'm sorry. I thought – I didn't mean –'

Zach said, 'You just don't care any more, do you? About me? About anything?'

The worst thing was, he was really *asking*. She thought, *It would be easier if he was trying to get at me. But he isn't. He really wants to know.* She said, 'Of course I do – it's not my fault, I can't help being so happy –'

Zach frowned, pushing his hair off his face and leaving a streak of cigarette ash on his forehead. '*Happy?*'

'Oh, come on, Zach, you know what it's like.'

240

Silence. There was something funny in the way Zach and Pete were looking at each other. She thought, *They've been talking about me. There's something going on . . .* but that was paranoid.

Pete put the kettle on, pressing the switch with a crisp tap that made Zach blink and look away. He said, 'OK. What do you fancy, Annis? Earl Grey, lapsang souchong, peppermint, English breakfast, or – er – *rose pouchong*? God, what's *that*?' And then he added, in the same breath, 'Why don't you get into your shadow's head, find out where she is, and how she's getting on? That's how it works, isn't it?'

It caught her off guard. 'Because I don't *want* –' She stopped, just too late.

That *look* again; like conspirators. What was going on? Zach said, 'Yeah, Anz, Pete's right. Find out what your shadow's up to. Maybe she's found mine by now.'

No, she thought. *No. I don't want to. I can't. And there's no point, anyway. I can't help him. It's all gone wrong.*

They were watching her; both of them, even Pete, even though he was making a pot of tea, slopping hot water all over the worktop. She said, in a kind of panic, 'I don't think that's a good idea. I don't want to – distract her, if she's –'

'What's the matter?' Zach's voice was very quiet.

She caught herself glancing towards the door, as if she was checking out her escape route. 'Nothing – but –'

'Then *do it*.'

There was a kind of intensity in his expression that she couldn't read. It wasn't that he wanted to find his shadow – or not just that . . . Something else as well . . . She thought, *Oh God, he hates me.* It hardly hurt at all; except that she knew her shadow was feeling it.

'Please. *Please.*'

She thought, *What if my shadow has found his? What if I was wrong?* She heard a little gulping noise and realised it was her, trying not to giggle. *Maybe I was just overreacting. Maybe I'll get into my shadow's head, and I'll know exactly where Zach's shadow is. It could happen.*

And of course Zach's getting worked up about it. He's got to track his shadow down, and destroy him, before anyone dies.

She stared back at him. He'd said *please.*

All right. For Zach.

She closed her eyes and watched the orange light behind her eyelids. *Just for a few seconds*, she thought, *and then I'll come back to myself. It'll be OK.* She took a deep breath and felt for the lever in her head, the one that could flip her over like a coin, spinning and spinning until she landed –

Oh God. Oh God. Oh . . .

She pulled away instinctively, the way she'd take her hand out of a flame. She was back, nearly, trying to grasp slippery handholds of light. But the impulse wasn't strong enough to hold her there: a flicker of sunlight, a flash like a camera, a snapshot of the kitchen, every outline drawn in silver and gold, impossibly beautiful; like a last breath before she went under again –

Oh God. Oh, shit, shit . . .

But she could bear it, just, after the first shock had
faded. It was almost easier than it had been a few days
ago: still dark and painful, like a cloud of black gas,
but . . . There was something inside her that felt like
relief, as if it was something she'd needed. That didn't
really make sense – she thought, *Why would anyone
need pain?* – but it explained why she could breathe
into it, relaxing until it was endurable.

She wasn't in Kensington Gardens any more. She
didn't know where she was. It was too dark. There
were waves of panic and horror sweeping over her.
She didn't know why; they felt as impersonal as a
storm, battering her, chilling her to the bone.
*Something's happened to me, has something hap-
pened?* she thought. *Where am I?*

She tried to think logically. If she'd had any sense
she would have got as close to Zach's shadow as she
could, just in case. But when she reached out with her
hand, listening for the barrier between them, there
was nothing. No resistance. *Why . . . ? What's going
on? Come on. Try to remember . . .*

And there was just so *much* darkness now. It felt
heavy on her skin, like water. She pressed her hands down
on the floor. Concrete, cold and damp on her palms.
But there was something odd about it; it took her a
second to realise it was just more *solid* than it should
have been. She was more substantial than before. She
thought: *I'm stronger. I'm getting more* – real.

*Where am I? I can't think straight . . . Where's
Zach's shadow? Shouldn't I be looking for . . . ? What
am I doing?*

She was huddled in the dark, hugging her knees to her chest. Another surge of fear rolled over her, making the hairs on her arms stand up. Annis closed her eyes, trying to work out what it was that was scaring her so much, but it was too hard to identify. Maybe it wasn't anything at all. Maybe it was just what you felt, when you'd been a shadow for too long, and the blackness was taking you over.

She tried to ignore it, determinedly taking stock of her other senses. She could smell damp, piss and decay. And the concrete under her fingers was silky with moisture in some places, pitted and roughened in others. She could feel, from the stillness of the air, that there were walls on every side of her. There was a faint glimmer of pale light, slanting across her vision. She knew it was broad daylight, but she had to squint, trying to make out what was there. Broken joists of wood, jagged edges, one flaccid carpet tile draped over a beam. She felt dizzy, disorientated, as if she was in the wrong time zone. All this darkness, when it's been light for hours . . . She could taste the rottenness in the air, the faint tang of ammonia. There was a noise like rain, and the sound of distant traffic. God, that *smell* . . .

I'm in a ruined house.

A ruined house . . . for a horrible, flinching moment it made her think of the ruins in France. But this one was different: just a normal, nasty, abandoned building, where drunks came to piss. She couldn't remember why she would have decided to come here; the weight of the dark sat on her thoughts, paralysing her. She could feel from the ache in her bones that she'd been there a long time. She thought, *Why am I here? What's happened?*

She tried to get to her feet, but she was so stiff and cold she could hardly move. She'd been leaning against a wall and her back was damp. There was something pattering round her, hitting the floor with hundreds of tiny noises. *Oh*, she thought, *of course. Rain. That's why I'm here. I'm sheltering from the rain. Stupid – I should be looking for Zach's –*

But – wait –

It hadn't been raining. It had been a beautiful summer morning. She remembered – very faintly – standing in the kitchen, the sunlight coming through from the garden, faint reflections dancing on the ceiling . . . But it was raining here, wasn't it? That noise . . .

She looked round, peering through the dark. Her eyes had adjusted; not much, only a fraction – but enough for her to see the endless movement, the vertical lines that kept on drawing themselves, over and over. Like rain, but not rain . . .

Flecks of dark pattering down from the walls, the ceiling. No, it wasn't rain. It was an endless shower of insects, crawling helplessly out of the woodwork to die.

She thought, *I'm here because I needed to be alone. I can't leave, in case – I knew that if I got too close to anyone –*

The horror rose in her throat like something rearing its head. She turned to one side and vomited.

She'd never been so glad to see daylight.

Somewhere between retching and spitting she'd come back to herself. She was shaking. Her face was wet.

245

Zach and Pete were staring at her. She was on the ground, for some reason. She dragged herself to her feet and looked from one to the other. She said, 'What?'

Neither of them replied. Pete looked almost as white as Zach; although it wasn't shining, glamorous white, it was just that he looked ill.

She felt water slipping down her chin and wiped it off with the back of her hand. She thought, *I know why I feel weird, but why do they look so shaken?*

Zach said, 'So . . .' His voice sounded rusty. 'Where was she, then?'

It was taking longer than usual, for the feelings to drain away; like dirty water going down a clogged sink, sluggishly. She turned to look out of the window – not the brown-papered one, but the other – letting her eyes unfocus. She said to herself, *It's all right.* This *is real – the dazzle, the singing in my ears. So much light.*

Pete cleared his throat. 'Annis? Are you OK?'

'Fine. Fine.' She felt the last dregs of nausea sloshing in her stomach. 'She was in a derelict house, waiting for . . .'

'And where's my shadow?'

Suddenly she felt too tired to lie. As if being the shadow had reminded her body that she hadn't slept for three nights – was it three? Not that it mattered . . .

She said, 'I don't know.'

She'd thought Zach would seize on that, like a crocodile, locking his jaws and shaking the truth out of her, but he didn't. He looked at Pete, with a blank, neutral look on his face, so you couldn't tell if he was even seeing Pete at all. Then he said, 'And what was wrong with your shadow?'

246

'Wrong?'

'*Something* was wrong. Wasn't it?'

If only she didn't still have this misery congealing inside her. She knew it would go, eventually, but for now it made it so hard . . . She thought, *It's all right. Just get through this, and soon you won't give a damn about anything.* She reached up deliberately and took her hair out of its ponytail. She ran her fingers through it, peering sideways at a tangle below her ear. 'Why would anything be wrong?'

'You cried,' Pete said. He slurred the word slightly, as if he thought she'd be embarrassed.

'Did I?'

'Good Lord, Annis . . .' He darted a glance at her, and then wrapped his arms round himself as if he was cold. 'Something happened, and you started to cry, like . . . I dunno, like someone had died . . . and then you stopped and looked around and there was this look in your eyes, like, I don't know, I can't describe . . . like you were *lost.*' He swallowed.

Zach said, 'Yes. The look in your eyes.' He sounded empty.

'I just – I – I just –' She couldn't think of anything to say. Her shadow . . . So much dark, everything round her dying, and all the time the blackness building inside her . . . She felt the sickness and tried to push it away, but it was harder than it normally was. She could still see a few shadows here and there, like tarnish. She tugged at her hair. At least *that* didn't hurt.

'And you still don't know where my shadow is.'

She looked at him; and saw him properly, for the first time in ages. It hit her, hard, like someone had punched her in the stomach. Oh *God* . . .

He was so white: almost as white as she was. And there was a sheen on his skin, like cloudy glass, the light shining through . . . He was nearly transparent. It wasn't just that he didn't have a shadow, it was like he wasn't *there*. His shadow was feeding on him. And his expression was strained and desperate; as if he knew what was happening.

Annis said, 'Oh, oh God, I'm sorry . . .'

Pete said, 'It's OK –'

At exactly the same time, Zach said, 'What for?'

She felt the answer struggling up through the black ooze in her gut, like a worm pushing up through mud. She thought, *No, no, I'll regret it* – but it was like the misery had a mind of its own. She heard herself say, 'I can't find your shadow, Zach. I'm sorry. I can't.'

A pause, so deep she almost heard the sucking noise, the *gloop* as the last of the darkness drained away. Then she was as bright and still as a shaft of sunlight.

Zach swallowed. 'You can't?'

Now the feelings had gone she didn't mind lying, but it wouldn't help. She said, 'No. There's a kind of barrier between them, the way there is between us. So my shadow can't get any closer. I could tell the direction, a couple of days ago, but it's not enough. And now . . .'

He stared at her, his mouth moving; she realised he was saying, *Can't get any closer*, the words silent and bare.

Pete made a noise that could have been the beginning of a question. No one looked at him. He shut up.

Zach nodded, as if he was drawing a line with his nose, carefully, up and down.

Pete said, 'So you can't help Zach . . . ?'

'No.' She liked the feel of the word in her mouth: uncompromising, round, complete as an egg.

Zach stared at the brown-papered window, his face quiet and attentive as if he was looking at a picture in a gallery. His body was sagging in odd places; for the first time ever, Annis thought he looked ugly.

After what seemed like hours he took a deep breath. Some of the tension came back into his shoulders, like someone had tightened the strings that held him together. And when he spoke his voice was low and controlled.

'So you're going to call your shadow back.'

'Well, I –' She heard the defensive note in her voice and swallowed, methodically. 'There's no reason to worry about it, yet. I mean, we might find another way to –'

'Might we?'

She swung his tone back to him, like a tennis player. 'I think we might.'

Pete said, 'Look . . . I don't want to intrude or anything, but –'

She said, 'Shut up,' without taking her eyes off Zach.

But – surprisingly – he *didn't* shut up. 'No, sorry, Annis, it's just that we were worried about you. I know Zach's worried about you. It's best for everyone, the sooner you get back to normal –'

'And leave Zach to fend for himself?' She turned round, enjoying the way he flinched. 'You're not much of a friend, are you, Pete? *I'm* trying to help him. I'm prepared to chance it, just in case we find a way –'

'Bollocks.'

It took her by surprise; for a second she thought Pete had said it. Then she turned back to Zach. 'What?'

'For *me*? You think all this is for *me*? That's bollocks, Annis. You know it is. This hasn't been about me, *ever*!'

Pete coughed. 'Hey, Zach, that's not – I mean, that's a bit unkind. I'm sure she was trying to help –'

'All right, all right! Maybe it was, once – yeah, OK, I concede, you *were* trying to help. But now . . . I don't know what's happened to you. You've gone whiter than I have, and you behave like you're high or something, all euphoric and selfish and not giving a shit about anything. And you've been hurting yourself, like . . . I wouldn't *recognise* you.'

She felt misery growing again in her stomach, like a fungus, but it was subtle, easy to ignore. 'Zach – all I'm saying is, maybe my shadow will find a way to –'

'Call her back. Call her back *now*.'

She stared at him. He was joking. He didn't *look* like he was joking, but . . . When she looked at Pete he had the same expression as Zach: terribly, comically earnest. She felt the corners of her mouth twitch.

Silence. She went over to the table, took a cigarette out of the nearest packet and lit it, making every movement as precise as she could. She put the packet down and stared at the health warning. *SMOKING KILLS.*

Pete said, as if he couldn't help it, 'You used to say every cigarette took five minutes off your – oh. Right.'

Zach said, 'Stop fucking around, Annis.'

She took a drag on her cigarette, rolling the bitterness over her tongue. She didn't look at either of them.

'*Call your shadow back.* Please.'

'I don't feel like it. Sorry.' She said it very smoothly, tilting her head to one side and staring idly at Mum's cookery books. She was fighting not to think about her shadow – about how it would be, to be human again, with all that pain, all that fear and misery. She thought, *I like being like this. I'm not going to call my shadow back. Why should I?*

Zach said quietly, 'How close is your shadow to killing someone?'

Very close. So close she's terrified to move, in case . . . 'How should I know?'

'Closer than mine is?'

Probably. 'I don't have a fucking clue, Zach. Why don't you send Pete to find out? If he dies, you'll know she's pretty damn close.' Another breath of smoke, sour, pleasant in the way the not-pain was pleasant.

'And you think there's nothing wrong with you.'

She rolled her eyes, clinging to the light. There was so much darkness now she was starting to feel it seeping into her veins. Why wouldn't it go away? It reminded her that her shadow was there, only a decision away, wanting to come back to her . . . Annis could almost feel her listening, clenching her hands in hope . . . *No.* 'Stop bossing me around, Zach.'

'I'm not bossing you around. I'm asking nicely. To start with.'

'What're you going to do, Zach? You can't even

touch me, just in case you forgot. And if Pete tries, he'll get hurt.' She did something to her face that was meant to be a smile. 'For once in my life, Zach, I don't care what you want me to do. And you know what – even if you and Pete have worked out a way for him to get near me – you *still* can't make me do anything. I'm totally fucking untouchable. Watch.' She took another long drag on her cigarette, hearing the rustle as it burnt down. Then she pressed the glowing end into the skin on the inside of her wrist. She heard Pete draw his breath in sharply, but Zach didn't move, only watched, his face neutral, as the not-pain blossomed and faded, the skin smoothing itself again almost immediately.

Pete said, 'Annis – correct me if I'm wrong, but I thought Zach said that all the pain comes back, with the shadow –'

She watched the burn heal, closing up, like a flower in reverse. She could sense the pain blossoming somewhere a long way away, her shadow crying out . . . 'That's exactly my point. Why should I call my shadow back? I don't want to.'

'But – your shadow will get stronger and stronger – isn't that right?' Pete held his hands out, appealing to Zach, but he wasn't listening.

'God, this is so *boring*.' She could feel the blackness slopping shallowly inside her, like bilge-water. Somewhere, a very long way away, her shadow put her hands over her ears, trying to block out the noise of things dying. 'I'm going to have a shower.'

'Oh no, you're not.'

Zach's voice . . . It was his fight-the-good-fight voice, the one that made even Mum and Dad quail.

Annis had always quailed, too. She'd have given way to it automatically, collapsing silently into a heap, until a few days ago. A few days – a long time ago . . .

She raised her eyebrows, and laughed. 'Really? How're you going to stop me?'

Zach looked at Pete. It was a brief, level look, like a signal. Then Pete squared his shoulders, like a man walking into the firing line, and stood in front of the door. He crossed his arms over his chest and stared at the air in front of her face.

It was his *eyes* that did it: that wide-eyed, out-for-a-Victoria-Cross look . . . She couldn't help it. She leant forward over the table and howled with laughter. She felt the tears roll down her face and into her mouth. She was sobbing with mirth; it was shaking her to pieces, like she was falling down an endless flight of stairs. Somewhere – it seemed a long way away – Pete was giving little uncertain bleats of laughter. *What a prat*, she thought, and giggled harder, helplessly, hearing her own voice go higher and higher like a singer practising a scale. *Honestly*, she thought, *how could I take this seriously?*

She stood up straight and made an effort to keep her voice steady. 'Pete, don't be ridiculous. Get out of the way.'

'No. You're going to stay in this room until you've called your shadow back.' He said it quickly, in one breath, so that she knew, all of a sudden, that they'd planned this together.

She said, 'That is absurd and you know it is. Get out of my way.'

Zach said, 'We're serious, Anz. I'm not going to let

this happen to you. We'll *make* you call her back.'

'Really. You and whose army?' A pause, while they looked at each other.

'You're going to stay here. We won't let you go until you have. Come *on*, Anz. It'll be OK, it's not going to kill you –'

'You won't *let me go?*'

'No. We can't touch you, but you can't touch us, either. I mean, you literally can't touch me, and you won't touch Pete because –'

She just looked at him. She saw him realise. For a second his mouth gaped, like a fish. He said, 'Jeez – Anz – *no* –'

She said, 'Pete – get out of my *way*.' And she reached out, like she was going to pick a flower. And touched him.

Crack.

He dropped like someone had chopped his legs off at the knee. Suddenly he was curled into himself on the floor, pulling his thighs into his chest so hard all the bones in his back were sticking out. He was convulsing silently; rocking backwards and forward, fighting for breath.

Zach had one hand stretched out, as if he was frozen. He looked sick.

There was such silence Annis had time to close her eyes and listen for the almost-music, the high aching sounds that were just loud enough to hear. *Like the stars*, she thought: *star-song* . . . She built the music into a shining wall, keeping her feelings outside.

She didn't know how much time went by. When she opened her eyes again her cigarette was singeing her fingers.

Pete wiped the back of his hand over his eyes. Then he looked up, his face deadly pale, the lips a faint shade of lilac that clashed with his hair. 'Jesus, Annis . . . oh God, please don't – don't do that again –'

Behind the dam of light, there was a great swell of dark, the kind of wave that could lift you off your feet. She thought, *I can't believe I did that. I did that, on purpose. Me. Annis Randall . . .*

She didn't move a muscle. Just flicked her gaze sideways to Zach's eyes – the only real black left in the world – and told herself this wasn't happening.

Zach said softly, 'You evil, *evil* bitch. What have you done with my sister?'

And the dark broke through.

She didn't know what was happening. She heard a noise like someone choking. There was so much dark – she could *feel* it, the overwhelming misery, the fury, the guilt like crude oil sticking to her skin . . . No, this was wrong, this was all *wrong* . . . She fought, trying to press it down, back to her shadow, saying, *No, no, no.* But there was so much of it – like a flood, uncontrollable, like Zach saying that was only the final straw. Everything, the anxiety, the fear, the shame that she'd been so useless, let Mum and Dad worry themselves sick, the – the – was all in a huge black wordless rush, smashing through her like a current . . . *No – help me – take it away* . . . There was some kind of resistance, but she fought against it, bundling everything sideways to her shadow as hard as she could, ignoring the way it sprang up again, burning her like acid. It was like a vortex: draining away, flooding back up, a mess of deadly thick dark . . . *Take it, please, I don't want it, I don't want –*

Her shadow said: **No. I can't take any more. Keep it.**

And then she wasn't there.

It was as if the rope had snapped; like watching someone drop away from you, sucked out of sight by gravity, falling so far and fast you didn't even hear them land. As if the shadow had taken too much, borne too much weight, so the bond wouldn't take it any longer, so the balance had gone. Or as if Annis had done something her shadow wouldn't forgive.

It didn't matter, anyway, Annis thought. It was like the details of an accident: so irrelevant you'd hate someone for asking. What mattered was what had changed.

And *everything* had changed.

Fourteen

There was no reason why Zach should know what had happened. But he did.

Annis thought her eyes were still closed. She thought the Zach she could see was her imagination, because in real life no one could look like that. No one could hold that much shock in their stare, except in a dream or a hallucination or something . . . But when she tried to open her eyes she discovered they were open already and Zach was real.

He said, 'Oh no.'

She struggled for the clear, bright haze in her head that she'd had before. But it wouldn't work. The misery sloshed around but it wouldn't go away.

She said, 'Zach . . . Zach, I didn't mean to . . .'

'Oh, Christ. Oh, bloody hell.' He licked his lips, as if he was going to say something more meaningful. Then he said, 'Oh, mother*fuck.*'

Pete had struggled to his feet. He didn't say anything; he stood absolutely still, frozen, like he didn't want to attract attention.

Annis said, 'I promise, I didn't mean to do that . . .'

Now, now that it was too late, she could feel the gap that shouldn't be there, the horrible gaping space. She understood, now, why Zach had called his shadow his *soul*. 'Please, Zach . . .' As if he could make it all right. As if he could help.

Zach dragged his hands through his hair. He said, 'Anz . . . no, you can't have . . .'

It would have broken her heart; but now all it could do was drive a wedge between the pieces. She said, 'I'm sorry.'

He turned away.

Pete wiped the back of his hand across his face, wiping the spit and mucus and tears away. Annis watched him because she didn't have anything better to look at. He looked as if someone had killed him and brought him back to life: sick, shaking, blue-lipped. But he was alive, and human. That was something, wasn't it?

She didn't want to think about her shadow. But it was like a wall of mirrors across her vision: she couldn't help but meet her own stare. *That's it. There's nothing I can do. Now I'm like Zach: I can't find her* . . . And now that she couldn't pass everything on – the fear, the unhappiness that was already growing, that would get worse – she saw it clearly. The light made her eyes ache.

Zach turned back, his fists clenched at his sides. He said, '*No*. I won't let this happen. *I won't.*' There was something childish in his voice; something defiant. He stared into her eyes, leaning so close she could feel the pressure on her eyeballs. 'Listen to me.'

'Zach –'

'Not you. Not you, Annis. Can you hear me?'

'What are you –' but she felt the answer; felt the faint, faint tug of something as her shadow raised her head. But as soon as she tried to get hold of it she felt the darkness dissipate. 'Zach –'

'*Not you*. I'm talking to the shadow. Shadow? Please – are you there? *Please*.'

She stared at him. It wasn't any good – she knew it wasn't any good . . . When she felt for the old thread – she only realised now how it had held her, suspending her over the darkness – it was gone; it was no use Zach talking, when she'd felt the shadow drop away . . .

But he wasn't looking at her. He was looking into her eyes, but not at her; as if he could see someone else. She felt the world lurch sickeningly. For a second she was in two places, somewhere dark, somewhere full of dying . . . **Yes. Yes, I'm here . . .**

It was ridiculous. If she couldn't find her shadow herself, how could *Zach* . . . ?

He said, 'Please. Please, you can hear me, can't you? I won't let you do this to Annis – *please* –'

And . . . what was it? Something in him, that made her shadow pay attention, even though Annis herself couldn't find her. For a moment she thought she knew what it was, but it slipped away.

'Where are you? Please, shadow, Annis needs you back, please, *please* . . .' His pupils were so black she couldn't take her eyes away. He frowned, so close he was almost touching her, and the space between them was pulled tight as a bowstring. 'Shadow – if you won't come back for Annis, please, for me . . . you have to come back, before it's too late . . .' His voice was low and taut and desperate, like he was praying. 'Please, listen to me, you have to come back. She can't call you but she would, I promise, *please* –'

Annis shut her eyes, squeezing her eyelids together so hard it stung, and thought, *Shadow? Shadow, are you listening to him? Why would you listen to him, and not me?* She felt a rush of jealousy and bitterness, because even her own shadow would rather listen to Zach . . .

'Please – she didn't mean to cut you off – oh, come on, please . . .' Zach's voice cracked, then set itself again like a bone. 'I know, all right? I understand – you can't forgive her, you've been so hurt – but you have to come back, otherwise . . . you have to. Please.'

She thought, *This is stupid.* When she looked round the edges of her mind, her shadow had gone. Even if it felt like someone was listening, a long way away . . . well, she was just imagining things. Because Zach and her shadow had never even met, there was nothing to make her listen –

Except love, Annis thought. She opened her eyes.

Zach carried on speaking as if she wasn't there. 'I don't care what I have to do, listen to me, you're stronger than you think, just come back to her. You can, I know you can –' and somehow the shadow was there, at the back of Annis's mind, looking straight back at him. **I can't. I want to but I can't.**

Zach saw her. Something leapt in his eyes – a flicker of triumph – and he leant even further forward, until it felt like something would give way. '*Yes –*'

And the shadow met his eyes. There was a strange, excruciating moment as they looked at each other; so intimate, so direct, as if Annis wasn't even *there*. And she knew she was right: that what made the shadow listen to Zach was – love. *Love. Something so pathetic, so simple and . . . and human*, she thought.

260

Just because my shadow was there, all my life, just because she loves Zach as much as I do . . . She was suddenly so angry she could have cried. It wasn't fair. *She* was Zach's sister; the shadow didn't have any right –

Zach stared and stared, as if he'd never look away. 'Anz . . . shadow . . . listen. Please come back. Please. I know you can hear me. Please. Please. *Please*.'

And the last *please* was almost a sigh – because he knew, he'd seen . . . He'd sensed the way everything flipped, how the darkness drew itself up to its full height, the light tilted its chin, the shadow gave in with something that was almost a smile, the nerves in Annis's mind jolted and swung sideways like compass needles, the whole world nodded and said *you're right* and rearranged itself, clicked into the right configuration like a game of solitaire, the pain smacking back into her like a bullet, the way the whole bloody thing just – *put itself right*.

And that was all it took.

There was a wave of black misery that rebounded, punching back into Annis harder than anything she'd ever known, the rush of air back into her lungs, pain – *real* pain – flaring in her hand and her wrist and all over her body, the thread between her and her shadow alive again, thickening and shortening so fast it pulled her off balance like a lasso, jerking her to the ground, breathless, blind . . . Sudden shadows everywhere, and the pain, oh God . . . *No – no, please* – but someone was saying, *Oh yes, thank goodness, yes, yes*, and she didn't know which one was her.

She tried to open her eyes. The world was so dark she could see everything.

Zach said, 'Annis? You're back – aren't you – you're back . . .'

And then the black of his pupils spun and opened like mouths and all the darkness in the world flooded in and swallowed her.

Everything hurt. Like there was a huge backdrop of just general back-in-her-body hurting, and in front of that there were splodges and flashes of real pain, in one ankle, like she'd twisted it, her hand, every separate knuckle outlined by a sharp demanding ache . . . the other wrist – *Oh Lord*, she thought, *what did I do?*

She sat up, catching her breath involuntarily. Ow, ow – bloody hell –

She was in bed, fully dressed, except for her shoes. Her room was full of sunlight, but gentle, shadowy sunlight, and everything looked more solid than she was expecting. *I can* see *it*, she thought. *Properly. Details and textures and everything – like it's really there* . . . She looked down at the floor. *That carpet is more carpetty, more essentially carpet-like, than any carpet I've ever seen* . . . she could have spent hours staring at it, marvelling.

'You're awake, then.'

She looked up. Pete was leaning on the door frame in an odd dangly sort of way. She said, 'Yeah, I seem to be.'

'Painkillers on your bedside table.'

She nodded and reached for them, hissing through her teeth as her body screamed at her. 'Thanks . . . how did you know I'd need –'

And stopped, looking at her hand. It was swollen, purple across the knuckles, covered with cuts, like streaks of rust. She could hardly flex her fingers. It looked like she'd been in a fight or something – no. Like she'd punched a window . . .

And . . . there was a plaster on her other wrist. She pulled at the corner, digging at it with her nails, until it peeled away. There was a round, angry burn, just starting to scab over. That cigarette she'd stubbed out . . .

She just looked at it. She could feel the long cut on her arm tingle and burn, like something waking up. *Everything*, she thought. *Everything I did to myself, while I was – while my shadow was – it's all come back. No wonder it bloody hurts.*

And the way I behaved – the things I said to Zach – the things he said to me –

She rolled over on to her side and started to cry.

She didn't hear Pete leave, but he must have done, because after a while he came back and knocked softly on the door. She said, 'Go away,' but he came in anyway.

'How's it going?'

'How do you *think*, you tosser?' She stared at him until more tears started to come. She flopped back down and pressed her face into her pillow, hating herself.

He cleared his throat. 'Do you want more painkillers?'

She rolled her head from side to side without looking up. There was such a long pause she thought he'd gone. Finally he said, 'Are you trying to smother yourself?'

She snorted. Then she had to sit up, because she'd

got snot all over her pillowcase by mistake. She wiped her nose on her duvet cover and stared at Pete, daring him to laugh.

To his credit he didn't, although he did chew his bottom lip and look down determinedly. 'Do you want something to eat?'

'No.'

'Something to drink? There's water by your bed, but if you want something else –'

'How's Zach? Is he OK? Has anything –'

'It's all right,' he said, shoving his hands into his pockets. 'I mean, don't worry, nothing's –'

'Good,' she said, as quickly as she could, while she could still trust her voice. Then she gulped, in spite of herself, and started to cry again.

'Er – hey . . .' He shuffled towards her, holding out a hand. 'Er . . . look, um, Annis, please don't cry –'

'I'm not *crying* –'

'Er – 'course not.'

'– it's just all the stuff I didn't feel before, you know, all at once, and I feel so *dreadful* –'

''Course you do – don't worry, it's OK –'

'– and I was so *horrible*, and Zach hates me and I don't blame him, I'm so useless, I never meant to get like that but – and I hurt you and he must despise me, I mean, *I* would, I *do*, I despise me –'

Then she ran out of words and just cried. She felt Pete put his arms round her, tentatively. It was a bit like being in the middle of a cat's cradle, but she didn't mind. It was so lovely, just to be held. She shut her eyes and pretended he was Zach.

He said, 'Don't worry, you're bound to feel a bit rubbish, after all that.'

'Yeah.' She thought, *Why the hell are you being so nice?* But she wasn't complaining. Pete just *was* nice.

'You were out cold for ages . . . and then we saw all these things appear on you, like cuts and bruises and stuff, all together, like magic, it was really nasty . . . and you've been asleep for ages, nearly three days . . .' He patted her on the back.

'I was so horrible. I'm so sorry.' She felt him shrug, in a comforting sort of way, but it didn't make her feel much better. Then she said, into his chest, 'Three *days?*'

'Yeah.' He drew back a bit, disentangling himself, peeling his T-shirt away from her face.

'Shit. What've you been doing?'

He clenched his jaw, and shrugged again, but this time it wasn't meant to be especially comforting. 'I've been lying to my mum, telling her I'm at a mate's house, and looking after you. Well, mainly just waiting for you to wake up. And Zach . . .'

'Yes? Zach?' *Please*, she thought, *tell me he's been here, with you, at my bedside. Worrying himself sick about me.* She felt bad, but she couldn't help hoping he'd been there.

'Zach's been in his room, most of the time.'

The disappointment hit her as sharply as a slap. 'Not – not here? I mean, didn't he . . . ?' She meant, *Didn't he care?* but she was too scared to ask.

Pete met her gaze, then looked away.

She dragged her hands down over her face, feeling the cool of her skin. Zach hated her. Well, it made sense, didn't it? After the way she'd been . . . The only surprising thing was that Pete *didn't*. She wanted to take her hands away from her face and give him a

265

wonderful, warm, grateful smile, but she wasn't sure she could remember how. She pitched her voice as low and controlled as she could. 'And – how is he? Zach? Has he –?'

'Killed his shadow? No.'

A pause. She didn't look at Pete, but she knew that even if she did he wouldn't be looking back. Of course Zach hadn't killed his shadow – because he couldn't find him. *I was his only hope. And I screwed up*.

She said, 'Pete – nothing's happened, has it? I mean – you said he was all right, just now – has his shadow got out of control?'

'I don't think so. He won't talk to me. I'm not sure he'd know, anyway. But – I think . . . soon. I'm guessing, but from the way Zach looks . . . We're – *he's* – at deadlock, Anz.'

Yes. She could see that. She wrapped her arms round her knees, wincing at the sparks of pain that seemed to spring up everywhere. It was so quiet: that kind of dead summer mid-afternoon silence, the time of day when Zach should have been just waking up with a monumental hangover, crawling round the house trying to avoid Mum and Dad. *Deadlock* . . . It fitted, somehow. This flat, empty quiet, like the calm after a storm; not a crisis, just a dead end.

She said, 'Is he OK? I mean . . .' She stopped, because it was a stupid question, then said it again.

'He's – well, he's . . . er . . .' Pete spread his hands out on the duvet and stared at them.

'Not.' A pause. 'He's not OK, is he?'

'Not really.' He didn't meet her eyes.

'What's he like?'

266

'Hard to look at. Sort of blurry round the edges. Fading.'

'Right.' She sneaked a glance at him, but now he was tying his shoelaces together and didn't look back at her. 'What should we do?'

'Why are you asking me?' He pulled at the end of one shoelace, undid the knot, then started tying it again.

'Because –'

He interrupted her, his voice suddenly loud. 'Guess what? I don't know. I haven't got a clue what we should do. *You* don't know, *I* don't know, and *Zach* certainly doesn't know. So it looks like he's stuck, doesn't it? His shadow starts killing people, Zach fades away into nothing.' He gave his shoelaces a sharp little tug to even up the loops. 'He'll get brighter and brighter and thinner and thinner until he's a kind of ghost. And the electricity will be like a kind of shield, keeping him away from people and hurting them if they get too close, so he'll be completely cut off. He'll lose his sense of time, the way you did, and he says it's getting hard to see . . . He won't even be a person any more. Just a kind of leftover. And the shadow will do exactly the opposite, getting darker and darker, sucking life out of people.'

Annis swallowed, tasting a sudden tang of salt. 'Pete . . .'

'I've had a lot of time to think about it.'

She turned to look at him properly. He was gaunt, with purple shadows under his eyes and round his mouth. He was biting his lower lip, frowning in a determined, furious way that Annis recognised, because that was what she did when she was trying

267

not to cry. For a moment she just watched him, imagining what it would be like, sitting with someone you hardly even knew for three sleepless days and nights, not sure whether they'd wake up, while your mate shut himself in his room and descended into a kind of private hell. She said, 'I'm sorry.'

He made an odd spitting noise, like someone getting out of a swimming pool. 'Not completely your fault, is it?'

'You got sucked in, and it wasn't fair. I'm sorry.'

His fingers were still busy with his laces. She watched him pick the knot apart with his fingernails. 'It's OK.'

She put her hand on his shoulder. He was very warm; she could feel his sinews through his T-shirt, but somehow that wasn't a bad thing. He turned to look at her, finally; held her gaze and then smiled, and for a moment she forgot about Zach completely. Then he said, 'He's such a stupid dick, it's so like him.'

She laughed, sorely.

He laughed too, and she could hear the same painful note in his voice. 'I never worked out how your mum and dad could have you two. One of you has got to be adopted.'

It was stupid, how angry that made her, suddenly. It was just so *familiar*: Zach, the clever charming one, Annis the stupid boring one. She said, 'Fuck off, Pete.'

He frowned at her, startled. 'No, I meant –'

'I don't give a damn. Forget it.' She levered herself off the bed, still shaking with resentment. Stupid Pete . . . she'd been so close to liking him, and then he had to compare her with Zach. She limped to the door, swearing every time she had to use her right foot. Behind her she heard Pete say again, 'No, really, Anz, all I meant was . . .'

She ignored him. She dived for the banister and used it as a support while she hopped along the landing to Zach's room, adjusted her stance outside his door, and knocked. 'Zach!'

'Go aw— *Annis?*' She heard a kind of clatter, and the door opened. Zach peered round the edge of the door frame, blinking as if he was walking into sudden sunlight. He looked awful. 'Anz . . . You're OK?'

'Yes – I think so . . . Zach, I'm so sorry about –'

'Forget it.' He stared at her, letting his eyes drop to her bruised hand, the long inflamed cut on her forearm. That was when he should have said, *God, Anz, I was so worried* . . . but he didn't. She tried to think of something to say, to cover the pause. He looked at her until the silence got too long, then he started to close the door in her face.

'Zach . . .' She took a hobbling, painful step forward. 'Please – please don't be angry . . . I'm sorry . . .'

'I'm not angry.' Zach's voice was only just recognisable; as if someone had hollowed him out, scraping at his voice box until it hardly sounded like him.

'I don't know what to say – I was only trying to help you –'

'And you failed, OK?' The door swung decisively open again like it had a mind of its own. 'No one can help me now. So thanks for trying, and I'm glad you're OK, but that's *all*. Now leave me alone.'

'Zach – it's not too late – not yet – is it?'

He shook his head; although she wasn't sure if he meant *no* or just *go away*.

Pete said, from somewhere behind her, 'Come on, Zach, please, talk to us.'

'What's the point?'

'Look, we're worried –'

'No kidding.' Zach looked round at him, then back at Annis. There was something sharp and strange in the way he moved his head, like an animal about to bite. 'You and Annis can talk, if you want. Just leave me out of it. Leave me *alone*!'

Pete took such a deep breath Annis could hear it from three metres away. 'We need to figure out if there's – I mean, what we need to do. We're running out of time –'

'Nothing. *Nothing. Nothing* –'

His voice cracked. He spun round into his bedroom and slammed the door.

Silence. Annis leant her forehead against the wall, squeezing her eyes shut. *I am* not *going to cry again* . . .

Pete said, 'It's not you, Annis. I'm sure it isn't you. It's just . . . the pressure . . .'

She swallowed hard. She said, without opening her eyes, 'Of course it's me. Because I mucked everything up. I could have helped, but I blew it. He hates me, because *he* had to rescue *me*, after everything . . . I don't blame him.'

'But – look, come on . . .' He patted her forearm. 'He just wants to be on his own, that's all –'

'Now he knows I can't help him any more. Like he said. No one can.'

Pete gave her a final, limp-fingered pat, and stepped awkwardly away. He didn't say anything. There was a sudden blast of music from Zach's room, like he was trying to drown them out.

Annis went back into her own bedroom, not caring if Pete followed or not, and sat down on the bed. The hopelessness had got into her bones like cold; it sat there with her, weighing her down. She didn't even have enough energy left to cry.

Pete said, 'Look, it's not your fault.'

'Yes, it is.' A pause. 'I'm useless. I should have been able to help him.'

He didn't contradict her. They sat without speaking, side by side, staring at the wall. Over the wail of Zach's music the alarm clock ticked, like something counting down.

The front door slammed.

For a second she thought it was Zach, on his way out; she was already on her feet, furious with herself, because she should have been waiting outside his bedroom door, ready to follow, not letting him get away –

'Annis? Zach? *Zachary!*'

Oh God. Mum.

The noise of something heavy – a suitcase – hitting the floor, then footsteps on the stairs, taking them two at a time, one long scuffling bound across the landing, and then –

Mum flung the door open so hard it hit the wall and rebounded, hitting her on the hip, half knocking her off balance. It would have been funny, if she hadn't already been shouting. 'Annis? *Annis!* You are in so much trouble – I have never been so angry with you in my entire –'

She stopped. For a moment it was very quiet; no

sound except the booming discordance of music from Zach's room. And in the pause Annis had time to feel a huge, childish rush of relief, because Mum was a proper grown-up, she could sort everything out . . .

Mum smoothed her hair, very deliberately, and turned to Pete. 'Pete. What are you doing here?'

'Hello, Mrs Randall – I came to water the plants, Mum asked me to . . .'

'I'm sorry, but I'm afraid I'd like you to leave.'

Pete nodded. 'Er . . . no problem . . .' He looked at Annis – a tiny, subtle look, but it said, *Shall I go? Do you want me to go?*

Mum said, 'It was kind of you to pop in, Pete. I expect it must have given you quite a shock, to find Zach and Annis in the house.'

Oh no, Annis thought, *it's her I'm-a-lawyer voice. She's being all polite and calculating – she's trying to get Pete to admit –*

Pete was only half listening, still watching Annis. He said, 'Yeah, well, it was at first, but –'

'How long have you known they were here?'

Pete looked round at her. 'Er . . .' Then his face said, *Shit*, as clearly as if he'd said it aloud.

Mum said, 'I phoned and *phoned*. Didn't your mother tell you?'

'She – well, the thing was – I –'

'I've been worrying myself sick. I hope you're ashamed of yourself.'

Annis stared, thinking, *Why's she angry at Pete? That's not fair – if anyone's behaved really decently, it's him . . .*

'Get out of my house. Get *out*.'

And then she knew, perfectly, wholly and unnego-

272

tiably, that Mum wasn't going to solve anything. Mum was just as furious and miserable as anyone else.

Pete nodded slowly. He could have said, *I think you should know, Mrs Randall, that I've been looking after your daughter for three days while her brother shut himself in his room and refused to talk to anyone. I think you should know that I listened to them when their own parents wouldn't. I think you should know that I behaved like an adult.* But he didn't. Annis admired him for that. He said, 'I'm very sorry.'

'Yes, now if you would very kindly leave us alone . . .' Her voice was rigid, trying to claw back the politeness.

Annis would have taken one look at her face and run. But Pete went over to the desk and scribbled something on a bit of paper. He didn't even look at Mum as he held it out to Annis. 'Anz . . . if you need me, OK? If there's anything I can do –'

She held his gaze. *Don't leave – please, don't leave me – please* . . . She said, 'Pete – please don't go. I need you. Zach needs you –'

Mum hissed sharply through her teeth. 'Annis, that's *enough.*'

Pete glanced at her, then back at Annis. 'I'm so sorry, Anz . . . look, I mean it, anything, any time –'

'*Out!*'

Pete pushed the bit of paper into her hand, gave her a sudden fleeting kiss on the cheek, and went.

The quiet was even louder than Zach's music had been, pounding in Annis's ears. She scrunched the bit of paper in her fist and held on to it, tightly, as if it was the most important thing in the world.

Mum shut the door with a bang. 'You two . . . We have been worried *sick*. I couldn't get a flight until this morning, and no one answered the phone here . . . If it hadn't been for Zach's note I swear I would have called the police. If you ever, *ever* do something like this again . . .' She turned away, her fists clenched. 'Has that young man been staying here?'

Annis's bones subsided, giving way underneath her till she was sitting on the bed. She said, 'Yes.'

Mum drew in her breath, slowly, letting the air whistle through her teeth. 'I see. And what else have you and Zach been up to?'

'Does it matter?'

A tiny, tiny pause, then Mum grabbed her shoulder, hard, pulling her back up to standing. '*Up. Now.*' For a second Annis thought she was going to hit her. But Mum kept hold, her grip so tight it hurt, pulling her towards the door. 'Right. Where's Zach? In his room?'

'Mum – *ow* – let go –'

But she strode down the landing without answering. Annis lurched painfully after her, breathless with shock and outrage. Mum was never like this.

'Zachary!' Mum grabbed the doorknob and went to open the door. It opened a few centimetres. Then there was a clunking sound and it jammed. '*Zach!* Open this door, *now*.'

Silence. Annis rubbed her shoulder.

'All right,' Mum said. She gave the door a long, level glare, as if she could see Zach on the other side of it. 'That's fine. We'll play it your way.'

Annis said, 'Mum . . .'

Mum ignored her. She turned sideways to the door, braced herself, and flung herself sharply against it. There was a sort of crack, and a thud, then the door gave way and Mum staggered through into Zach's bedroom. Annis followed, stepping over the chair on the floor, one strut broken where it had given way.

The room was empty. Zach wasn't there.

Mum went over to the open window, glanced down into the front garden, then closed the window. The noise of the latch was very loud. There was a pause, while Annis stared at her back.

'Where is he?'

'I don't know.'

Mum turned. The look on her face made a shiver of cold run down Annis's spine. 'Are you telling me the truth?'

'Yes. Mum – I promise, I really don't know where –' She felt her throat tighten. Zach was gone, and she really didn't know where he was.

'I see.' There was no way of telling if Mum believed her.

'He didn't say he was going – and . . .' She took a faltering step forward, hearing her voice crack. 'Oh God, it's my fault – I don't know what to do – he hates me, Mum, he really *hates* me, that's why he's gone – I'm sorry, I'm so sorry, it's all gone wrong –'

'All right, Annis. Tell me what happened.' Mum was making a real effort, but you could still hear the anger grinding beneath the surface. 'Talk me through it. Why did you two run away in the first place? Was it – I know things haven't been easy between your father and me –'

Annis shook her head, trying to swallow a sudden

275

sob of laughter. 'No! It was . . . Zach – he –' She knew she had to say it quickly, or she'd never say it at all. 'We were . . . he was . . . Do you remember, he told you he was being followed, that he was in danger? Well, he *was* – and we had to –'

'Oh, for goodness' *sake*!' Mum slapped her hand down on the window sill, hard. The window juddered in its frame. 'Annis, please don't tell me you've been taken in by . . . ! If you're trying to tell me that you ran away – and we've been sick with worry – because you believed Zach's ridiculous stories –'

'They're not – Mum, I *saw* –'

'Is he on drugs again?' She didn't give Annis time to answer. '*Is he on drugs?*'

'No – no, Mum, it isn't like that, please, I'm trying to tell you –'

'Then – if it's not drugs – he's ill, he must be, these childish fantasies, paranoia – Annis, how could you run away with him like that? How could you be so irresponsible? Can't you see he's *ill*? He needs professional help –'

'Mum – *listen*, why won't you –'

'You stupid, *stupid* little girl, how could you? And now he's gone. I can't believe you didn't realise how selfish and reckless . . . Do you have any idea how much *damage* –?' She stopped, breathing hard. Her whole body was shaking.

Silence.

Annis heard her own voice, clear and cold and deliberate, as if it came from a long way away. 'But *you* didn't even try. You wouldn't listen to him. He asked you for help. Remember? He *begged* for help! And you said no. *You – said – NO.*' She tried to

276

swallow her fury, but it rose up again like bile. 'At least I *tried*.'

Mum's mouth moved, soundlessly. There were bright patches of red on her cheekbones, and her face was wet. She turned abruptly and walked past Annis. She said, without looking back, 'If he hasn't come back by tomorrow morning I really will call the police.'

Annis watched her leave. Then she sat down on Zach's bed, huddling herself into the duvet, and pressed her face into one of his pillows. She could smell his shampoo, and his skin.

She didn't cry. The misery was too deep for that. It was under her skin like a bruise, covering her whole body.

Zach had gone. Alone. He hated her; he thought she was useless . . . and he was right. So what if she'd tried to help? She'd failed, hadn't she? Failed Zach so badly he never wanted to see her again; so badly that he'd left, without a word . . .

Somewhere, she thought, *Zach's shadow is getting stronger, breathing darkness into the air like a poisonous gas. He can't help it. Even if he hides, the way my shadow did, sooner or later people will start to die . . . and somewhere Zach is fading into a dazzling insubstantial ghost of himself, giving off lethal sparks if anyone gets too close . . . and I'm here, and there's nothing I can do.*

She stood up. Pete's phone number was still in her hand, the paper creased and moist from her palm. She unfolded it, looked at it for a moment, rolled it into a little ball and dropped it into the bin. What was the point? It wasn't as if he could help.

But she couldn't leave it there. She crouched down and picked it out again, straightening it between her fingers. Then she stood up, cracking her head on the edge of Zach's desk drawer. She swore and leant on his bookshelf to steady herself, blinking down at the mess on his desk. Either Zach had left in a hurry, or he just didn't care what he left behind . . . He hadn't even bothered to put the lid back on his fountain pen. His notebook was closed; there was a pencil caught between its pages like he'd flipped it shut without paying attention. It made the cover bulge. She reached down, opened the notebook, and took the pencil out.

It said:

Wake up. For God's sake, wake up. You've been asleep for more than twenty-four hours. Just lying there. I'm not sure you've even moved.

She didn't mean to read it. But once she started she couldn't stop.

. . . Thank God. Thank God, thank God, thank God . . .
I knew you'd wake up. I knew it. But I knew it in that
unsure, scary sort of way that means you have to keep
telling yourself you know it . . . You were here, just a
second ago, banging on my door, and I opened it and
looked at you and I was *this* close to bursting into tears.
I slammed my door in your face, because that's the last
thing you need.

And Pete was there, staring at me over your shoulder,
with a look on his face that said, No thanks to *you* . . .

I was so afraid. I can admit it now. I thought, What if
that's it, and she never wakes up, and it's all because I
interfered? I kept telling myself it was better to sleep for
ever than fade away, turning into someone you're not,
which is what was happening to you . . . and I believed
it, I still believe it, but . . . oh, thank God.

Now there's only me to worry about.

There's so much space, now. I know I don't have very

279

long, but it feels like I've got for ever. Time's started to do weird things. A second ago it was an hour ago. I can't get the hang of it any more. I've put my music on as loud as it'll go (well, almost) but even so it doesn't drown out the silence in my head. When I look at the page I can see little glittering things swarming on the white. Like lice, only they're in my eyes, not my hair. And I can't look at my reflection in the mirror. It's too bright. My brain keeps telling me I can't possibly exist. Jesus, even my *own brain* thinks I don't exist . . .

I was looking back over the stuff I've written. There's a bit, right at the beginning . . . I said you didn't actually help, that you didn't actually do anything useful at all. I said you made a sweet, valiant attempt to help and ended up comatose and covered in minor injuries, and it didn't do a blind bit of fucking good.

I was so angry with you. For ending up like that, hurt, asleep, making me feel guilty. I wasn't being fair. You *did* help. I don't think you even realise. It wasn't exactly what you had in mind, but –

I know what I'm going to do. It's obvious. It's been obvious since that night, when I called your shadow back to you. I didn't really believe that it would work, but I was so desperate. I thought, She's going to end up like me, and it'll be my fault . . . But when I looked at you . . . it was like I knew, all of a sudden. I saw your shadow in your eyes. She hadn't gone, at all. Something had changed – the bond between you had broken – but she was still there, still listening. It wasn't that she'd left you. It was the other way round. *You* were the obstacle. I could still get through to her.

And your shadow was so familiar. I *recognised* her. She was as much you as you are. Which means that mine . . . he'd go where I'd go. I'm trying to find myself. And I know where I'd be.

So . . .

What I want most in the whole world is sleep.

And shade. I want shadows. I want colours, especially green. I want sunlight to be something outside my head, not inside. I want normal life, like a hangover on a Sunday morning and trying not to let Mum and Dad notice and drinking so much multivitamin stuff my piss goes fluorescent. I want to touch people – I want to kiss Mum goodnight and give Dad a mock-manly handshake and scuffle with you or Elliot, just fooling around, and I want to play a really rough game of football and walk down the high street and bump into someone without giving off a spark like a Van de Graaff generator. Oh, and I want to get off with Vanessa McKay. No, actually, I want to *shag* Vanessa McKay. Lots and lots of times. *Again*, I mean . . . Ha. Bet you didn't know that, did you, Anz?

I want to get drunk. I want to get high. I want to go back to France and do a really hard day's work helping Dad clear the rubbish out of the barn. I want to go to Dury College, even if it is a school for drop-outs and losers whose parents have more money than sense. I want to finish my A levels.

I want to go outside and smell grass and hot pavement and Flora-next-door's roses. I want to play on my games console. I want to go through the wine rack and smash every bottle against our beautiful white kitchen wall – that, I could do – and I want to burn every single one of Dad's precious half-a-crown paperback classics. I could do that too. I want to phone Cecilia (may she rot in hell) and tell her I borrowed Dad's mobile and sneaked a look over his shoulder for his PIN and now I know *exactly* what colour knickers she's wearing and *exactly* what's under them.

I want to go somewhere with trees and grass and water and birdsong. I want to feed the ducks. And I want to lie down somewhere where no one will trip over me and just *go to sleep*.

I want, I want, I want.

I want this to be over.

I'm scared. I've got this sick weight of fear sitting on my lap, like some horrible snotty-nosed child that won't leave me alone. It's been here with me for days now, whining at me, hitting me with its fists to get my attention. I can't get rid of it.

Remember the first night of *Peter Pan*, in December? 'Course you do. I was scared then, too – almost as much – but it was different. I was scared in this incandescent, *powerful* way, like knowing I was going into battle. Like I was running towards a cliff. And I ran and ran and I managed not to falter and suddenly there was air instead of grass underneath my feet, tiny seagulls and dunes and sunhats between my toes. And I took off.

It was like flying. I mean . . . I'm not being clever. I

know I *did* fly – that really hurt, actually, the harness was too small – but I don't mean that. I mean, somewhere on the stage, something happened to me. All the lights, and the heat, and the smell of Vanessa's eyeliner that I'd borrowed . . . and I was so happy, feeling the whole audience listen, the whole dark bank of them watching, and I knew nothing could go wrong. It was like one of those dreams, like a drug, like the way I felt when my shadow left me . . .

And it was because I'd been so nervous. If it hadn't been for the fear, I would have been dull and competent and faintly charming and you would have said, Zach, that was really good, instead of looking at me speechlessly and going bright red, which is what you did.

If it hadn't been for the fear. The fear made it an adventure. And I like adventures. Don't I?

That's what I keep telling myself, now.

Oh hell. The front door – Mum – oh, shit. Mum . . .

I don't have long, then. I should go, but I'm procrastinating. I got up and wedged a chair against the door, but that'll only get me thirty seconds or so. I can hear Mum shouting at you. I'm sorry. If I were an older brother worth his salt I'd be there defending you. But then, we both know I'm not, don't we? I'll let Pete do it. He's much better at the whole chivalry thing, anyway. Oh, and he fancies you like mad. Don't ask me why – but you've got my blessing. He'll be a good person to have around. Tell him I'm grateful, for everything.

* * *

283

Oh, for fuck's *sake*! Why is she trying to be a good parent *now*? And where's Dad? Couldn't he tear himself away from sorting out the guttering?

And thank *you*, Anz. If it hadn't been for you . . . Thanks. I mean it. I'm not any good at thanks, any more than I'm good at apologies, but – well, it's easier to write it down, isn't it? You *did* help. You did. Don't forget that.

I'm going. I'm really going. I have to face my shadow, I have to –

Fifteen

Annis stopped reading. She didn't have time to read the rest, not now. She slammed the book shut and pressed it between her hands, feeling the pulse racing in her palms. She was breathing hard, as if she'd been running, crying with relief and a strange skewed kind of joy, because Zach didn't hate her. Whatever happened – he didn't hate her . . .

But there wasn't time to think about that. She raced back into her own bedroom, grabbing a rucksack, her wallet, travel card, spare change, shoving the notebook in with everything else, because she was going after him. She knew where he'd be. It was like it was the only place on earth: his favourite place, and hers, because it was his . . . Kensington Gardens, of course – and not just Kensington Gardens, but the heart of it, the place they always went to glare at the tourists and the people taking ridiculous arty photos, the statue that they both agreed didn't look anything *like* Peter Pan . . .

It wasn't far, thank God. She didn't know what she'd do if she was wrong, and he wasn't there, after all, but she didn't let herself think about that. She had enough to worry about, anyway, because if Mum saw her leave there'd be hell to pay . . . She crept down-stairs, grabbing things as she went – anything that might be useful: A–Z, Zach's cigarette lighter, her mobile, the Swiss Army knife out of the drawer in the hall. She hovered for a few seconds outside Dad's room, thinking, *Hammer? Chisel?* What if Zach didn't have the right weapon – if he was going to face his shadow . . . ? But she couldn't think straight. What was he going to do? He'd worked it out, he knew how to find his shadow – and she had to be there, because she didn't know what he was going to do, and he might need her . . .

She took the tube, because she couldn't walk very fast, shifting furiously from foot to painful foot as she waited on the platform, swearing through gritted teeth when the first train went to Barking and not High Street Kensington. Oh, come on, come *on* . . . When the train did come she counted down the stops in her head, trying not to wonder what Zach was doing or whether she'd be too late.

She got off at the other end and hobbled desper-ately down Kensington High Street, feeling everything jolting and jumping in her rucksack like it was urging her on. She cannoned into a woman on the pavement and flinched, expecting the flash and arc of light, before she remembered. Then she stumbled away, laughing breathlessly, while the woman stared after her. *If only I was giving off electricity*, she thought, *at least people would move out of my way* . . .

It was further than she'd thought: along the high street, down the road with the embassies on it, right again . . . until she was there, through the gate, running over the grass through the trees, down towards the Long Water, gritting her teeth at the pain in her ankle. Down the path, left, and towards where she knew Peter Pan was, out of sight behind the trees.

And she stopped running, because Zach was sitting huddled on a bench in front of her. He was smoking, his arms wrapped round his knees, his head bent. It was hard to look at him straight on: there was something flickery about him, dazzling, like a TV with bad reception. Annis thought, *If I hadn't been looking for him, I wouldn't have seen him* . . . Even now her mind was bending under the strain, trying to tell her he wasn't there.

She walked over to him. He didn't look up until she was a little way away; then he glanced up and leapt to his feet in one movement. 'Annis – *Anz* . . . Go *away*. What the hell are you doing here?'

'I found your notebook.'

He took a half-step backwards, walking into the bench and almost losing his balance. 'No – you can't stop me, Anz, please don't try – it's no good –'

'Stop you? I don't want to *stop* you, Zach, I want to help . . .' She swung one arm out of her rucksack and dug around in it for the things she'd brought, dropping them one by one on to the grass. 'Look – I didn't know what to bring – but *something* might be useful.' The Swiss Army knife thunked down next to the coil of string, her mobile, a roll of sticking plaster, the A–Z. 'Maybe –?'

There was a pause. Zach was staring down at the roll of sticking plaster. He ran a blurry, glowing hand across his forehead, then he looked at Annis. He didn't say anything.

Annis said, 'What?'

'No paracetamol?' His voice was so flat and hollow she wouldn't have recognised it.

'What?'

'To go with the plaster? A couple of paracetamol? Or maybe some cough mixture might do the trick . . . What do you think, Annis? Eye drops? Antiseptic? They'd be pretty fucking useful, too, wouldn't they?' He closed his eyes for a long moment. 'Anz . . . I don't want you here . . . really . . . I don't want you watching, while . . .' Then he sat down on the arm of the bench and gave an odd, jerky laugh, like a hiccup. 'For God's sake, Anz – *plasters*?'

She sat down too, perching carefully at the other end of the bench. Her legs were shaking, as if she'd been running all day. 'I just grabbed it. Whatever I thought might be useful. I didn't *know*, Zach – we don't know what'll happen, if you kill your shadow, whether you could get hurt, or . . .' She shrugged. 'If it was a fight, and –'

'If I kill my shadow? Whether I could get hurt?' His voice sounded very thin, as if he didn't have enough breath.

'I guess, once you destroy it, that'll stop you fading any more – but you might start to feel pain again, or something, we just don't know . . .' She put one finger in her mouth and turned to look up at him, gnawing at the nail. He was staring at her. She said, 'What?'

His mouth moved, but it was a second before any sound came out. He said, 'Anz . . . you read my notebook, didn't you? You said you did.'

'Yes. No. I stopped – when you got to the bit about – I realised where you'd gone, so I . . .' There was

288

something in his expression . . . She felt something cold trickle upwards from her stomach, defying gravity. 'Why?'

'Because I –' He clasped his hands in front of his face and started to laugh, like he was choking. 'Oh God, Anz . . .'

She sat, frozen, one hand still clenched on the strap of her rucksack.

'Annis . . . I thought, for ages . . . and I realised . . . I *can't* destroy my shadow. No one can. I tried, remember? I threw that knife at him, and it didn't touch him. You can't kill death, it just doesn't work . . . He's as immortal as I am.'

'But . . .' No, she thought; *no, because if that's true – that can't be true –*

'I know I have to stop him. He might kill someone. He won't mean to, because he's *me* – I get that, now – but . . . but I can't *kill* him, not like that.' For a second he sounded nearly like himself. 'And I'm *glad*, because I don't want to kill him, he's *mine*, my death, and . . . it would be like killing my soul. I don't *want* to destroy him.'

'But . . .' She took a deep breath. 'But you said, you have to stop him . . .'

'Yes. I have to stop him.' Zach looked at his hands. 'I can't go on like this. Even if it didn't hurt anyone else.'

Annis closed her eyes.

'Anz . . . I have to get him back. That's the only way . . .' He swallowed. 'And when you broke the bond between you and your shadow, and I called her, and she came back to you, even so . . . I knew what I had to do. Somehow, even though I don't know where he is . . . my shadow's listening. He's still there, still mine . . . He'll listen to me. If I call him back, if I really *want* him, he'll come, the way yours did. He has to.'

Annis could hear the tourists yelling at each other, and trees swaying in the breeze, and birdsong, but they were just different kinds of silence. There was only silence, surrounding her, cutting her off from everything. And when she spoke, her voice was part of it: just part of the silence . . .

'If you call him back you'll die. Won't you?'

More silence; so much that she thought it would overflow, and deafen her.

'Yes.'

She opened her eyes and looked at him. He was still staring down at his hands, with a set, stony expression on his face. She could almost see him fading, the light rising like a tide, drowning him . . .

'You can't,' she said. 'Zach, you *can't* – you can't just – no, *no*, you *can't –*'

He didn't answer. He didn't have to.

'Zach!' She reached out to grab his shoulder and stopped herself just in time. 'Please, don't be stupid. This isn't – this can't be . . .'

He gave a small, twisted smile. 'I should be glad there's *something* I can do. It's better like this – better than having to go on. You know what it's like, Anz. It's horrible.'

'But you –' She wrapped her arms round her ribs, trying to keep herself in one piece. 'Zach, you *can't* – you'll *die*, you can't – please . . .'

'I know. I *know*!' He turned to look at her, finally, his face blazing. 'I fucking *know*, all right? I know, I know, but – what am I supposed to do? What else can

I do? I don't *want* to, OK, and I'm so scared, shit-scared, but –'

'What about *me*?' It was an awful thing to say, and she knew it. 'What about me, Zach? I couldn't live without you, I wouldn't know where to start – and Mum and Dad – *you*'re the brave one, the brilliant one, I'm just – please don't leave, *please* . . .' She couldn't bear to look at him any more. She covered her face with her hands and talked through her fingers, feeling the trickle of water running down between her knuckles. 'I'm so useless – everyone will think it ought to have been me, and they'll be *right* – I'm so pathetic, I mean, *look* at me –' She sobbed, half laughing.

'Is that what you think? Oh, Jesus, Anz . . .'

'All I ever do is follow you around, tag along, like this scared little, *stupid* little girl, and now you're going to –' But she couldn't say it.

'Oh, for God's *sake*!' His voice was suddenly so full of irritation Annis looked up. 'You *are* pathetic. Of course you can live without me. Don't be ridiculous.'

'But –'

He shook his head in disbelief. 'You think *I*'m the brave one? This is the first brave thing I've ever tried to do, and I'm so scared . . . Anz, I ran away – that's all I ever did, I saw my shadow and I practically wet myself, I was so frightened . . . I couldn't face him. I couldn't think, I went to pieces . . . but *you* . . . Do you remember the night my shadow came to find me? You went up to him – you tried to protect me, you got so close you nearly blacked out . . . And then you sent your own shadow away, to help me. You risked everything – you knew what you were doing, and you still did it! So don't talk to me about being *brave*.'

She blinked.

'*You*'re the clever one, the sensible one, the survivor . . . Anz, I'm just a fuck-up.' He laughed, painfully. 'Mum and Dad will be glad it's me and not you. I'm a mess. I wish I was more like you.'

'But . . .' She swallowed. 'I'm boring. Nothing ever happens to me. And –'

He gave another snort of laughter; but this time it sounded real. 'Yeah? You think?'

'I mean –'

'Anz, will you *listen*!' He bit his lip. 'Look . . . I should have said this a long time ago . . . I thought – you're right, I *did* think you were just a kid. I thought I *was* the interesting one, because I could pass exams and act in plays and everyone loved me . . . but I was wrong, OK? I realised that. I'm sorry.' A tiny pause. 'I'm not saying you'll be better off without me, because, well, you're never going to be able to do your own maths homework . . . but you'll be OK. *You'll be OK*. I promise.'

She held his look. Then she nodded, slowly, trying to smile. She said, 'And – what about you?'

He dragged his hands though his hair. 'I don't have a choice, do I? This is only . . . it's only what should have happened, that day in the ruins.'

For a moment she tried to imagine Zach, dying . . . but her mind flinched away. He was right. He didn't have a choice. So . . .

'Are you – are you going to call your shadow now?' She made herself take deep breaths.

'I was sitting here for ages. Before you turned up . . . trying to work up the courage . . .' He shook his cigarette packet. 'This was full, an hour ago.'

'Give me one.' She reached across, met his eyes, and stopped where she was, with her hand outstretched. He took a cigarette out of the packet, put it on the wooden slats between them, and threw his lighter across. 'Thanks.'

'God, if you knew how much I miss just *touching* people.' There was a silence. He waited until she'd lit her cigarette, then scooped the lighter up and lit one for himself. 'I hope this isn't going to be a habit, Anz. It's very bad for you.'

'No.'

He nodded, then blew a smoke ring and gave her a sidelong look. 'Ah, well . . . The condemned man had a final cigarette, right?'

She laughed, choked on the smoke in her mouth, struggled for breath, and started to sob.

'Oh, shit . . . Anz, I'm sorry – don't . . . please, don't . . .'

She shook her head, trying not to make any noise, but she could hear herself gasping and coughing as her whole body shook. She tried to say, 'I'm sorry, I'm sorry,' but her mouth wouldn't make the right shape. She thought, *Stop crying, for God's sake, that's all you've done for a whole day* . . . She forced herself to take a short shaky drag on the cigarette. It tasted so horrible it helped, a bit.

'I should go.'

She looked up, wiping the tears out of her eyes. 'Go?'

'I won't go far. But I want you to stay here, OK?'

'But – you can't be on your own –'

'I don't want you to see. Please, Anz . . . I've never

293

been brave in my life, so let me try, just this once. I don't want you there.'

'But – Zach, I could call an ambulance – why don't – maybe there'd be a chance, please –'

'*No.*' He clenched his fists. 'I don't want you to. I don't want to pretend to myself . . . I don't want sirens and flashing lights, and I don't want you there. I need to do this on my own. *Please.*'

But – I want to be with you – you can't die alone . . . It was the hardest thing she'd ever done, not to say it, but she didn't. She concentrated hard on being businesslike. 'All right. You know what you're going to do? Wherever you're going?'

'I think so. I hope so.' He swallowed. 'I think . . . if I *want* him, if I call him back and really mean it . . . Pete said he thought – when I called your shadow back – he thought it worked because I was so desperate, that she heard me because she could feel me *wanting* so hard . . . and it didn't matter that it wasn't you, because I love you, which means I love her, too, in a way . . . I'm babbling. Sorry.'

'Don't worry.' She didn't want her cigarette, but she took another drag of it anyway so she wouldn't have to look at him. *I love you.* She said, in a rush, 'By the way, I love you too. Just so you know.'

He looked at her and nodded, jerkily, pushing his hair back. 'Oh – and at my funeral – can you make sure they play something decent, I really don't want any –'

She couldn't bear it. She said, 'Zach, for fuck's sake! Will you please just *go*?'

They looked at each other, both trying to smile.

'Right.' He opened his mouth as if he was going to say something else, but he closed it again. Then he raised his hand to her, in a kind of salute, and started to walk away from her.

She followed him with her eyes until he disappeared into the sunlight. She thought, *What do I do now? How long do I wait? How do I know when he's –?* She took her mobile out of her pocket, to phone Mum, or 999, or Pete . . . but she couldn't bring herself to turn it on. *He wants to be on his own. That's the last thing I can give him. And maybe there's a chance – maybe, maybe . . .*

She stayed where she was, letting her cigarette burn down and lighting another, watching the sun slowly dip until every hillock had a long fin of shadow. She didn't know what time the park shut, but she didn't care. She wanted to sit there for ever. She closed her eyes.

When she opened them, Zach was coming down the slope towards her, half running, his skin bright as neon.

She was on her feet, running towards him, her heart as swollen and light as a helium balloon. For a second she thought she was dreaming. He'd done it – he was still alive, still on his feet . . . He was saying something but the words didn't mean anything. She shouted back, 'Zach!' and reached for his hands.

The electricity threw her backwards so violently the breath came out of her lungs with a thud and the sky rolled down like a blind until it was hanging vertically in front of her face. Then she realised she was flat on her back on the grass. For a second she was just surprised; somewhere in her head someone said, quite clearly, *Oh*. And then the pain kicked in and she curled into a ball, gasping and helpless, and all she could think about was enduring it.

When it faded Zach was crouching a little way away, looking into her face. The sun was behind him but his skin was like a winter moon, blazing with a fierce white light. Annis turned her head away, hearing the air rattle in her throat.

He said, 'I tried to stop you, but you didn't hear, and then it was too late. I'm sorry.'

She stared at the edge of the railings and the dark shrubs behind. She'd wanted to hug him more than anything in the world. The disappointment was so strong it swamped everything else, like black ink.

'Annis? Are you OK? Oh, *shit* . . .'

'I'm OK.' She didn't bother to wonder whether she meant it.

'Anz . . .' He cleared his throat. There was a rustling sound, as if he was sitting down, but she didn't have enough energy to look. Then he made a noise like someone treading on a punctured tyre. 'I expect you're wondering how come I've come back.'

'I saw you, and I thought – it's over and you've won, somehow you've –' But really she knew it wasn't true. Her throat closed, cutting off her voice as neatly as a pair of scissors.

'No. I'm sorry.' The noise of someone pulling up a handful of grass. 'It's . . . it didn't work, Anz. I couldn't do it.'

Silence. The shadows in the undergrowth were so thick she could hardly tell what was solid and what wasn't.

'Annis. Did you hear me?'

'Yes. You said you couldn't do it. So you were wrong, about being able to call the shadow back.' She let her head roll round until she was looking at him. 'There's nothing you can do, then, is there?'

He clasped his hands together in front of his face and stared at his fingernails. 'No. I wasn't wrong. I *can't* be wrong. It's not that. It's just . . . that I couldn't do it.'

'It's the same thing, isn't it?' He didn't answer. She sat up cautiously, and linked her hands round her knees. 'What happened?'

'I tried . . . and he was listening, I could tell he was there, somewhere. You know, I'd never really *believed* I could find him, before, and suddenly I could feel him, and I thought, this is going to be so easy, all that fuss and it'll be so easy . . .' He reached out and picked a blade of grass, twirling it between his fingers. 'But then . . . even though he was there, I couldn't make it happen. I tried to call him back, but . . . I think you need to *want* it so much. And I *don't* want it . . . I'm too cowardly to call him back and mean it.'

A sudden, defiant spark of happiness leapt down Annis's spine. She stood up. 'Well, anyway, that's it. You tried and you couldn't do it. Let's just go home.'

'No.'

'What?' He was shaking his head, his shoulders hunched. He didn't look at her. She said again, '*What?*'

He said, very quietly, 'I said *I* couldn't do it.'

'Yes. You said.' She swung her rucksack to and fro, watching him, until the momentum drained away and it hung still again. 'Zach . . . ?'

'I couldn't make myself mean it. I wasn't brave enough.'

The gladness in her stomach flickered and faded, like an ember cooling. She said, 'Well, maybe that'll change. I mean, if you think about it for a few days, then really put your mind to it –'

'It doesn't have to be me.' A pause, no longer than a heartbeat, then he looked up, his face pleading. 'Anz . . . please, I did it for you, so you could –'

'No.' She stared at him, frozen. 'No.' It took all the breath she had.

'You could do it, I know you could, you're braver than me – please, it's the only way –'

'I am not – I – am – *not* . . .' Her mouth was full of words but she couldn't get any of them out. 'No – I'm not going to –'

'I need you to help me. Please.'

'But – Zach, I can't – I wouldn't mean it, either, not if –'

'Just try. Please.'

She couldn't stop staring at him. She said, 'You can't ask me to – Zach, you *can't* fucking ask me –'

She wanted him to swear back at her, or shout, or even explain, in a tight, furious voice, why she had to do what he said. But he just looked.

She turned away, dropping her rucksack and covering her eyes with her hands. She pushed her palms against her forehead, feeling the strength of her skull, the pressure of bone on bone. She said, 'But if I call your shadow back to you, and you die, then that's – it'd be –'

'Finishing something that's gone on far too long. I should have died in the ruins. You know that.'

'I can't believe – I don't believe you *want* this –'

'I *don't* want it. Anz, for God's sake! I *need* it, I need your help, I need . . .' He cleared his throat. 'Annis – you said you understood. And the longer it goes on, the worse it gets. I'm not – *alive*, I'm not human any more, not properly . . . I just want to get it over with.'

She dropped her hands and opened her eyes, blinking in the sudden flare of light. The sun was low, now, almost setting, so that it looked as if the sunlight was passing straight through Zach, like he was made of glass. She thought, *If he looks like that, what does his shadow look like?*

'Anz?'

'All right. I'll try.' She didn't recognise her own voice. She wanted to touch him more than she'd ever, ever wanted anything.

He was shaking. She saw that from the way he shoved his hands into his pockets, but she stared at the setting sun and pretended not to notice. Then she sat down opposite him, at arm's length, so that she could have reached out and touched him. She focused on the space between his eyes. 'OK, shadow. Come back.'

Nothing. She wasn't expecting anything, but it was still a relief. She said, 'Oi. Shadow! Hello? Hello? Are you listening? We need you to come back. Please.'

Zach said softly, 'You're not trying.'

'Yes, I *am*! Jesus, Zach, what am I meant to do? Really *want* you to die? Well, it's not going to happen.' She stood up.

Zach leapt to his feet, but not to follow her. He moved into her path and stood glaring at her. 'Annis, you said you'd *try*. Please.'

'I did try. I just don't want you to die, any more than you do. I don't see why that surprises you.'

'Sit down.'

'Don't tell me what to do.'

'*Sit down.*'

She sat down. The last of the sunlight had gone, and the world was suddenly chilly, tinged blue at the edges. The only noise was distant traffic and the trees whispering to each other. She thought, *It's late. There's no one else here. The gates must be locked by now.*

'Look at me.' She turned her head and stared at the space in front of him until his face blurred into a white blob of light. 'Annis! *Look at me*. Look into my eyes.'

She breathed out slowly, until her lungs were empty; then she looked into his eyes. He was watching her, his gaze absolutely steady, with such a level, intimate look on his face she felt her cheeks burn. She let her eyes slide away, tracing the shape of his face, learning it by heart. When she raised her eyes to his she knew she'd never, ever forget what he looked like at that moment.

He stared back. His pupils were black, so absolutely black that it made her heart give a funny kind of jolt. The rest of him glowed, like sunlight coming through a sheet of paper, but his pupils were completely dark, not just the absence of light but the opposite . . . As if the shadow was still there, and it wasn't Zach looking back at her at all, but his shadow . . .

Annis felt her lips move, but no sound came out. She

thought, *No, that's stupid, of course it's Zach* . . . But there was something alien in that steady black gaze – not hostile, but *different*, something not quite human. Just holding his look made her feel uneasy, right to the pit of her stomach. She said, 'Shadow . . .'

Something happened. She didn't know what it was: something rising to the surface of Zach's eyes, something suddenly *there*, as if the darkness itself was paying attention. It made her feel giddy, panicky, so she had to dig her hands into the grass to hold herself steady. Zach was biting his lip, but the rest of his face was blank.

'Shadow . . .' Her voice was just on the edge of audibility, so quiet she could hardly hear it herself. But the darkness was listening. 'Shadow, please . . .' She wished, abruptly, that she knew its name. But that was stupid. How could a shadow have a name? She swallowed, taking deep breaths. 'Come back to Zach. Please.'

It didn't say *no*. It didn't say anything. But suddenly it was glaring at her, throwing fury and misery back at her like a punch. She rocked backwards, caught off guard. Zach squeezed his eyes shut, then opened them again, like someone determined to keep awake. He said, in a whisper, 'He's there, isn't he? He's listening.'

For a second when she looked at him he was Zach again; then the darkness flicked on behind his eyes and he wasn't. She clasped her hands together and pressed them against her solar plexus, trying not to shake. She said, 'Come back to him . . . I know, I *know* –' she raised her voice, trying to block the anger in his eyes – 'he sent you away, but he was *scared*, he still is, it doesn't mean he doesn't want you back –'

She almost *saw* her words break against him, like waves on a rock. She thought, *I can't do this, Zach's hurt him too much, I haven't got the strength to call him back . . .*

She leant forward, almost close enough to touch, concentrating on Zach's pupils until all she could see was black. 'Please . . . come back . . .'

But she didn't mean it. Or, at least, she didn't mean it enough. She felt her teeth starting to rattle uncontrollably in her head. She felt sick and dizzy and cold; and when she looked away she could still feel the shadow staring at her, all the force of his resentment and unhappiness stinging her skin like windburn. She was too weak. The shadow was there, but she didn't have the words, or the power.

She said, 'Zach . . . it's no good, I'm sorry . . .'

'Please – Anz, he was there, listening, I could feel it –'

'Yes, I know, but . . .' She wrapped her arms round herself, trying to stop shuddering, feeling her bones jerk. 'I can't . . . he's too angry . . . and I don't want him to come back to you, how can I, if it means . . . ?'

A second, then he shook his head, looking down, so that she couldn't see his eyes. 'I just . . . I thought you'd be able to. I thought you could do it.' A flicker of an almost-smile. 'You're the competent one, after all.'

She held on to her own body, hugging herself, as if she was in danger of falling apart. She waited until Zach raised his head again, and forced herself to look into his eyes. 'Come on – please, come *on* . . .' She was talking to herself as much as to the shadow.

No good. The blackness stared straight back,

waiting for her to mean it.

She felt herself rocking. It was so hard to hang on, when all that darkness was filling her mind, claiming her. She held her gaze, staring the shadow out. If she could stop being scared, and *understand* . . . *But I can't*, she thought. *I don't have the strength. I don't* . . .

She tried to look away, but she couldn't. For a horrible moment she felt as if she was falling. There was a flash of blackness, a lurch like waking up after a nightmare, and something shifted in her head, answering the shadow's gaze, unafraid. It said, **But I do.**

Silence so deep she felt as if her heart had stopped; and a kind of peace, deeper than sleep.

The fear drained away. She wasn't quite herself, any more. She was looking out through her own eyes, calm and still and quiet. No, she *was* herself . . . But she was someone else as well, someone who could meet Zach's gaze without blinking. She thought, *My shadow. I'm my shadow. I always was. My death, my soul, my shadow . . . she's just* me.

And so Zach's shadow, she thought, *is only Zach. That's all.*

She leant forward and said, very gently, 'Zach. I want you to be whole again.'

Sixteen

He understood. She saw the look on his face change, the darkness leaping in his pupils, so that for a second she didn't know who she was looking at, Zach or his shadow. And then she knew she'd done it, because they weren't separate any more, they were both there at once . . . He looked back at her with a kind of real-isation – something like elation and fear and regret all mixed into one – and his lips moved, echoing what she'd said – so that she never knew, afterwards, if it had been his words or hers that had brought the shadow back . . . For a moment they looked at each other, and she thought, *Thank God, he is, he is whole, now. Whatever happens, he's himself again.*

He glanced up, over her shoulder, as if he'd seen someone coming towards him, running across the grass; and for a moment he half smiled, as if it was someone he knew, an old friend. Then blankness dropped over his face like a mask, his eyes suddenly blind.

The shadow. She'd done it.

She felt the breath go out of her, as she realised what she'd done. No – *no* . . . but it was too late. The pause, the last second of white light gleaming on his skin – and then his in-breath as the darkness hatched, sliding into place around him, under his eyes, the tiny curls of dark where his hair fell over his forehead, under his fingertips . . . as if, suddenly, he was three-dimensional again. The colour of his face was back to normal, his eyes unfocused, staring painfully, but human, alive, *human* . . .

He gasped, and met her gaze. He really was smiling.

The shadows deepened as the light from his skin faded. Suddenly it was dusk. She could only just see the outline of his cheek, the pale seams of his jeans, his trailing shoelaces.

She could only just see that he was dying.

But it wasn't as if the injuries *appeared* on his body. There was no invisible hand, pressing him out of shape like something made of clay; the injuries didn't develop, or emerge like a skilful piece of animation, the way they'd healed. It was more as if . . . as if they'd always been there, and she was only just seeing them. The head at the wrong angle, the unnatural twist in his ankle, the deep graze on his temple that had knocked his face out of shape . . . like she'd been staring at a line of writing, and suddenly she knew how to read. He was dying. As if he'd *always* been dying, all along . . . And yet he was still looking at her, still – impossibly – smiling . . .

She reached out, her mind empty, and took his hand, the one that wasn't trapped beneath him. It was warm and dry and didn't move when she pressed it. She said, 'Zach . . . ?'

Perhaps . . . later, she wondered – thought, perhaps – that she'd seen the shadow in his eyes, a sort of ease and peace, and she'd thought how strange that was, when he was in so much pain . . . but she never knew, for sure. She never knew, either, exactly when the moment was, when his eyes weren't looking at anything, any more; or when she knew that the hand she held had started to get cold. She never knew how long she'd been there, before she finally drew away.

It was dark. She should have been frightened to be on her own, with Zach's body so close and only the high night sky and the almost-silence of the distant traffic for company, but the darkness was like a friend. She knew, somehow, that soon she'd start to feel unhappy; sooner or later she'd understand about Zach being dead, and that would . . . but she couldn't begin to imagine what that would be like. And right now she couldn't feel anything but peace. He was safe: safe from his shadow, safe with his shadow. It was the only thing left; it was *right*.

She lay back on the grass, feeling the chill soak through the back of her T-shirt, and touched Zach's hand with the tips of her fingers. He was cold, too, but she could almost imagine that he was still alive. She looked upwards into the great globe of the sky and listened. She found the someone inside her that understood the dark, that remembered what being the dark was like.

She thought, *I'm not scared, any more. I won't ever be scared again.*

It was going to be a clear day. She watched the sun rise over the trees, huddled with her knees to her chest. She was cold, shivering so much she'd forgotten how to be still. She still didn't feel very much, but that was all right, even though she knew it was ordinary

306

human numbness, not the euphoric no-pain of before. She could think perfectly clearly, though; for example, she knew that it was too early to phone Pete. She could have phoned for an ambulance, or phoned Mum, but she wanted to hold on to the last hour of peace. She wouldn't have space like this for a long time; and she'd never be able to sit like this again, with Zach.

Once, when they'd been camping a few years ago, she'd woken up early and read almost the whole of a book, lying beside Zach in her sleeping bag. She felt the same way now: wanting and not wanting him to wake up, glad she wasn't on her own but glad he was asleep . . . Soon everything would ruin it, she knew that – the grief, the anger, the endless questions from Mum and Dad that she'd never be able to answer, not properly . . . She heard Zach's voice in her head: *You'll be OK*; and she thought, *Yes. Yes, I will. Not happy, not for a long time – but OK. Yes.*

She bent down and kissed Zach's forehead, the way she would have done, when they were camping, except that she hadn't dared, in case he woke up. Then she brushed his hair off his face, because, after all, she'd always wanted to do that, too.

It was four-thirty; she'd phone Pete at five, so she had half an hour to kill.

When she shifted her weight she could feel something hard pressing on her hip. It took her a long time to notice it and to reach into her pocket, and even longer to work out what it was, when she did. A wodge of paper, so cold it felt damp. She opened it out with stiff fingers, and stared. The pages from the book Zach had torn up, such a long time ago. 'A Lecture

307

Upon the Shadow'. 'A Valediction: Forbidding Mourning'. She looked at them all, methodically, without taking anything in. *Death, be not proud . . .*

Edward Randall, June 1978.

She knew that at some point the pages would be important, somehow. She knew she'd read them over and over . . . *From rest and sleepe, which but thy pictures bee . . .* but the words didn't mean anything yet. And everything was spelt wrong.

She got Zach's notebook out of her rucksack and hugged it to her chest, feeling the cardboard covers bend under the pressure. She thought, *This is mine. Mine, from Zach.* She breathed in the smell of ink and paper, and, very faintly, the musty male smell of Zach's bedroom. Then she put the pages of poetry carefully between the cover and the first page, pressing them like flowers, to keep them safe.

And she held the book up to the sunlight, and flipped to the page where she'd stopped reading.

I'm going. I'm really going. I have to face my shadow, I have to get it over with.

The word I'm trying not to use is *die*.

Any minute now, Mum's going to burst through my door, shouting about – oh, I don't know, something about leading poor impressionable you into danger. It'd be true, of course, but all the same I don't feel like hearing it.

No. That's not true. I do feel like hearing it. I want to stay here and get shouted at. I want Mum to do her Responsible Adult act for all she's worth, until I start to believe it. I want to swap surreptitious glances with you and wink back at you when you roll your eyes. I want it all to be normal – even normal-post-Cecilia. I want to tell Mum everything and burst into tears like a five-year-old and sob in her arms. Which, to be honest, is probably what I should have done a long time ago. She might have forgiven me if I had.

I want to lose it completely with both of them, Mum and Dad. I want to scream and swear and then, yes, cry my eyes out. I want to tell them what's happening and for them to believe me. I want to go back to how it was, when I was small and I thought that Mum and Dad were brilliant. When I thought they could do anything.

But I'm older now and wiser and I'm not fucking stupid. I know that if I stay here until Mum barges in she'll do something crap, like lock me in or send me to a psychiatrist. So I have to go. Even though all I really want is for someone to put their arms round me and tell me I'll be OK.

And Dad didn't even come home.

I'll never see Dad again.

Anz . . . if he ever asks . . . if Dad ever asks whether I was angry with him, can you tell him I forgave him? And said I was sorry, and not to feel bad?

No, of course it isn't true. But that's not the point.

I used to get this feeling, when I'd been drinking. It only lasted a few minutes, but . . . suddenly I'd realise I was going to die. This sudden wave of something that wasn't quite horror. I'm going to die. Me. I will be – nothing. I'll be nothing, I won't be anything . . . Knowing I couldn't escape.

But sometimes, when I carried on drinking . . . I'd find this gap. Like inside the terror there was a little quiet room, just big enough to hold me if I didn't kick off. It was very still, and very peaceful. It wasn't bravery exactly. But it worked. I wasn't scared. I *trusted*. Not anyone or anything. Just – *trusted*.

And some of those nights, I actually *wanted* to die. To find out what it was like.

I'm tired of cheating. I'm tired of trying to wriggle out of the rules. I'm tired of running away.

When I called your shadow back to you, there was a second before you collapsed. You were looking at me but you weren't seeing me. You had this expression on your face like you were watching someone walk towards you. You were in love. You weren't afraid.
I need to remember that.

I have to go. I really do have to go.

I'm quite looking forward to it, actually.

ACKNOWLEDGEMENTS

I'd like to thank Rosemary Canter and Jodie Marsh at United Agents; everyone at Bloomsbury, especially Emma Matthewson; Malorie Blackman; Lee Weatherly; the Arvon Foundation; and, as always, my family. Thank you.